Beautifully
BROKEN SPIRIT

THE
SUTTER LAKE
SERIES

CATHERINE
COWLES

Dedication

This book is for Emma, a.k.a. my wormhole twinsie. I'll be forever grateful the universe brought you into my life and that I get to go on this crazy writer journey with you. And because you were excited for Tuck and Jensen before I'd written a word of their story.

And, as always, for my dad. I carry you with me on every step of this journey. Eternally grateful to be your daughter.

Prologue

THE WIND LIFTED MY HAIR OFF MY NECK, SWIRLING IT around my face. It carried with it the calls of birds overhead and the scent of the surrounding pine trees. I stared out at the fields around me. They dipped and rolled, meeting up with forests that ran into snow-capped mountains.

My palms pressed into the rock beneath me. This was usually one of my two favorite places in the world. My boulder on the five hundred or so acres that my parents had gifted me on their ranch in the hopes that I would make my home here. This was the place I came to when I needed to think. To get away. To daydream. To feel peace.

Now, I felt nothing. Just a radiating numbness that seemed to make my fingers and toes tingle, the same way they would if they'd fallen asleep after sitting in the same position for too long. God, I wished I were sleeping. That the past three months had been nothing but a nightmare.

Tears tracked down my cheeks. I did nothing to try and staunch the flow. I kept hoping that, eventually, I'd be all cried out. That there would be no more tears left to cry. And when that happened, I'd miraculously know what I was going to do.

"Little J, I didn't know you were back from college."

The rough voice jolted me out of my thoughts, and I quickly did my best to wipe my face. I stretched my mouth into a bright smile—the same expression I'd been forcing so often lately, it felt as though my face might crack in two. "Hey, Tuck. Surprise trip."

Tuck's gaze traced over my face, and his angular jaw, dusted with dark blond stubble, went hard. "What's wrong?"

"Nothing's wrong. Just getting a little peace away from the crowd at the ranch house."

Tuck rounded the boulder, his broad frame crowding me, dominating the seemingly infinite space. "Little J…"

I gave him my best mock scowl. "Stop calling me that. I'm not exactly little anymore."

He ran a hand through his hair, tugging on the strands. "I'm well aware. Now, stop trying to change the subject. You've been crying." He glanced in the direction of the ranch house. "Do you want me to go get Walker?"

"No!" Of course, he would offer to get Walker. My brother had been Tuck's best friend since before the two could talk. And the three of us had practically grown up together. But the last thing I wanted in this moment was my brother.

Tuck settled himself next to me on the rock. "Jensen." His use of my full name had tears pooling in my eyes again. He pulled me into his side and wrapped his arm around me, giving my shoulder three quick squeezes. "What's going on?"

"I'm in trouble." The words came out in a hiccupped staccato beat as I tried to hold in the sobs.

"Whatever it is, we can fix it."

I shook my head. "I'm pregnant."

Tuck's body went as rigid and still as the stone we sat on. "What?"

"I'm pregnant," I whispered.

Tuck shot up. "I'm going to kill that fucker."

The sobs came in earnest then, wracking my body.

"Shit, I'm sorry, Little J. Come on, don't cry." Tuck wrapped both of his arms around me this time, holding me tight to his chest. "It's going to be okay."

"Cody left me." I sucked in a breath. "He doesn't want me or the baby." I curled myself into a ball against his chest. Tuck's warmth enveloped me. He was comfort. Home. I never wanted to leave this spot. Because here, there was no judgement about the fact that I hadn't even completed my freshman year of college, and I was pregnant and alone. No judgment that I'd fallen prey to the pretty words of a handsome senior boy. That I'd thought he loved me.

Tuck's lips brushed my hair. "That makes him one seriously dumb fuck." He kept his voice quiet, but I could hear the rage simmering beneath the surface.

I burrowed deeper into Tuck's hold. "I don't know what I'm going to do."

He pulled back, tipping my face up to his with a single finger. "What do you want to do?"

I looked into his pale blue eyes, having no answers. Our gazes held, the seconds ticking by. "I want to go see the herd."

Surprise flickered across Tuck's expression before a gentle smile pulled at his mouth. "You got it." He stood, offering me a hand. "Come on."

Tuck led me towards his truck, parked just on the other side of the fence that separated our families' ranches. The same two families who'd founded the town of Sutter Lake a century ago. I loved the history of this land, and that it held all my roots. I'd always planned to build a home and family here, and I'd thought I found the man I was going to do that with. But I was so wrong.

I squeezed my eyes shut, attempting to force the thoughts from my brain. My lids opened as Tuck released my hand to launch himself over the fence. I shook my head. Always the show-off. I opted to duck between the rails. Tuck was there to offer me a hand as I straightened.

We were silent on the hour drive to the national forest, Tuck seeming to sense that I needed more time to put my thoughts into words. That was the thing about my friendship with Tuck—we always accepted each other just as we were. No pretense or pressure. When we were together, we could just *be*.

As paved roads turned to unmarked gravel paths, I still didn't have any answers. Tuck pulled off the lane, shutting off his truck. "You up for walking?"

I couldn't help the laugh that escaped. "I'm pregnant, not dying."

Tuck rubbed the back of his neck. "I don't know what all pregnancy affects."

I reached over, giving his shoulder a pat. "It doesn't affect my ability to walk."

"Then let's get walking." Tuck jumped from his rig and rounded the vehicle before I could fully get my door open. "Careful."

I rolled my eyes. My brother and Tuck had always been overprotective. No bullies on the schoolyard dared turn their cruelty towards me. Boys rarely asked me out for fear of the threats Walker and Tuck had leveled on the one who had. I went to prom with my AP bio lab partner, who was more interested in dissecting frogs than what might be under my dress.

Maybe if Walker and Tuck hadn't been so overprotective growing up, I wouldn't have been so damn gullible, falling for the first guy with pretty words and a charming smile that I came across. And if I'd thought they were overprotective before,

I had a feeling pregnancy would take things to a whole new level. I sighed. It wasn't their fault. There was no one to blame for my situation but me.

I lowered myself to the ground without Tuck's help. He scowled. "I'm fine, you grumpy grizzly." His scowl deepened, and I laughed. "Let's go."

Tuck studied the forest around us. He'd always had a special relationship with nature. He seemed to hear voices that didn't reach anyone else's ears. Maybe it was the fact that tracking had been passed down through Tuck's family for generations. But I thought it was a connection that was uniquely his.

He inclined his head towards a hillside. "This way."

Silence reigned again as we walked. Tuck led, careful to point out any downed logs and hold back any tree branches that obstructed my path. Twenty minutes later, he slowed, coming to a stop at the edge of a clearing.

My breath caught. It didn't matter how many times I'd seen a similar sight. They were just that beautiful. Across the clearing, I counted at least a dozen mustangs. Wild, like they had been for generations. The stallion studied us, trying to decide if Tuck and I posed any threat. We ducked our heads, breaking eye contact, showing that we didn't intend to challenge his authority here.

Tuck tugged on my hand. "Let's sit." He pulled me towards a downed log, and we settled there.

It was Tuck who had introduced me to these creatures. In middle school, I'd been having a tough time with some mean girls, and he'd brought me out here, just like his grandfather had done for him. I'd fallen in love. Whenever life felt out of control, this was where I wanted to go. To see the beauty the world had to offer. The magic. The wildness that still reigned free.

My eyes caught on the tiniest of creatures behind one of the mares. Still wobbling on his new legs, the foal couldn't have been more than a couple of days old. I fisted Tuck's shirt. "Look."

"They're puttin' on a show just for you today." I could hear the grin in his voice but couldn't force my eyes away from the foal.

"He's perfect."

Time flew by as I lost myself being with the horses. Let them remind me what family should be. Protection, loyalty, love, care. I stilled as a curious mare approached.

"Steady now," Tuck whispered, keeping his head lowered while fixing an eye on the mare.

"I know." I didn't move a muscle as the horse drew closer. She sniffed the air around me, my hair, my shoulder, and then zeroed in on my belly. At three months along, there was no bump, but she sensed something. The horse sniffed my middle and then nuzzled my stomach. I sucked in a breath.

"She's pregnant, too." Tuck's voice came quietly from my side. "She wants to show another mama some love."

Tears pricked the corners of my eyes as I took in the mare's swollen belly. I resisted the urge to stroke her, to throw my arms around her neck and bury my face in her coat so I'd know that I wasn't alone in this. The stallion let out a whinny, and my new friend backed away, returning to her family.

I met Tuck's Arctic blue stare. "I'm scared." I ducked my head, unable to keep his gaze.

Tuck lifted my face with a single roughened fingertip under my chin. "Being scared just means you care about something. Nothing there to be ashamed of." Our eyes locked. Held. Tuck dropped his hand and balled his fist.

I bit my lip and nodded, my palm traveling to my belly. "I love this little person already."

"I know you do." Tuck gripped my neck lightly, giving it a squeeze. "You're not alone, Jensen. Families can take any shape, and sometimes, the unique ones are the most beautiful."

CHAPTER
One

Jensen
PRESENT

I GRIMACED AS I SWALLOWED A MOUTHFUL OF COFFEE. I hated coffee, but I was desperate. I needed all the caffeine I could get these days, and I would take it in whatever form was the most potent.

Footsteps thundered on the stairs. Noah swung around the corner, almost taking out a vase of flowers on his way.

"Hey there, Speed Racer, what's with the zero to sixty?"

Noah's adorable little nose twitched. "Do I smell pancakes?"

I grinned. "You do."

Noah threw his arms around me, his face burrowing into my belly. "Thanks, Mom. You're the best. It's not even the weekend."

I soaked up his easy affection. I knew it wouldn't always be this way. At nine years old, he'd soon be too cool to tell me that he loved me or to give me a hug. He'd be asking me to drop him off down the block from school instead of right out in front. So, I would try to create as many of these moments as possible, no matter how little sleep I got. And I would do everything I could to hold onto the feel of his little-boy arms wrapped around me.

I ruffled Noah's hair. "What do you think? Banana and chocolate chip?" This earned me his beaming smile and an enthusiastic nod. "You make sure your backpack is all ready to go and then head to the table."

Noah took off down the hall. He had two speeds—full-out, and slow as molasses. Pancakes meant full-out. "Mom, I can't find my hat."

"Did you check in your karate bag?" Our house wasn't large, only two bedrooms and a den, so there were a limited number of options as to where things could hide. But Noah always amazed me with how he could lose stuff. I let my gaze travel over the space that was supposed to be temporary, wondering if it was time for us to find somewhere new.

The house wasn't even really mine. It was the guest cottage a few hundred feet from the ranch house that was home to my parents and grandmother. When I'd gotten pregnant, this had seemed like the perfect setup. Close to help and support. But now, I wondered if it was just pathetic that I still basically lived at home.

Noah charged back into the kitchen. "Found it!" He pulled the hat over his head as he scooted onto a chair at the kitchen table.

I tilted my head in his direction. "What's the rule about hats at the table?"

"I just don't want to lose it again."

I stifled a giggle. "Hang it on the hook with your coat, then you won't forget it."

He looked up at me skeptically as he trudged to the coat hooks by the door, as though the hat might run away on its own, never to be found again.

I plated a stack of pancakes for Noah and a single one for myself and then sat down at the table. Noah immediately began shoveling food into his mouth. "Fank you these are so gooh." His words were barely intelligible around the food.

I disguised my laugh with a cough. "Why don't you swallow before you talk, mister?"

Noah took a gulp of milk and grinned, white mustache and all. "I can't help myself. They're too good." He shoved another bite into his mouth.

I cut off a bite for myself. Slowly, I chewed. It tasted like everything else had lately. Bland. No flavor. I wondered if lack of sleep caused all your senses to dull.

I looked over at Noah to find him studying me. "Not hungry?"

I forced a bright smile. "I had some before you came down," I lied.

Noah's gaze narrowed, but he nodded, continuing to chow down. My little boy was far too perceptive, and I needed to get my shit together.

A knock came from the front of the house. "Come in," I called.

The door pushed open to reveal a scowling Walker. "You have no idea who's there, and you just say, 'come in?' And why isn't your door locked?"

I took another sip of my coffee. "And good morning to you, too, brother dearest."

Tuck appeared behind him, dark blond hair looking almost brown as though it were still damp from a shower. "Morning, Little J. You got any more of those for me?" he asked, eyeing the pancakes.

I inclined my head towards the platter on the counter. "Help yourself."

Walker pulled out a travel mug and filled it with coffee. "You just inhaled three donuts, how are you still hungry?"

Tuck shrugged, patting his flat stomach. "I'm a growing boy." He shot me a grin that had girls all across the county dropping their panties as he sat with a plate full of pancakes. "And J's pancakes are the best."

Noah nodded furiously. "They're my favorite, too."

"Good taste, little man." Tuck took a peek in my mug, his brows pulling together. "Since when do you drink coffee?"

I took another sip of the bitter liquid, trying to fight the grimace that wanted to surface. "Since I needed more caffeine than tea could offer."

Tuck and Walker eyed each other, and my teeth clenched. Walker pulled back the last open chair and dropped onto it. "Tuck and I wanted to see if you could meet us for a late lunch at the saloon. We have SWAT training this morning, but we could meet you at two."

Tuck and my brother were not only the best of friends, but they also served on a tri-county SWAT team that had all different branches of law enforcement on it. So, while Walker was the deputy chief of police in Sutter Lake, and Tuck worked for Forest Service law enforcement, they still got to work together on a semi-regular basis.

I set down my mug. "I wish I could, but I've got too much going on at work. Then I need to pick up Noah and take him to karate." In reality, I was happy I had an excuse to miss lunch with them. It wasn't that I didn't love them both, but I was so damn tired of all the assessing stares and carefully couched questions.

Walker's jaw worked. "You need to get some more help there."

My grip around the mug of coffee tightened. "I know how to run my business, Walker." I'd proven that time and again. Even when the economy had suffered, my tea shop had flourished.

He sighed. "I know that. I just don't want you overextending yourself."

Sometimes, it seemed like my brother thought I was a moron. I forced my voice to remain even. "I'm looking for someone. There just haven't been any good applicants yet." The Tea Kettle was my pride and joy, and I wasn't going to hire just anyone. The Kettle needed the right employee.

Tuck set down his fork. "They might not be as good as Tessa

was, but you need someone. You're running yourself ragged lately, and you look exhausted."

I fought the urge to throw the remainder of my pancake at Tuck. "Thanks for letting me know I look like shit." One of my best friends and most valuable employees had recently quit so she could pursue art full-time, and I missed her presence on a whole bunch of levels. But I didn't need to know that I looked like shit while trying to make up for Tessa's absence.

"Ooooooh, Mom. That's a bad one. You gotta put a quarter in the swear jar." Noah stuffed another bite of pancake into his mouth.

"You're right, baby. I shouldn't be saying those words." I glared at Tuck.

Tuck scowled. "That's not what I meant, and you know it."

"Sure." I focused on my half-eaten pancake. His comment had cut more than I wanted to admit. I was trying so hard to show everyone that I was fine and that I had everything under control. During the day, I did a pretty good job. But the circles that rimmed my eyes told the truth about the nights.

That was when it all came crashing down around me. The voices that railed against all the horrible choices I'd made in my life. But it was the most recent that stole the greatest amount of sleep. I had let a monster into all of our lives. A man I'd thought was kind, caring, and shy. Really, he had been sick, twisted, and sadistic.

And my actions had nearly gotten my brother and his girlfriend killed. I didn't know how to live with that. Each night as I lay in bed, I remembered how I'd let Bryce in. How I'd told him all my worries and fears. How I'd seen nothing but kindness in him. I'd close my eyes and feel his hand cupping my cheek, his fingers running through my hair. Then my eyes would fly open, and I'd dart into the shower, rubbing my skin until it was raw, praying that it would erase the memory.

It never did.

Between Noah's father and Bryce, it was safe to say that if I became interested in a man, the only thing I should do is run in the opposite direction.

CHAPTER
Two

Tuck

WALKER'S TRUCK RUMBLED TO A START, AND HE THREW it in reverse. My eyes lingered on Jensen's front door. Things were not good in her world, and I had no idea how to make it better.

Walker's phone buzzed in the cupholder, and he snatched it up. A dopey grin took over his face, and I chuckled. "Taylor?"

His eyes narrowed in my direction. "Yes."

"How are things in relationship land?" My best friend had finally been taken down, and he was staying there. I was thrilled for him, happy that he had that kind of love and loyalty in his life. A prickle of something that felt a lot like jealousy flitted through my chest. Not at him being with Taylor, but envy that he had something I never would.

Walker pulled out of the space he'd filled in front of Jensen's guest house. "Things are great. How are things in manwhore alley?"

"Well, Carrie Kilpatrick learned how to do this thing with her tongue—"

Walker smacked me upside the back of the head. "I don't want to hear that shit."

I chuckled. "You asked." I was single, I might as well enjoy the variety life had to offer. I was always honest about what I was looking for—and what I wasn't. I treated the women with respect. Hell, I took a lot of them on dates. But I rarely saw a woman more than three times. Three seemed to be the magic number where most started to think they could be the one to change my ways. And I was not down for that.

Walker glanced back at the guest house as he guided his truck down the drive, the leather of the steering wheel squeaking as he tightened his hold. "I'm worried about her."

I ran a hand through my hair, giving the ends a swift tug. "Me, too." And it wasn't just the circles rimming Jensen's eyes, it was the dullness within them. The amber used to glow and dance with mischief, burn with wildfire. Now, they had no life in them at all.

"She won't talk to anyone. Not even Taylor has been able to get through to her."

I looked up at the rearview mirror and saw Jensen corralling Noah into her SUV. "Taylor makes her feel guilty. *You* make her feel guilty. Hell, your whole family probably makes her feel guilty."

"What are you talking about?"

I continued watching Jensen through the mirror. "You got shot. Taylor almost died. Your family nearly lost you. She blames herself for bringing Bryce into all of your lives."

Walker's jaw worked. "That's bullshit. We all knew Bryce for years. None of us had any clue. The pain he caused is Bryce's fault alone."

"I know that. You know that. The whole town knows it. But J doesn't believe it."

Walker switched on his blinker and turned towards town. "How do I get her to believe it?"

That was a question I'd asked myself a million times. I hated how powerless I felt to help her. For as long as I could remember, I'd always been able to make things better for Jensen, but everything I'd tried recently just seemed to piss her off. I wanted to help, but I also wanted my friend back. "I'm not sure." But I sure as hell planned to keep trying.

Silence overtook the cab as we wound through the country roads. Ranches and rolling hills gradually gave way to smaller homes and flat, paved surfaces. Walker slowed for a stop sign.

My entire body locked up at the sight of a figure exiting a house on the corner.

Bastard. It wasn't enough to be a cheater. Apparently, he wasn't even going home anymore. Wasn't even making an attempt to hide his indiscretions.

"Isn't that your dad?" Walker's voice held a puzzled curiosity.

I cleared my throat, forcing levity into my tone. "Yeah, my mom mentioned he was going to help a friend of hers with a leaky sink this morning."

"That's nice of him."

I let out a snort of derision. "That's Craig Harris, nicest guy around."

Walker stole a sidelong glance at me before accelerating through the stop. "Tuck…"

"It's fine." It damn well wasn't, and we both knew it. Walker just didn't know why I seemed to hate my father so much. *"You're just like me, Tuck. Two peas in a pod."* I refused to let myself become the man my dad was, forcing his son to lie for him, treating his wife like garbage.

My mom had done her best to cover for him. She made excuses, tried to hide her worry, but she didn't know the depth of his betrayal. She thought he abandoned her most nights for the bottle. I knew the truth. His real drug was women.

At least growing up, he'd fished outside of Sutter Lake waters, but lately, he'd been getting bolder. And I knew that my mother would find out eventually. And it would kill her. A woman who had wanted nothing but to build a family with my father. To make him happy. And this was how he repaid her?

Craig Harris's blood ran through my veins, but I would never let myself become him. I would never leave a wife and child at home waiting for me, because there would never be a wife and child to begin with. I rubbed my sternum, trying to alleviate the phantom feeling in my chest.

My life was full. I was happy. I had a job that I loved. People in my life who loved me. And I never hurt for female company. It might not be a typical life, but it worked for me. I was fine.

CHAPTER
Three

Jensen

T HE BELL OVER THE DOOR TO THE KETTLE SOUNDED AS
a blast of cold air shot through my warm and cozy
space.

"Hi, baby girl. How's your day treatin' you?"

I took in my mom, her dark brown hair swept up in a bun
that somehow managed to look both casual and elegant. Just
like the rest of her. The sight of her put-together outfit and ex-
pertly applied makeup had me brushing crumbs off my rum-
pled shirt. "Hi, Mom."

She gave me the patented, assessing *Sarah Cole* stare. The
same look she'd been giving me for months. "Why don't you let
me cover the full shift tomorrow? You can take a day off."

"I don't need a day off." My words came out more harshly
than I'd intended. I grimaced as hurt filled my mom's eyes. I
gentled my tone. "There's too much I need to get done around
here. You're already helping enough by covering these two
hours so I can go take care of the horses." I had enough guilt for
how much my family stepped in to handle my responsibilities. I
didn't need any more.

"I wish you'd let your father delegate one of the hands to help you with all of that."

I pushed down the instinct to snap at her again. "I don't need the help. I like doing it." Aside from my son, my rescued mustangs were the brightest part of my day. And I wasn't giving that up for anyone.

My mom rounded the counter, brushing back strands of hair that had escaped my ponytail over the course of the day. "I know you like being with your herd, but you have to stop taking everything on yourself. You look dead on your feet."

"Why does everyone feel the need to tell me I look like shit lately?" I couldn't hold in the snap of my words this time.

My mom gave a little jolt. "Jensen." The single word was half chastisement, half concern.

My shoulders slumped. "I'm sorry. I haven't been sleeping very well, and it's got my fuse a bit shorter than usual."

My mother's eyes narrowed in an even more careful study of my face. "Talk to me. Tell me what's going on in here." She tapped the side of my head. "And, more importantly, in here." She placed her palm on my chest over my heart.

My mouth opened. I wanted to tell her. I craved dissolving into tears, laying all my burdens at her feet, and letting her tell me it would all be okay. My mouth snapped closed. I couldn't. It was time I shouldered more of my own load. Stood on my own two feet.

My mom's face fell. She pulled me to her, wrapping her arms tightly around me. "I know this whole thing with Bryce is killing you. I'm here whenever you're ready to talk."

A burning sensation scorched the back of my throat, but I fought the tears and nodded against her shoulder. "I love you."

"More than words, baby girl. More than words."

I let myself crumple to the ground, leaning against the boulder. Work was done. The horses were fed. I had an hour before I had to be home to make dinner for Noah. This was my time to fall apart. To let out all that I'd held in for the other twenty-three hours of the day.

The tears that came were hot. Full of frustration and exhaustion, not sorrow. Sorrow was never part of the equation. What I'd lost had never been real to begin with. What those around me had almost lost was so much more. I'd have given anything to protect them from the destruction my careless decisions had nearly caused, but I couldn't. It was too late. Now, all I could do was move forward, carrying more of my own weight.

A warm muzzle nuzzled the top of my head. I tilted my face to meet the horse's dark, probing gaze. "Hey there, Phoenix. You not hungry?"

The mare huffed and pressed her face against mine. This trust and intimacy had taken a long time to build. Of all the wild mustangs I'd rescued from auctions and holding pens, Phoenix had been the most damaged.

I rubbed my hands along her neck and down her side, my fingers lingering on a scar there. She'd been taken down by either a stray bullet or a careless hunter. Someone who hadn't stuck around long enough to find out who he'd almost killed.

But God or the Universe had been looking out for Phoenix that day because Tuck had heard the shot and had gone to investigate. He'd saved her life. The recovery had been long, and there was no way Phoenix could've been released into the wild afterwards. So, she'd found a home with me.

I'd taken a portion of the land my parents had gifted me and created a safe haven for mustangs who had been ripped from their homes for one reason or another. Sometimes, the cause was humane, they were injured or ill. Sometimes, it was sheer greed, the desire for more land for cattle to graze. Regardless of the why,

I gave them a safe place to rest. And the horses gave me somewhere to be totally myself.

I patted Phoenix's shoulder. "I'll be okay. I promise. I'm getting stronger every day." The mare blew air out between her lips as if to say "*bullshit*." Okay, maybe I wasn't stronger yet, but I'd get there eventually. I had to, right?

CHAPTER
Four

Tuck

"HEY, MOM, YOU HERE?" MY VOICE ECHOED OFF THE high-beamed ceiling of the massive ranch house. It had been upgraded and expanded over the generations but still held so much history. And you couldn't beat the view. The panoramic windows that filled the entirety of the back of the house displayed rolling pastures, dark green forests, craggy mountains, and even a glimpse of the lake our town had been named for.

Heat filled my gut, along with frustration that I couldn't come here more often. And a good dose of anger that someone had stolen the magic of my family home. I turned at the sound of approaching footsteps.

"Tuck, I didn't know you were coming by." My mother smoothed back her blond hair that had begun to show threads of silver running through it. She looked exhausted. My father's nights out weren't exactly rare, but even with his excuses of staying the night in town so he wouldn't have to drive, they still took a toll on my mom.

I worked my jaw back and forth, trying to keep the frustration off my face. "How are you?"

She reached up on her tiptoes to kiss my cheek. "I'm good, honey, busy as ever. Why don't you come on into the kitchen and have some of the cookies I just pulled out of the oven?"

I patted my stomach. "That sounds perfect."

My mom led the way through the open-plan living space that poured into a bright and airy kitchen. "You don't have work today?"

I settled myself on a stool at the counter. "We had SWAT team training this morning, so I thought I'd swing by after I had lunch with Walker."

A gentle smile tipped her lips. "How is Walker?"

"He's good. Nothing but trouble, as usual."

My mom shook her head. "It seems to me trouble abounded whenever the *two* of you got together."

"Must have been his bad influence. You know I'm an angel."

She laughed. "You'll always be perfect in my eyes, but I have no illusions that they'll be nominating you for sainthood anytime soon."

I clutched my heart in mock affront. "How can you wound me so?"

My mom pushed a plate of cookies across the marble counter. "I love you just as you are, trouble and all. So, how are Taylor and Walker doing? Should I be thinking about wedding gifts anytime soon?"

I'd taken a bite of my cookie and promptly began choking. My mom filled a glass with water and handed it to me. "You okay?"

I swallowed a mouthful, clearing my throat. "Yeah, sorry, wrong pipe. I don't think there are any wedding bells in their future anytime soon. At least not that Walker's said to me."

A little twinkle sparked in my mom's eye. "I don't know. He's head over heels for that girl, and she's a keeper. If he has a lick of sense, he'll lock that one down."

I guess she had a point. I knew that Taylor was the one for Walker, had known it from the moment he'd mentioned the new tenant at his family's guest cabin. I just hadn't thought things would move this quickly. Life would look differently when everyone around me started to settle down.

My mom poured some coffee into a mug. "What about you?"

"What about me, what?"

"Any ladies catch your eye lately?"

I was glad I didn't have another bite of cookie in my mouth. "Lots of ladies catch my eye," I said with a grin.

She grimaced and shot me a disapproving look. "You need to settle down. Find a woman you can build a life with. Someone who won't let you get away with everything most of those girls do. You know who I always thought you'd be good with—?"

"Mom," I cut her off, "I'm not looking to get serious with anyone." I didn't have the heart to tell her that would be the case forever.

Her face fell. "I know your career is important, but so is a happy life."

"And are you happy?" I regretted the words as soon as they left my lips.

Pain flitted across my mother's face. "When you've been in a relationship as long as your father and I have, there are bound to be ups and downs."

I gripped the edge of the countertop, the marble edge cutting into my palm. "I don't remember a hell of a lot of ups." My gaze bored into hers, begging her to really hear me. I gentled my tone. "At some point, isn't it time to call things a loss and move on?"

Her face hardened. "Tuck, I made vows. And I intend to keep them. Marriage is meant to be forever."

Whatever my father was doing now had shot those vows to shit. And I found it hard to believe that they'd ever mattered much to him to begin with. "He treats you like crap."

I didn't have the heart to tell her the depth of it. I couldn't bring myself to say that I'd known since I was eight years old and had walked in on him and some woman in the barn. I wasn't sure what would destroy Mom more: Dad's betrayal or my own. But I'd been keeping the secret for so long, I couldn't seem to let it out now. And I wasn't sure it would matter if I did. She seemed to have an excuse for it all.

My mom busied herself cleaning an invisible mess on the counter. "Your father works hard. He likes to blow off steam. Do I wish things were different? Sure. But I love him, faults and all." Her gaze met mine. "None of us is perfect."

I shut my mouth with a snap, my teeth clacking together. Whatever I wanted to say wouldn't be helpful at this point in time. I inhaled slowly through my nose, changing tack. "I love you, Mom. I'm here if you ever change your mind. And you know you can always come stay with me if you need to." I glanced down at my watch. My dad usually got home in about an hour, and I didn't want to risk any run-ins if he was early. "I need to get going."

"Oh, honey. Don't. Please stay for dinner. I'm making pork tenderloin and potato leek au-gratin."

My stomach rumbled at the mention of one of my favorite meals. "I really can't tonight." *Or any night Craig Harris will be at the table.*

My mom's shoulders fell. "All right." She rounded the counter and wrapped her arms around me. "I'm sorry we argued. You know I love you, right?"

I engulfed her slim frame. "I know. I just want the best for you."

When she pulled back, there were tears in her eyes. "I could say the same. And I'm not sure the best is alone."

I stood from the stool. "And, sometimes, alone is exactly what's best."

I pushed open the door to the Cole Ranch house. Noah's squeals of delight were followed by an array of deep chuckles. As I moved through the entryway littered with a variety of family photos, jackets hung haphazardly on a coat rack, and a few of Noah's toys scattered on the floor, warmth flooded my chest. This space was home. More than the three-bedroom craftsman I'd bought in town. More than the sprawling ranch I'd grown up on. This place was comfort and chaotic peace.

"Tuck!" Noah flew towards me at a speed that seemed otherworldly for a nine-year-old. I lifted him high into the air as he launched himself at me. "Liam taught me a new song on the guitar. Can I play it for you?"

"Of course, you can. You getting rock star lessons, too?" I glanced into the living space, giving our resident superstar a grin. Liam grimaced. He might be a multi-platinum-selling musician, but he was much more at home here in Sutter Lake with his girlfriend, Tessa.

Noah nodded rapidly. "Yup. I'm gonna be a rock star, fighter pilot, karate superstar."

I held in my chuckle. "I guess it's good you're practicing."

I greeted Liam, Walker, and Walker's father, Andrew, with backslaps and half-hugs as Noah pulled out his guitar and proceeded to play a barely recognizable rendition of *Twinkle Twinkle Little Star*.

My gaze caught on Jensen. She looked on from the kitchen, adoration filling her amber eyes. Her hair, so dark brown it was almost black, fell in loose waves framing her heart-shaped face. There was something about the shape of that face that always had my eyes zeroing in on her perfect lips. Plump and pouty, without her trying. Lips that could enchant and entice. And they did.

That mouth was not one I needed to be thinking about. I blinked rapidly, forcing my gaze back to Noah as he hit the final chord. "That was great, little man."

He beamed up at me. "I'm getting better."

Liam ruffled his hair. "You've been practicing."

"Tucker Harris, I didn't see you come in. Don't you think you can sneak by me. Come over here and give me some sugar." The voice that called out above the din of the various conversations was roughened with age but still clear as a bell.

A smile spread wide across my face. "Now, Miss Irma, I would never neglect you." I crossed to the kitchen where Walker and Jensen's grandmother leaned against the counter, sipping a glass of wine, surrounded by the other ladies. I plucked the glassware from her hand, set it on the bar, and pulled her into my arms, dipping her back. "When are you finally going to run away with me?"

Irma cackled, smacking my chest with her hand until I righted her. "I'm too much for you to handle, cowboy." She took a step back, giving me an exaggerated once-over. "But that doesn't mean I can't enjoy the view."

Laughter erupted around us. Jensen rolled her eyes and took a sip of her wine. I slipped behind her, giving a strand of her hair three quick tugs. "How are you, Little J? Get some rest?" At first, I thought she had, the circles under her eyes seemed somewhat muted even if the eyes themselves still looked tired. But as I studied her more closely, I saw that makeup disguised the dark blooms of color. A muscle in my cheek ticked. She still wasn't sleeping.

Jensen swatted my hand away. "What? You're not feeling the need to tell me I look like crap?"

My hands fisted at my sides. The urge to grab her and kiss that smart mouth was overwhelming.

"Jensen! Language," Sarah chastened.

"Sorry, Mom." Jensen sent a scowl in my direction.

I held up my hands in mock surrender, backing away. "I was just asking how you were." I rounded the counter to brush my lips against Sarah's cheek. "Hey, Mama Sarah."

Sarah set down the spoon she held and wrapped me in a hug. "It's so good to see you. It's been too long."

Jensen refilled her wine glass. "You saw him last week."

Sarah released me and returned to stirring her pot of chili. "And that is much too long to go without my Tuck fix."

I turned my grin from Sarah to Jensen. "It's a difficult cross to bear, being this desired, but someone has to do it."

Tessa and Taylor giggled, but Jensen picked up a carrot from the salad fixings and pelted it at me. I caught the veggie before it could hit. "You didn't."

Jensen arched a brow. "Sometimes, it takes drastic measures to bring someone back to reality."

I shrugged, taking a bite of the carrot, but as soon as Jensen turned back towards her wine, I made my move. Darting around the counter, I grasped J by the waist and threw her over my shoulder. She let out a high-pitched shriek that I swore almost pierced my eardrum. "I think someone needs her own dose of reality. What do you think, ladies? Would a dip in the pool do it?"

Tessa and Taylor tried to hide their laughter behind their drinks with minimal success. Irma raised her glass to me. "You show her, sweetheart. But you gotta go in after her. And you gotta take off your shirt so I can get the full show."

"Grandma!" Jensen hissed.

Irma shrugged. "What? A woman's got needs."

"Tucker Harris, you put me down."

I gave her pert ass a little pat. "Oh, I'll put you down." I strode towards the door. "Noah, can you open the back door for me?"

Jensen fisted my shirt, trying to wiggle out of my hold. "Tuck! It's forty degrees out there."

Noah bounded over and opened the door. "Where are you taking Mom?"

"I'm taking her swimming, little man."

His nose wrinkled. "Isn't it kind of cold to go swimming?"

"Her temper needs a little cooldown."

Noah nodded as if he understood, and I headed out the back door.

Jensen let out a series of *oomphs* as I jogged down the back steps. At the center of a large, manicured yard that led up to rolling pastures dotted with a variety of animals was a pool. One that hadn't been closed up in preparation for winter yet.

Jensen pinched my side. "If you throw me in that pool, my revenge will be so epic, you will be paying for it for decades."

"You talk a big game for a very little girl."

"Stop calling me little, I'm five-eight."

"Still tiny to me."

She tried to wrench herself from my grasp, but I held firm. "That's because you're a giant. An unnatural behemoth."

I chuckled. "Now is that any way to talk to someone you're trying to convince *not* to throw you in a pool?"

"Tucker..."

I paused at the edge of the water that did, in fact, look freezing. "What'll you give me if I don't?"

"I won't murder your ass."

"That's not very nice." I started to tip Jensen towards the pool.

Her fingers dug into my back. "No, no, no! Okay, fine, whatever you want."

"That's better." I backed a few steps away from the pool. "Now, what could I possibly want? Free scones at the Kettle for life?" I slowly eased Jensen down the front of my body. I should have tossed her in the damn pool. Having her come after me hellbent on revenge would've been a lot safer than the delicious friction of her curves sliding down my front.

My muscles tightened as her face came level with mine, that tempting mouth just a breath away. She leaned in closer, her lips skimming the shell of my ear. "If you come around my shop asking for free food, I'll make sure yours is laced with ex-lax."

I let out a strangled laugh as Jensen gave my chest a hard shove and headed back towards the house. I rubbed a hand over my stubbled jaw and grinned. She might be pissed as hell at me, but at least there had been some life in those eyes again. The dullness that had been plaguing them lately always made me want to punch something.

The girl I'd known all her life had a wildness to her. An unnamable quality that couldn't be tamed. She'd lost that over the past year, that wildfire in her eyes, gone. And I'd do whatever I could to help her get it back.

Walker moved through the back door as I headed up the steps. "What was that all about?"

I shrugged. "Just trying to startle some life back into her."

Walker chuckled. "You're lucky she didn't knee you in the balls."

I winced. "I know how to protect the family jewels."

We made our way inside to find everyone taking seats at the massive dining table. Walker gave my back a slap. "Good luck, man."

As he headed for an empty seat next to Taylor, I saw that the only other vacant chair was next to Jensen. I grinned and headed for it.

Jensen scowled as I lowered myself onto the seat. "One wrong move, and I'll stab you with my fork."

My grin widened. "Why, Jensen, are you doubting my table manners?"

She let out a snort. "You're a caveman."

Dinner passed in its usual fare of five different conversations happening all at once until Noah commanded our attention with a story he desperately needed to tell everyone. As things began to wind down, Sarah turned her attention to me. "How are your mom and dad, Tuck? I haven't seen them around much lately."

I stiffened. Of course, she hadn't seen them around much. "They're good. Just busy."

Sarah took a sip of her wine. "Walker said your dad was helping a friend of your mom's in town with a plumbing issue. That's so kind of him."

My jaw clenched so hard it was a miracle I didn't crack a molar. I couldn't seem to utter a word of agreement. The man wasn't kind. He was cruel. I forced my head into a jerky nod and turned my attention to my beer. A hand reached under the table and gripped mine, giving a quick succession of squeezes.

"Mom, I'm going to head over to Rock Springs in a couple days to check out some of the mustangs Lee told me about. Want to come with me?"

I let the conversation fade out to background noise as Sarah answered Jensen. I never looked Jensen's way, but her fingers stayed linked with mine, holding tightly. Jensen had always seen more of me than anyone else. Knew the secrets I held deep inside. Every single thing I hid away from the view of the world. Every single thing...save one. And that was one secret she'd never know.

CHAPTER
Five

Tuck

I TOOK A SIP OF COFFEE AS I STRODE UP THE PATH TO THE Forest Service station and wondered if it would be possible to get an IV so I could mainline the stuff. I scowled down at my travel mug when I remembered *why* I was so damn tired this morning.

Jensen.

I'd woken up at four a.m. with a racing heart and a pulsing dick after the most vivid dream of my life. I could've sworn that I tasted her on my tongue. I gripped my mug tighter. It was getting harder and harder to resist her.

And last night had been my own damn fault. Letting those luscious curves press up against me, of course, I'd dreamt about her. The more significant problem had been shaking myself out of the stupor it'd caused. Returning to sleep had been impossible. So, here I was, running on four hours of shuteye and having to face a meeting with one of my least favorite people.

I pulled open the door to the station and found a way-too-chipper officer manning the front desk. "Morning, Carl."

"Hey, Tuck. How are you? How was SWAT training yesterday? I bet it was awesome."

I fought the grimace that wanted to surface. Carl was simply enthusiastic about his job. This morning it was just a little more than I could handle. "It was good, man. Is David in yet?"

Carl's gaze darted to the right. "He's in his office. He told me to send you in whenever you got here."

Great. David would probably bitch and moan about me being late when I was actually fifteen minutes early. Nothing I did or didn't do would ever make the man happy. I gave Carl a chin jerk and headed for David's office, opting to bypass my desk. I gave the door two quick raps.

"Come in."

I pushed open the door to find David hunched over papers at his desk, a donut in one hand, and a coffee mug in the other. Talk about a law enforcement cliché. "Good morning, sir."

"It's about time you got here." He placed the donut on the plate and wiped his hand on his uniform-clad paunch.

I didn't even bother pointing out that I was, in fact, early. It would only piss him off. Instead, I took a seat in one of the chairs opposite David's desk. "What's on the docket this week?"

I headed up a team of four officers. Three men and one woman. Each team leader had a weekly meeting with the boss to discuss the cases they'd be focusing on and what areas of the forest they'd be patrolling.

"There're a few things I want you to check out. First, I want you guys to go by the campground on the north end of Creekside trail. We've had a few calls about kids partying up there."

I pulled out my phone and started taking notes. "Got it."

"Then, we've had some poaching on leased grazing land I want you to talk to Rich Clintock about. Someone stole two of his sheep from right under his nose. We can't have that."

A fair amount of state and national land had been leased out for animals to graze on. But because the ranchers didn't live on the same land their animals did, there were occasionally issues. I tapped out a few more notes on my phone. "I'll send Dominguez and Hightower to the campground, and I'll go with Mackey and Rhines to Clintock's place."

David leaned back in his chair and nodded. "Next is more about lip-service than anything. Gotta say I sent someone to check it out. Two campers called in complaining about someone shooting off a gun and scaring the wild horses away up by county road twenty-three."

I sat up straighter. "Were any horses injured?"

David shook his head. "They're fine. It was probably just someone hunting deer. But you know how touchy those tourists are when they hear gunshots. It was probably nowhere near them or the wild horses."

The statement was true enough, but I wanted to make sure the horses were okay. If someone had been messing around up there and accidentally killed a horse, it would devastate Jensen. "I'll go check that out while I have the rest of my team on the other two cases."

David straightened. "I want you on the Clintock case. You can check out the horse business afterward. If there's time."

I gritted my teeth but nodded. "Anything else?"

"Nope. Go find that poacher."

I rose from my seat. "Will do." But as soon as I could, I was heading for Pine Meadow. Because if Jensen heard about someone scaring off the mustangs, her crazy ass would be out there investigating, and she'd get herself into some sort of trouble I'd end up having to get her out of.

I headed down the hall to the main room and found Dominguez and Mackey settling into their desks. "Morning."

"Morning, boss." Dominguez placed his sidearm in the top drawer of his desk.

Mackey, already seated, gave me a wave as she bit into a breakfast burrito. The girl was all of five foot two and one hundred and ten pounds, but she could pack away more food than I could.

I set down my mug and leaned against my desk. "We're gonna have a busy day today. Dominguez, you and Hightower are on Creekside North campground, looking into kids partying up there. Figure out if it's worth sending a couple officers out there late-night to try and catch them in the act."

I turned to Mackey, who was chasing her burrito with a swig of Coke. "Mackey, you, me, and Rhines are on a poaching case."

"Aw, man," Dominguez whined. "Why you gotta do me like that, boss? Stick me with teenagers just looking to have a little fun while you guys are doing the cool stuff?"

I chuckled. Unlike David, I fostered a casual relationship with those under me. They needed to know they could talk to me. They needed to blow off steam. In my mind, respect should be earned, not demanded. "Next interesting case is all yours."

Dominguez cheered slightly at that, and we shot the shit until the rest of the team arrived.

My truck rocked to a stop outside the grassy pasture. Mackey and Rhines pulled in next to me. Rich Clintock was already waiting. I hopped down and crossed to the weathered man in his fifties. "Mr. Clintock."

He swiped off his cowboy hat and extended a hand. "You know you can call me Rich, son."

"Rich. These are Officers Mackey and Rhines." I inclined my head in turn to each. Rich nodded at both. "Can you walk me through what happened?"

Rich glowered at the pasture, and I caught sight of a younger man working to fix a fence. "At first, I thought it was those damn horses that tore down my fence and that a few of my sheep just got loose, but when I took a closer look, I saw that the wire'd been cut. We're still counting, but so far, we've got four missing. Four that got snatched, I should say. Luckily, we'd already been planning to move them this week so I don't have to worry about someone stealing more. But you gotta find this asshole." His gaze flicked to Mackey. "Apologies, ma'am."

She waved a hand in front of her face. "I've heard worse."

I studied the field and noted its close proximity to the road. In all truth, there wasn't a lot we could do. "You have anyone who's been giving you trouble?"

Rich ran a hand over his balding head. "Not off the top of my head. I've got a good relationship with the other ranchers who have livestock up this way. Like I said before, the most trouble we've had was with the horses."

I ignored the latter part of his statement. Ranchers and animal rights activists were at an impasse when it came to the wild horse population. Ranchers were frustrated that the mustangs often ate the grass they held grazing rights to and sometimes tore down their fences. In my mind, they were here before we were, and we should try to find a happy medium.

I looked back to where Rich's workman was repairing the fence. With only a handful of sheep missing, I had a feeling the perpetrator was someone local. There were several poorer communities scattered around Pine Meadow, and it was possible that someone had been driving by and the need to feed their family had outweighed their knowledge of right and wrong. I'd investigate, of course, but I wasn't overly optimistic.

I pulled a card out of my wallet and handed it to Rich. "I'm gonna have Mackey and Rhines drive around and talk to folks today to see if anyone's seen or heard anything. But you let me know if you hear anything in the meantime."

Rich nodded, shoving the card into his pocket. "I appreciate you coming out."

"Anytime." I turned to Mackey and Rhines. "I have something else to check out, but I want you to make the rounds and update me with any developments."

They nodded, and I took off towards my truck. Turning over the engine, I backed out and headed to where the campers had called in gunshots. I needed to put my mind at ease, and I needed to be able to tell Jensen that all was well if she heard about the complaints.

It only took twenty minutes for me to reach the pull-off, and then another fifteen to hike up to the ridge that would give me the best vantage point. I took a deep breath as I reached the top, letting the cool air and the stillness of nature center me. I gazed down at the meadow below. The tension seeped from my shoulders as I took in the herd.

After a few minutes of scanning and counting, I let out a long breath. Everything was fine. My phone buzzed in my pocket. It was only because I stood atop the ridge that the call had come through. Five minutes down the trail, and I would've had zero service.

Walker flashed across the screen. I tapped accept. "Hey, man. What's up?"

"Hey. Where you at?"

"I'm standing in one of my favorite places on Earth."

Walker chuckled. "You're either up at Pine Meadow or at the saloon surrounded by women. But since it's a workday, I'm guessing the former."

I sat down on a log, extending my legs. "You'd be right. We had some complaints about gunfire up here, so I was just checking it out."

Walker's tone sobered. "Everything okay?"

"All looks good. Don't mention anything to J, I don't want her to worry."

"I won't. She'd be up there in a flash, and she's already running herself ragged these days."

I made a sound of agreement in the back of my throat. "So, what'd you need?"

"Well, I was hoping to tell you in person, but time's gotten away from me." He paused. "I'm gonna ask Taylor to marry me."

I stared out at the horizon, letting my gaze go unfocused. "That's great, man. I'm happy for you."

"That's it?"

I let out a chuckle. "What were you expecting, exactly?"

"I don't know, some bitching and moaning about losing your wingman. Maybe something about how I'll be missing out on all the other women out there."

A grin pulled at my mouth. "Walker, just because I don't want to settle down doesn't mean I think you shouldn't. Taylor is a catch. How you conned her into falling head over heels with your ugly mug is beyond me. But if you let her get away, I'd be the first to tell you that you were a fucking idiot."

Walker cleared his throat. "Lucky to have you, man. You know you're my brother in every way that matters."

I swallowed against the burn. "I know. And same goes."

"Will you be my best man?"

I smiled against the wind. "She's gotta say yes first."

Walker let out a laugh. "She will. I'm asking tomorrow night. I want all our friends and family there afterward."

"You just tell me where to be and when."

"I'll text you the details when I have them all ironed out. Tuck?"

I watched as the stallion heading the herd below tipped his head back in a long whinny. "Yeah?"

"You're gonna find this one day."

I forced a chuckle. "Gotta be looking to find it." The horses below started to run, in formation but wild and free. Just as it should be.

CHAPTER
Six

Jensen

"ARTHUR, YOU'RE GOING TO HAVE TO MELLOW OUT YOUR game if you want to keep playing at the Kettle." I ushered my favorite patron toward the front door of the shop. I was totally lying. I would never kick Arthur or the rest of his bridge cronies out, but as heated as their games sometimes got, I worried that one of them might have a heart attack one of these days.

Arthur shuffled towards the door. "Clint cheats."

I bit my lip to keep from laughing. "Last week, he accused you of the same thing."

Arthur jutted out his chin. "He cheats, *and* he lies. Maybe you should kick him out."

I pulled open the front door. "You wouldn't have any fun without your best competition."

He mumbled something under his breath that sounded something like, "I'd win a lot more money, though."

I leaned over and kissed Arthur's papery cheek. "You be careful on your walk home. Will you text me when you get there?" Arthur only lived four blocks away, but I still worried. He didn't get around quite as well as he used to.

He scowled down at me. "I'm not senile, you know."

"I know." I held up my hands in acquiescence. "I'm just a worrier. Humor me?"

His scowl melted into a gentle smile. "You're lucky you're so pretty. You get away with damn near anything."

I gave him one more peck on the cheek. "Good to know." I watched as he navigated the front walk and moved out to the street, not leaving my post until he disappeared from sight. I sighed as I flipped the sign on the door to *Closed*.

I had the overwhelming desire to let my body sink to the floor so I could curl up and take a nap. "First, you need to clean. Then, you can try for a ten-minute power nap." Maybe ten minutes would be short enough that no nightmares would be able to find me.

I surveyed the space around me. Without a second pair of hands during the day, more dishes had piled up on tables and in the kitchen sink. I needed help, but the two people I'd interviewed this week would be more trouble than they were worth.

Tessa had offered to come back until I could find someone to replace her, but she was leaving on tour with Liam in a few weeks anyway. I might as well get used to tackling the Kettle's workload mostly alone. Plus, it had taken Tessa so long to finally go after her passion, I didn't want to be the one that took her away from her art now.

I headed for the kitchen and grabbed the busboy bin. Methodically, I made my way around the café. The tub got heavier and heavier with each table I cleared. When I finished about half of them, I lost my grip on the teacup I'd grasped and it went careening to the floor, smashing into bits. "Fuckity, fuck, flipping fudge sticks."

My cursing always straddled the line between things that would come out of a sailor's mouth and the made-up curse words I tried to use in front of my son. Today, my brain was apparently short-circuiting and combining all of the above. I bent down, setting the container on the floor and trying to pick up as many of the shards as I could before I got the broom.

The bell over the door jangled. I shot up at the sound, not realizing I hadn't locked the door.

"Hey, Little J."

My entire world seemed to tunnel as my vision went black, and my knees buckled.

"Shit!" Strong hands caught me before I could hit the floor. I blinked rapidly as Tuck's face came into focus. His expression was full of worry. "Are you okay?" He settled me into one of the café chairs.

My stomach pitched. "I'm fine. Just got up too fast. You startled me."

Tuck's brow furrowed. "The door was unlocked."

"Well, I thought I'd locked it."

Tuck let out a sound that was a cross between a sigh and a growl of frustration. "You need to be more careful. Anyone could've come in here, and you wouldn't have even known. Just because we live in a small town doesn't mean you shouldn't take precautions."

I pinned him with a stare that should've had him taking a step back. "I know that. Believe me, I of all people fucking know that."

Tuck winced. "I didn't mean it like that."

I waved him off. "I know." I pushed up to stand, but the world turned wobbly again, and Tuck pressed me back into the chair.

"Oh, no, you don't. When's the last time you had something to eat?"

I tried to think back. I guess I had missed lunch. "A granola bar in the car on the way to drop Noah off at school?"

This time Tuck did growl. "You need to take better care of yourself."

My skin prickled. "I take fine care of myself, you big behemoth."

"I'm not seeing a whole lot of evidence of that lately. You take care of everyone *but* yourself." I opened my mouth to argue, but he kept right on going. "You stay right here while I go fix you a snack." Tuck pinned me with a hard gaze. "You move a muscle, and I will paddle your ass."

My jaw came unhinged, but simmering heat pooled low in my belly. My hands fisted. *What the hell?* Before I could regain any semblance of the ability to speak, Tuck had turned on his heel and strode towards the kitchen. Had I actually hit my head? Was I now in some sort of coma-induced alternate universe where Tuck threatened to spank me? And why the hell did some part of me like the idea?

I was clearly in some sort of hunger-induced brain misfire. That was the only reasonable explanation. I did all kinds of crazy stuff when I went too long without sustenance. Yes, those crazy things were generally something like eating an entire pan of brownies in one sitting. They weren't typically the burning desire to climb one of my best friends since birth like a tree. But hunger could make you do lots of insane things.

Tuck emerged from the kitchen juggling a plate with the largest sandwich I'd ever seen and a tall glass of what looked like apple juice. He came towards me with what I could only describe as a swagger. Had his hips always moved like that when he walked?

Don't get me wrong, I knew Tuck was attractive. Hot even. I'd had the requisite crush on him throughout my middle school years and even into high school. But he had always treated me like a little sister. Someone he liked hanging with. But never once had he given me even a single hint that he was interested in more than friendship. And I'd grown up. I'd put him firmly in the big-brother category. So, why, all of a sudden, was my body reacting to him?

It had to be my dry spell. Could it even be called that if it was as dry and vast as the Sahara? I needed to get laid and stat. Because the last thing I needed was to fall for a guy who was a walking one-night stand.

Tuck set the plate and juice down in front of me. "Eat."

"Apple juice?" My voice squeaked on the second word.

Tuck studied me carefully. "You need sugar."

I took a small sip. "I really just keep this in the fridge for Noah."

Tuck shrugged. "If I have to come here and feed you an afterschool snack every day to make sure you're eating enough, I will."

And there went the flicker of lust. I narrowed my eyes at him. "The day got away from me, that's all. I'm sure even the all mighty Tucker Harris has forgotten to eat once in a while."

He shot me that infamous grin. "I am pretty mighty." He winked. He freaking *winked* at me. Then his expression sobered. "But I've never forgotten to eat for so long that I almost passed out." He paused. "I'm worried about you, J."

There was something in his tone that made my eyes burn. It was so damn earnest. I swallowed against the emotion clogging my throat. "I'll make sure I remember to eat."

Tuck pushed the plate closer towards me. "Thank you."

I picked up the sandwich. "What are you doing here, anyway?"

"Did you forget what tonight was?"

I searched through the filing system in my jumbled brain and then promptly dropped my sandwich. "Shit. Walker's proposing. How could I forget that? I'm a really crappy sister."

"You are not." Tuck's words had a bit of a bite to them. "You've had a lot going on lately. That's why I dropped by. To make sure you remembered."

"Thank you." I glanced around the halfway tidied room.

"I have to finish cleaning up and then pick up Noah at karate and—"

Tuck reached across the table to grab my hand. He tapped the back of it, bringing my attention to him. "I'll clean up. You eat. And you're not driving anywhere. I'll take your SUV, and we can get Noah together."

"I'm fine, Tuck." I made an exaggerated show of biting into my sandwich.

"You just almost passed out. You are not getting behind the wheel of a car. I'll drive you and then get someone to bring me back to get my truck after."

"Fine." I stuck out my tongue at him. "You can be my chauffeur. I'll sit in the back with Noah, and we'll call you Jeeves. And you'll be required to speak to us only in a British accent."

He shook his head. "Lord save me from smart-assed women."

I had to fight the burn of tears as I crested the rise. Walker had proposed to Taylor under a tree on top of a hill at the edge of our ranch. It was a place we'd come to as a family to watch sunsets and have picnics, and now Taylor would be part of that family.

Noah barreled ahead, launching himself at Taylor and Walker. He was absolutely ecstatic to be gaining an aunt. When Tuck and I told him what would be happening tonight on the drive over, I'd thought he was going to bounce out of his booster seat and right out of the SUV.

Tears filled my eyes as I watched Walker and Taylor laugh with my son. I was thrilled for them. I couldn't think of anyone who deserved happiness more. But I also couldn't help the trickle of longing that danced down my spine, settling somewhere deep in my gut.

I shoved it down. Locked it away somewhere no one would find it—not even me. Because if I didn't reach for more, it couldn't break me. I'd opened my heart to someone twice. And both times, I'd had my heart destroyed. I wasn't sure I'd survive a third time.

And I had more important commitments. My first responsibility was to Noah. I had to build a safe and secure life for him. That meant not risking letting someone into our lives who had the potential to hurt us both. I looked around me at all the faces. I had plenty of love in my life. I could be good with just this. It was more than most had.

An arm wrapped around me, pulling me into a solid body. "You okay?"

I tilted up my face to meet Tuck's Arctic blue gaze. "Yeah. Just some happy tears." I wiped under my eyes. He didn't look like he believed me, but he said nothing as we watched the couple greet everyone around them. Yes, this could be more than enough.

CHAPTER
Seven

Tuck

I COULDN'T GET IT OUT OF MY HEAD. THAT LOOK OF SOUL-deep pain in Jensen's eyes after the proposal. As though she were giving up. That and her almost passing out on me at the Kettle had been playing on a near constant loop in my head for the past week.

Which was why I currently wandered by all the shops in town, searching for...I didn't know what. Something that would bring a smile to Jensen's face. Something that would make her laugh. *Fuck, I have no idea what I'm doing. This is a bad fucking idea.*

I turned on a dime, about to head back to my truck, but I nearly crashed into Taylor as I did. I grabbed her shoulders to steady her. "Sorry about that, gorgeous."

She pushed her blond locks away from her face. "Glad you have quicker reflexes than me, or I would've landed on my ass."

I chuckled. "I got your back." I released her and took a step back. "So, how's it feel to be the future Mrs. Cole?"

The smile that graced her face could've lit an entire room. "I don't think I've ever been happier."

"I'm so glad you guys found each other."

Taylor reached out and squeezed my arm. "Thank you. So, what're you up to?"

Heat crept up the back of my neck. "Well, I…uh…"

Taylor's brow knitted as she studied me. I didn't want to tell her, but at the same time, maybe she was exactly what I needed. "I wanted to get something for Jensen. She's been so stressed lately. I just wanted to do something nice for her. But I don't know shit about all this girlie stuff."

Taylor's eyes widened ever so slightly. "I think that's a wonderful idea. Want some shopping assistance?"

"That would be great."

Taylor linked her arm through mine. "Follow me. I know exactly what we need." Taylor pulled me down the street at a speed that was shocking for someone so tiny. "I'm worried about her, Tuck."

"Me, too. And I'm not sure what to do. She won't let anyone help shoulder the load. Won't talk to me like she used to."

Taylor slowed her pace and looked up at me. "I love how close you two are. I guess it comes from basically growing up together, huh?"

I chose my words carefully. "I've known her since she was born. I've always looked out for her."

Taylor stopped moving altogether, releasing her hold on my arm. "I feel like it's more than that."

I swallowed against my suddenly dry throat. "We've just always been able to talk about the tough stuff, you know? Were able to show each other all the pieces of ourselves, even the ugliest parts." I ran a hand through my hair roughly. "But now, she's hiding from me. From everyone." I hadn't realized how much that pissed me off until I said the words. Like Jensen had stolen something that I needed to breathe.

"Tuck." Taylor reached out and grasped my forearm. "She'll come back to us. We just have to be patient. Show her that we're here for her, that we see she's hurting, and let her know we're not leaving her to deal with it alone."

I nodded. "Any ideas for a present that will say all that?"

Taylor let out a laugh. "I've got you covered."

I held two bags stuffed with tissue paper and a variety of items. Maybe this was a bad idea. I could always climb back into my truck and head home. I heard a scream from inside Jensen's guest house. My body jolted forward.

Just as I pushed open the door, Jensen's voice, louder than I'd ever heard it, filled the space. "Noah Nolan Cole, you go to your room right now. You're in time out until I tell you otherwise."

Noah's face, red and blotchy, scrunched up. "I hate you!" He stormed past me and up the stairs.

Jensen's gaze followed him, catching on me. The hurt, pain, and exhaustion that filled her face were quickly replaced with irritation. "You don't even knock anymore? You just let yourself in now?"

"Whoa. I was outside and heard screaming. I just reacted."

"Well, maybe pause to knock next time."

I would've been annoyed at Jensen's tone, but I could see tears glittering in her eyes. "I'll try to remember to knock before barging in to save the day next time. But it really does kind of put a damper on the whole hero vibe I was trying for."

She let out a small laugh and wiped under her eyes. "Hero, breaker and enterer, same difference."

I grinned. "Brat."

"Behemoth."

I held up the bags, feeling like a total idiot. "I brought you something."

Jensen eyed the packages. "Is something going to jump out and bite me?"

She wasn't totally out of place to ask. Walker and I had played more than one prank on her growing up. "There's only one way to find out." I held out the bags.

Jensen shook her head and gestured with her hands to her shirt covered with splatters of food. "Let me clean up real quick." Her eyes flicked to a plate of food that now lay scattered across the floor and then to the stairs, her cheeks reddening. "Sorry about that. I told Noah I couldn't take him to this karate tournament he wants to watch next week, and he wasn't too happy about it."

I took a step forward, fisting my hands around the handle of the bags. The desire to pull Jensen into my arms was so strong. "He didn't mean it."

She let out a sniff. "I know." Crashing and banging sounded from upstairs. "Shit. I'd better go up there."

I set the bags on the table. "Let me?"

Jensen paused for a moment and then nodded. "Good luck."

I jogged up the stairs and headed for Noah's room. Pushing open the door, destruction greeted me. Toys, books, and stuffed animals littered the floor. "What's going on, little man?"

Noah glowered at me and threw himself on his bed. "I hate her."

I eased down onto the mattress. "That's a pretty ugly word, bud. I'd say the ugliest."

"She's ruining my life." The words were muffled since his face was shoved into a pillow. "All my friends are going to the tournament. Their moms can take them, why can't mine?"

My chest tightened. "I'm guessing your mom has to work?"

Noah slammed his little fist against the bed. "Yeah. I hate the freaking Kettle, too!"

I leaned back against the wall. "It sucks that you can't go to the tournament. There's no way around that."

"Yeah."

I pushed on. "But don't you think your mom wants you to go?"

Noah turned his head so that he could see me. I could read in his expression that he hadn't thought of that. "I don't know."

"Your mom loves you so much. And she wants all the good things for you. But to be able to give you all those things, she has to work." I paused for a moment, unsure what I was about to say. But Noah was getting older, and he needed to hear it. "When you have one parent instead of two, they have to work twice as hard to give you all the good."

Guilt flashed across Noah's expression. "I didn't think about that."

I reached over and patted his back. "That's okay. We all have times when we don't think about others as much as we should. All we can do is learn from it and try to do better. Think you can do that?" Noah nodded. "Why don't you pick up your room and then come downstairs and apologize to your mom?"

Noah's head bobbed up and down again. "Maybe I should make her an I'm-sorry card."

I bit back a grin. "I think that's a great idea. But clean this mess up first, okay?"

"'Kay, Tuck."

"Good man."

That brought a small smile to Noah's face, and he got to work. I headed down the stairs. As I rounded the corner to the kitchen, I froze. Jensen sat on the floor, the contents of the two gift bags strewn around her. In one hand, she held the bottle of wine, and in the other, chocolate.

She looked up at the sound of my footsteps. "You got me the good stuff."

I grinned. "Taylor might've helped."

"Sorry I was such a raging bitch when you barged in."

I lowered myself to the floor next to her. "You're entitled to a few raging-bitch moments. We'll call them a mom write-off."

Jensen took a sip of the wine straight from the bottle, then pointed at some of the contents of the second bag, a mischievous smile stretching her mouth. "You got me girlie stuff. Bubble bath. Body oil. Face masks. I'm impressed, Harris."

That familiar heat crept up my neck. "Taylor picked it out."

She bumped her shoulder with mine. "Thank you. I needed this more than I can say." She took another sip of wine and then handed the bottle to me.

I took a swig. It wasn't bad. For wine. "You know, all you have to do is ask for help. I would've been happy to take Noah to the tournament next weekend. And I know the rest of your family would have, too."

Jensen grabbed the bottle back so forcefully, wine splashed onto the floor. "I need to take care of Noah by myself." The mask that she had mastered over the past year, the one that I fucking hated, slipped into place.

A muscle in my cheek ticked. "Why?"

She stared straight ahead, her eyes fixed on some point I couldn't see. "I need to be able to do this on my own because that's the life I've chosen for myself. I need to learn how to handle it."

I forced my jaw to relax. "You're not alone."

Jensen turned to face me. "I am. And that's the way it has to be. I'm not opening myself up to that ever again."

I got it more than she would ever know. The choice to be alone. It was the last thing I wanted for her, but I got it. Still, I tried to talk her around. "You just need time. You'll find the right person."

Jensen took another pull of the wine. "I won't. Not if I'm not looking."

My back molars ground together. "Choosing to close yourself off from a shot at love isn't the answer for you—"

Jensen's gaze turned hot. "Oh, should I fuck half the state of Oregon instead?"

Her words cut deeper than they should've. I pushed on any-way. "But if you *do* choose that, it doesn't mean you have to live your life in isolation. You can still have help. Families, support systems, they don't always have to look the same."

I held her gaze, willing her to read between the lines. She knew. She understood better than anyone else the family I had created for myself when my own had been too fucked up for me to stand for long.

Jensen's gaze softened, and then the tension seeped from her body as she leaned into me. My arm naturally curved around her. "I don't know what the answer is. How to find the balance between being strong enough to stand on my own two feet and not shutting everyone out." Her voice hitched. "I'm so tired of being a burden."

I felt a tearing sensation in my chest. "You are not a burden." I held her tighter against me. "Not. Fucking. Ever."

"I feel like all I do is take. And I have nothing to give back."

I rested my chin on the top of her head. The familiar scent of jasmine and hints of tea from her shift at the Kettle filled my senses. "The only time you don't give back is when you hide yourself away from everyone who loves you. I've missed my friend."

Jensen burrowed her face in my chest. "I'm sorry." Her shoulders began to shake. "I just—I've put my family, so many people I love, through too much."

I couldn't take this anymore. We needed to have a come to Jesus talk, and I didn't give one shit that she hadn't wanted to talk about the elephant in the room for the past year. "Jensen. I need you to hear me. What happened with Bryce wasn't your fault."

She began crying harder. "It was."

"How?"

Her words came out on hiccupped sobs. "I'm the one who

gave him the gate code to the ranch. If I hadn't, he'd wouldn't have been able to take Taylor." Was this what she'd been carrying around so much guilt over? A damn gate code?

Jensen lifted her head, and her eyes held a ravaged pain I'd never seen in them before, one that socked me right in the gut. "Did you know she has scars? Ones that will never go away. Taylor has to live with the reminder of what that monster did to her every single day. And I let that happen. Because *I* trusted him."

I cupped Jensen's cheek. "Listen to me. Bryce would've found a way regardless. It wouldn't have mattered if Taylor were locked behind the walls of Fort Knox. He was determined and fucking crazy. The only one to blame is him."

Her gaze held mine. "I wish I could believe that."

I sighed, pulling her to me. "Is this why you've been pushing everyone away?"

Jensen's breath hiccupped. "I feel so damn guilty. And sometimes being around everyone just makes me feel worse."

I brushed my lips against the top of her head. "You have to forgive yourself, J. No one blames you. We just *miss* you."

Jensen's body began to shake again. "I'm sorry. I've missed you, too."

"It's okay. Just don't disappear on me again." I gave her arm three quick squeezes. "Promise?"

"I'll try."

It was all I could ask for.

CHAPTER
Eight

Jensen

MY SUV BUMPED OVER THE DIRT ROAD, BUT MY heart only got lighter the closer I got. I was doing my best to take Tuck's advice. Just because I didn't want a romantic partner didn't mean I was alone in life. I still wanted to stand on my own two feet, but part of that meant knowing when to ask for help. So, I was taking the afternoon off and going to my favorite place.

I rounded a curve in the road and spotted the pull-off I was looking for. I angled my vehicle off the lane and parked. Grabbing my pack from the passenger seat, I hopped out. I took a moment to close my eyes and inhale deeply, tipping my face up to the sun. The scents of pine and crisp early winter air mixed in an aroma that somehow managed to be both calming and invigorating.

This was just what I needed. An afternoon away from daily tasks and responsibilities. Nothing but me, nature, and hopefully, some time with my mustangs. I slung my pack over my shoulders and tightened the straps. The trail I headed down was off the beaten path, one Tuck had shown me in high school. It wove up a ridge and then down into the meadow that was one of the horses' favorite grazing grounds.

I struck off. Within ten minutes, the tension was already seeping out of my muscles. I wound my way up the incline, nothing but the sounds of birds chirping and critters scurrying in the underbrush keeping me company.

We were headed into the winter months, but there was no sign of snow, and the sun shone so brightly you would've thought it was the dead of summer. As I crested the ridgeline, a smile stretched my face. This place was magic. The rocky range dotted with trees dipped down onto what looked like a sea of golden grasses before rising up again into a series of mountaintops.

My gaze scanned the meadow. No sign of my mustang friends yet. I'd hike down and see what I could find in the forests that surrounded the grasses. I started down the ridge, but my step faltered. What was that? A dark form lay just off the path about one hundred yards ahead.

My heart dropped to my stomach, and I started to run. Rocks and dirt sprayed as I flew down the path. I lost my footing, my palms catching the worst of my fall. I scrambled to my feet and kept right on going.

I skidded to a halt, my heart hammering in my chest. *Please no, please no, please no.* I stepped off the path. Crouched. Placed my hand on the coat beginning to grow shaggy for the winter. I closed my eyes against the pain. Too cold. Too still. The mare was gone.

I blinked against the tears gathering in my eyes. Tears that turned hot with anger when I took in more of the horse in front of me. There, in the mare's chest, was a gaping bullet wound. My breaths came quicker as my head jerked in every direction, as though the murderer might still be lurking.

I wrenched my pack from my back, frantically searching

for my phone. I held it up. No service. I looked from the fallen mare to the top of the ridge and back. I had to leave her so I could call someone. I knew she was gone from this Earth, but it still tore at my heart to leave her alone. "I'll be back," I whispered.

I climbed as quickly as possible, my leg muscles burning by the time I reached the top. Two bars of service. I didn't hesitate. I hit Tuck's name on my list of favorite contacts.

Two rings later, his roughened voice came across the line. "Hey, Little J."

"I need you to come to the ridge at Pine Meadow. The place we always go."

Tuck's tone was suddenly alert. "What's wrong?"

I swallowed against the pain creeping up my throat. "I found a mare. She was shot, Tuck. She's gone."

"Fuck! How recent?" I could hear him slam a drawer closed.

"It's been less than a day, no scavengers have been at her, but she's not warm either." I stared down at the beautiful creature whose life had been stolen from her.

"Hike back to your car right now. I'm on my way." An engine turned over in the background.

"I'm not leaving her."

"Dammit, Jensen. The hunter could still be around. What if he mistakes *you* for an elk?"

I dug my nails into my already tender palms. "Whoever did this is long gone, Tuck. I'm not leaving."

I heard a muttered curse and something that sounded like "stubborn woman."

"I'm about thirty minutes out. Be careful."

"I'll see you soon." I hit end and headed back down the path. I settled myself on the ground next to the mare. "I'm so sorry this happened to you." I closed my eyes and sent up a prayer. My relationship with God was a complicated one, but I figured it couldn't hurt to ask that He welcome her home with open arms. It didn't hurt to ask for protection for the rest of my precious mustangs, either.

I hugged my knees to my chest and let time pass. I didn't know how long it took before I heard Tuck calling, but I couldn't bring myself to answer him audibly. I simply stood and raised my hand in a wave. He jogged down the path towards me, athletic and agile, unlike my bumbling attempt.

When Tuck reached me, he tugged me to him with a ferocity that stole my breath. "Are you okay?" He pulled back, grasping onto my shoulders, his gaze tracking over my face.

"I'm fine." I could hear the lie in my voice, and I knew Tuck could, too.

He looked away from me and to the mare a few feet away. A muscle in his cheek ticked.

"We have to find the bastard that did this."

Tuck's face hardened. "*You* aren't going to find anyone. That's my job. You're going to march your ass back to your SUV and go home."

My blood began to heat, and I shook off Tuck's hold on me. "You are not the boss of me."

Tuck scowled. "Well, this is now an active crime scene, so I could always arrest you for interference."

My jaw dropped open. "You wouldn't."

"Don't test me."

I threw up my hands in frustration. "You are the most infuriating—"

Tuck caught hold of my wrist, bringing my hand closer so that he could inspect my palm. "What happened?"

I swallowed, the heat from his hand seeping into my skin. "I tripped."

Tuck looked heavenward as though praying for patience. "Come on." He led me up the path.

"Where are we going?"

Tuck kept a loose hold on my wrist. "I'm taking you back to my truck, where I have a first-aid kit."

I rolled my eyes. So freaking overprotective. "It's just a couple of scrapes."

"They could get infected," he gritted out.

I opted for silence as I followed. Once Tuck had set his mind to something, there was no changing it. He was possibly the most stubborn man on the planet. We made it back to the vehicles in record time. Tuck let down the tailgate of his truck and hoisted me onto it as though I weighed no more than Noah. "Stay."

"I'm not a dog, you know."

"Believe me, I know. A dog would listen."

I stuck out my tongue at Tuck's back as he dug through the cab of his truck.

"I know you're sticking out your tongue at me."

I immediately retracted said tongue. "Was not."

He turned and headed back to me with a massive first-aid kit. "You know I always know when you're lying."

It was true. From the time I could talk, Tuck always knew when I wasn't telling the truth. It was infuriating. I shrugged. "Whatever you say."

"That's more like it." Tuck ripped open an alcohol wipe. "Give me your hands." I held them out, palms up. "This is going to sting." He began swiping the cool pad across one palm.

"Oh, frickedy freaking fuck!" It burned like the fires of Hell.

Tuck chuckled. "That's some creative cursing." He lifted my palm to his mouth and blew gently, taking away the worst of the sting. Our gazes locked and held. Something crackled between us.

No. No. No. This could not happen. I could not be having any sort of sexy feelings for my best friend. *My brother's* best friend. I opened my mouth to say something—I wasn't sure what—when the sound of tires on gravel sounded.

Tuck glanced over his shoulder. "My team." I nodded, still not quite able to find my words. He looked back at me. "I'm sorry you had to be the one to find her."

I swallowed against the emotion that crept back up my throat. "I'm just glad someone did." I gripped Tuck's arm, uncaring that the action stung my palms. "You're going to find whoever did this, right?"

"I'll try. But I'm not sure we'll have much luck. You know how many hunters there are around here."

I squeezed his arm tighter. "But you'll do everything you can?"

Tuck's eyes bored into mine. "I'll do everything in my power."

His words were a promise. And Tuck never broke a promise.

CHAPTER
Nine

Tuck

I WATCHED AS JENSEN'S SUV DISAPPEARED DOWN THE DIRT road. The tightness in my chest lessened just a fraction. She was safe. She was heading home and would be out of the way of any potential harm.

It had only taken a single word when she called. One word and I had known that something was wrong. My entire body had locked. Now, it could ease. I could focus on what I needed to do.

I hoped that this was just a horrible calamity—someone hunting where they shouldn't. Thinking a horse was an elk. Something. But my mind flashed back to finding Phoenix shot in a similar fashion. My gut said that none of this was an accident. But Jensen didn't need to know that until I was sure.

I turned to Mackey and Dominguez. "Let's go."

We hiked out to the fallen mare. A muscle in my cheek ticked as I took in the details of the scene, things I hadn't been able to process when I had been focused on getting Jensen gone.

I held up a hand to keep Mackey and Dominguez back. I needed the crime scene as undisturbed as possible. My experience tracking meant that I might be able to recreate what happened in my mind. I studied where the horse had fallen, did my best to estimate a possible range of trajectory. Then I searched.

My gaze traveled the ground and the surrounding under-brush for any sign of a shooter's nest. As I focused on the task at hand, the rest of the world melted away.

Time passed without me having any sense of it. Small glim-mers of hope flickered in and out as I thought I had found some-thing, only to realize they were animal tracks. My eyes caught on a broken branch. I crouched, studying a patch of compressed underbrush.

A tiny flash of color caught my attention. I pulled out a glove from my back pocket along with an evidence bag. I plucked the cluster of red threads from the bramble and placed it in the plas-tic bag. I tied a marker to a nearby tree.

I headed back to my team. "There's a shooter's nest about twenty yards in. I want you to measure the exact distance and take photos."

Mackey pulled a camera from her pack. "Got it."

Dominguez looked at me. "What are you doing?"

Dominguez was hungry. Part of it was a desire to learn and grow as an officer. The other part was impatience for advance-ment. The first piece I could respect, the second annoyed the shit out of me. "I'm assessing the scene. And checking for signs of other casualties."

Dominguez straightened. "I could help with that."

I pinned him with a hard stare. "I gave you your orders. Go help Mackey."

He held back whatever it was he wanted to say and followed after the female officer.

My gaze roamed the space, my eyes searching for anything that might provide a clue. A tree five feet away caught my at-tention. It seemed to have an explosion of bark on its trunk. I made my way towards it. Leaning closer, I examined the hole that appeared to have been drilled into it. A flash of metal shone in the sun.

"Gotcha." I pulled out my pocket knife and dug around the bullet. With my gloved hand, I carefully extracted the hunk of metal and placed it in another evidence bag. We were gonna get this fucker.

I turned to see David marching down the path. I met him halfway. "Sir, I didn't know you were coming out."

He grimaced at the mare. "I wanted to see what you were able to find. We can't have people hunting out of their allotted areas. We need to find this guy before they hurt someone."

I wanted to argue that someone had already been hurt. The mare wasn't human, but that didn't make her loss any less real. I bit my tongue. At least David was taking this seriously. "We've got some leads."

"Fill me in."

I walked David through what I believed happened and showed him the threads and the slug. "Between this and the bullet I'm sure they'll find in the mare, at least we've got something. When we get a suspect, we can compare ballistics to their firearms."

David studied the evidence bags, and then his gaze flicked to me. "Good work. But no one's going to approve of an autopsy for a horse. This bullet you found is enough."

I hated that the mare wasn't getting the respect she deserved, but David was right. One bullet was all we needed to nail this guy. "All right. I'll make sure they get logged, and the bullet gets sent off to the crime lab as soon as I'm back."

David made a beckoning motion with his hand. "I'll take them. I'm headed back now."

"Thank you, sir." I handed him the evidence.

"Keep me apprised of anything else you find."

"Will do."

I would find whoever did this. And I was going to nail them with everything I had.

I rolled my truck to a stop outside Jensen's guest house. The urge to check on her, to make sure she was okay had been too strong. I hopped down and made my way up the path. Rapping on the door three times, I waited. Her SUV was here, so I assumed she was home.

The door swung open, and Walker stood there. "Hey, man, what're you doing here?"

Jensen appeared behind him, her dark hair piled into a haphazard bun on the top of her head. And she wore an apron dotted with what looked like tomato sauce. "Hey, Tuck."

I forced my gaze back to Walker. "I just wanted to check on Little J, make sure she was okay."

Jensen's head fell back, and she let out an exasperated sigh.

Walker stiffened. "What do you mean, check on her? What happened?"

"She didn't tell you?" Of course, she hadn't.

Jensen threw up her hands. "*I* was never in any danger." She pinned me with a stare. "The only thing you need to worry about is figuring out who needs their hunting license revoked. Have you found any leads?"

I opened my mouth to answer her, but Walker cut me off. "Will someone tell me what the hell is going on?"

I took a few minutes to fill Walker in. The longer I talked, the redder his face got. He spun to face Jensen. "That was so fucking stupid."

She arched a brow. "Excuse me? One, watch your language, Noah is upstairs. Two, don't you dare pull that attitude with me."

I was pretty sure there was smoke coming out of Walker's ears. "You should know. Better than most. It is incredibly dumb to go out onto any of these trails alone. Anything could happen, and you would have had no one to help you."

Jensen's hands went to her hips. "I had a fully stocked pack and my phone. I'm not an idiot. I was less than a mile from my car."

Walker rubbed his temples. "There are about two places in a five-mile radius up there that get service. What if you had gotten hurt?"

Jensen's jaw hardened. "I didn't."

"Well, you could have. You can't pull this kind of shit. You have a son."

I sucked in a breath. Walker froze. He knew he'd crossed a line as soon as the words left his mouth.

"Get out."

"J, I'm sorry, I just want you to be careful."

"Get out!"

Walker stuttered back a step. "I'm sorry."

I clapped a hand on Walker's shoulder and ushered him towards the door. "Give her a bit to cool down." I followed him outside.

Walker scrubbed a hand over his face. "Shit, man. I didn't mean it like that."

"I know you didn't. And neither does Jensen. You just need to give her some time to see that."

Walker nodded. "I'll come back tomorrow morning. Apologize."

I slapped him on the back. "Good plan."

His gaze met mine. "Look out for her, will you?"

"Always." If he knew the thoughts that were traveling through my head about his little sister, I'd be the *last* person he would ask to look after Jensen. *Fuck.* I needed to get myself in check. I took a deep breath of cold, pine-scented air, and headed back inside.

Jensen was at the stove, stirring something that smelled amazing. "What are you still doing here? You think I'm an idiot who doesn't know what I'm doing, too."

I leaned against the counter. "Hey, now, don't lump me in with Mr. Open Mouth Insert Foot." I paused. "But you know he didn't mean it."

Jensen tightened her grip on the wooden spoon. "I needed some time alone. And I wanted that in my favorite place."

"I get it. I do." I reached up and wiped a splash of sauce from her cheek. "Just let someone know where you're going next time. Then your bases are covered."

"Mom knew where I was. I told her my exact path, and she knew when I'd be back, too. If my know-it-all brother would have reined in his temper for two minutes, I could've told him that."

I chuckled. "Walker doesn't always think before he speaks. And he loves you. But you'll always be the little sister he feels he needs to protect."

She scowled at the bubbling sauce. "Between the two of you, it's a miracle you haven't implanted me with a tracking device and wrapped me in bubble wrap."

I gave a strand of hair that had escaped her bun a couple of light tugs. "Hey, now, that's a good idea. We can inject you with one of those trackers that vets put in dogs."

Jensen reached out and pinched my side. "You come near me with any needles, and I'll knee you in the balls."

I chuckled. "If I promise not to inject you with any trackers, will you let me stay for dinner?" I gave an exaggerated sniff of the sauce.

"If you keep Noah entertained while I clean up, you can come for dinner anytime."

I wrapped an arm around Jensen, pulling her into my side and kissing the top of her head. "You've got a deal." At the feel of her against me, at the familiar jasmine scent, my body came alive. I released her immediately. "I'll go see what the little monster's up to now." Anything to get some distance from those curves and that smell. Being around Jensen was the most beautiful form of torture. And even though I knew I shouldn't, I'd always sign up for more.

CHAPTER
Ten

Jensen

I EASED OUT OF MY SUV, FLIPPING MY SUNGLASSES DOWN off the top of my head to fight the glare and hide the things my eyes would betray. I hated this place. I knew they were doing their best, but there was something so incredibly wrong about it.

Pens with metal fencing over my head. Not a blade of grass in sight. Just an endless sea of dirt and dust, scattered with piles of hay.

A group of horses in one pen ran from one end to the other, but the area was so small that by the time they picked up speed, they were forced to come to a screeching halt. My chest burned. It was all so very wrong.

"Jensen." Lee's voice cut in above the sounds of hooves and whinnies.

I gave the lean man walking towards me a wave. I was grateful that there was someone here who cared about these horses living their lives in limbo, caught between the wild and finding new homes. But it wasn't enough. These amazing creatures deserved so much more. "Hey, Lee."

He pulled me into a quick hug. "Thanks for coming out."

"Anytime. Can I see her?" Technically, I wasn't looking to take on any new horses. I had about all I could handle without hiring some additional help, but Lee had called about an elderly mare who was fading. She'd lived the last five years in one of these pens, and she deserved to live her last days in peace, in as close to freedom as we could give her.

"Follow me." He led the way through a maze of pens. "You have plans to head back out to Pine Meadow anytime soon?"

The mare I had found a few weeks ago flashed in my mind. I hadn't been back since I'd discovered her fallen form. I needed to. I couldn't let that experience color my favorite place in the world. "I'll probably go next week."

Lee nodded. "Let me know how the herd's looking, will you? I haven't been able to make it out there much lately."

Guilt pricked at my skin over my earlier thoughts. Lee was doing the best he could with the resources he had, and he cared about these horses. "Of course."

Lee gestured to his left, taking us in another direction. The longer we walked, the smaller the pens got until we reached those designed to hold only one horse. "She's not doing well. I knew her chances of being adopted were slim given her age, but I just kept hoping…"

I sucked in a breath as we rounded the corner. A dark bay horse stood shivering in the corner of her pen. The corner farthest away from any people and the other horses. An invisible fist squeezed my heart. "I'll take her."

Lee's steps faltered. "You've barely laid eyes on her. Haven't even heard her story."

"Doesn't matter." It didn't. There was something about this horse. I knew she needed me. Maybe we needed each other. That was the thing about horses, they tended to teach you way more than you would ever teach them.

Lee eyed me carefully. "I don't know how much time she has left. And she's definitely not rideable."

"You know that doesn't matter to me." Some of the mustangs were adopted and trained to be trail and competition horses. I took the approach that the horse would show me what he or she wanted to be.

I had a couple who seemed to be bored by what I more or less dubbed retirement. I'd trained them to be trail horses, and they loved it. Others didn't seem to want a human on their backs, and I respected that, too. Still more were too injured to ever be able to carry the weight of a person. Some people would've put a horse down for that. To me, it did nothing to lessen the horse's worth. Being able-bodied didn't have anything to do with how much you were able to give.

Lee shook his head but did it while grinning. "Glad I can always count on you for the tough cases."

I gave him a small smile. "Can you work on the paperwork? I'd like some time alone with her."

"Of course. I'll be in the office. Just come find me whenever you're done."

"Thanks."

Lee headed off, and I approached the edge of the pen. The mare's trembling intensified. I halted and slowly sank to the ground. Crossing my legs, I bowed my head, trying to show her in every way I could that I meant her no harm.

Nothing in this process could be hurried. It was a delicate dance. I needed to get her out of here as quickly as possible. The chaotic energy of the holding facility was only preventing her healing, but if I forced her too soon, I could do irreparable damage.

I tilted my head so I could see the mare out of the corner of my eye. She studied me, her head moving in jerky half starts and retreats.

It all came down to trust. A five-letter word that was so incredibly fragile. With others, but even more so with yourself.

This horse didn't know if she could trust her perception of what was happening around her. And boy did I ever know how that felt. Everything around you became a potential threat when you couldn't trust the way you interpreted the world around you.

"It's okay, beautiful girl. You take all the time you need." I crooned the words softly, willing her to hear hope in my words. The promise of a safe space to rest. To have a little bit of her freedom returned to her.

She sniffed the air, catching my scent on the breeze, but she didn't venture any closer. Instead, she chose to stay on the other side of the pen. I remained still, my head lowered as I kept talking. I told the mare about Cole Ranch. About the other horses.

I promised her that when we got to the ranch, no one would ever hurt her again. That she could set the pace for our relationship, and I would always respect it.

I lost track of time as I continued speaking in a low, comforting tone. Sharing with this beautiful girl everything that filtered into my mind. I wasn't sure how much time had passed when something shifted. The mare's energy calmed just a bit. She took a few tentative steps towards the fence.

I slowly extended my hand. The horse took another step, giving my fingers a sniff. Her whiskers tickled my fingertips, and I grinned. The first small step towards that fragile five-letter word. The greatest gift of all.

She was going to adjust beautifully. I had a feeling it was the noise and chaotic energy of the holding facility that had her so jumpy. She nuzzled my hand. This mare loved people. You could tell. I rubbed her cheek. "You'll be getting all sorts of attention when I get you back to the ranch."

My fingers eased up her face and then down her neck, so very slowly. "What do you say, beautiful girl? Want to come home with me tomorrow?" There was no discernable answer, but I liked to believe there was a flicker of hope in the horse's eyes.

"I'll be back soon." I would never lie to this mare. The potential gift of her trust was too valuable. "It's going to be scary. You're going to have to ride in a trailer again. And there will be some loud noises and a few new faces, but you're so brave. And I promise you, it will be worth it."

The horse let out a little huff of air. I could only hope that I was doing the right thing, choosing the right timing. I slowly rose, and she backed away. I did the same. But I would be back for her. She'd never be alone on my watch again.

The bell jingled as I pushed open the door to the Kettle. The scents of tea and baked goods were almost as comforting as that of horses and hay. Almost.

My mom greeted me with a bright smile. "So?"

I grinned back. "I'm bringing her home tomorrow."

Mom did a little jump and squeal, clapping her hands together as she went. "I can't wait to meet her."

"She's going to need a little time to adjust, but I can tell she loves people."

My mom sobered. "Poor thing. I hate that she's been stuck there for so long. We'll make her feel safe again."

I rounded the counter and wrapped my mom in a hug. God, I loved this woman. She approached every living creature, large or small, the same. It didn't matter if they were human, mammal, or reptile, they all got kindness and a safe place to rest in Sarah Cole's orbit. "I love you, Mom."

She gave me a squeeze. "I love you, too, baby girl." She released me. "So, you got a name picked out?"

"Not yet."

My mom let out a huff of air. "Everyone needs a name."

I chuckled. My mom was always hurrying me to name the horses I adopted, but I liked to give them a chance to show me who they were first. "I'll know when I know. But I have a couple ideas."

"Oh, fine." A timer buzzed from the kitchen. "Watch the register while I grab that batch of brownies, would you?"

"Of course." I eyed the bakery case to see how we were doing on supplies. I'd only been gone a couple of hours, but the scones were gone, and the brownies were running low. Good thing I could count on my mom to stay on top of it all. Now, if only I could find another employee as good as her.

The bell over the door jingled, and two men entered, pulling off their cowboy hats as they crossed the threshold. Their expressions were as different as night and day. One had a bright smile, the other wore a deep scowl. *Here we go...*

Kind smile walked up to the counter. "Afternoon, Miss Jensen. How're you doing?"

"I'm good, Bill, how about you?"

"Can't complain. Just grabbing some supplies at the feed store and had to get a stash of some of your treats for the road." He patted his stomach.

The man behind him mumbled something under his breath that I couldn't quite make out, but it had Bill giving him a warning look.

"Check out what we've got in the case, and my mom's pulling another batch of brownies out of the oven right now." I met Mr. Grumpy's gaze. "Can I offer you a sample of anything? On the house."

The man's stare hardened. "I wouldn't take food from you if you paid me."

"Tom—" Bill started.

I bristled. "Excuse me?"

Tom's hands fisted at his sides. "You think you're better than the rest of us. Throwing your family's money around to protect those horses that are no good to anyone."

My jaw clenched. Last year, there'd been a vote on whether to increase the lands for ranchers to lease for grazing. That increase would've cut into the area where the mustangs roamed. My family had been vocal in opposing the measure, and some people thought we were betraying our own.

I took a steadying breath. "I understand you might not agree with our stance, but that doesn't change the taste of the cookies we serve here. I'd be happy to give you some." *Kill them with kindness.* I repeated my mom's mantra over and over in my head.

Tom let out an unflattering curse, then turned on his heel and strode right out the door. Good riddance.

Bill shuffled forward, his cheeks red. "I'm real sorry about that, Jensen. Tom has a temper on him."

I waved a hand in front of my face. "Not your fault. I know it's tough when you're passionate about something and someone disagrees."

"That's true enough." Bill pointed out what he wanted and paid. "You have a good day."

"You, too." I stared out the front windows as Bill headed for his truck. I wished there were a more straightforward answer to maintaining the balance between the ranchers and the mustangs, but there didn't seem to be one. And at the end of the day, the horses had been there first, so that had to earn them some rights.

I startled as my mom squeezed my shoulder. "Everything okay?"

"Yeah, just an unhappy rancher."

Mom frowned. "He say something?"

I sighed. "Nothing I haven't heard before. You okay until closing? I was hoping to get some things set up for the new mare before Tuck brings Noah home from their manly man hang session."

My mom laughed softly. "Of course. Go make she-who-has-yet-to-be-named a cozy home."

I grinned. "She'll have a name when she's ready." And she'd have a new home tomorrow.

CHAPTER
Eleven

Tuck

"**O**KAY, WHAT DO WE DO NEXT?"

Noah's brow furrowed, his face scrunching slightly. "Get low and get quiet."

I grinned. "You got it."

We crouched, and Noah studied the outskirts of the clearing. "There are some broken branches over there."

"Good eye, little man. You lead the way."

His chest puffed out as he rose and gave me a smile that would have melted the coldest hearts. I loved getting this time with him. Teaching him to track the same way my grandfather had taught me.

Noah walked carefully towards the edge of the clearing, his gaze trying to figure out a path an animal might have taken. He made it a few feet into the trees and then halted. "I don't see anything else."

I gave his shoulder a squeeze. "When I can't figure out what's next, I try to look at the picture from a different angle."

Noah looked up at me. "What do you mean?"

"Well, think about it this way,"—I got on my tiptoes, towering over him—"when I look at you from here, I see one thing." I crouched down level with him. "From here, I see another." I laid down on the forest floor. "And from here, another."

Noah giggled. "So, I should lay down on the ground to see where the deer went?"

I sat up, smiling at him. "If that's what it takes. But try getting low again first."

Noah sank to his knees and stared at the brush all around us. His eyes squinted until they were slits, and he finally let out an exasperated sigh. "I still don't see anything." His head drooped. "Maybe I'm no good at tracking."

"Hey, now." I gave his back a pat. "No one is an expert their first few times out. I told you about the time your uncle Walker and I decided we were going to track a cougar and got lost, didn't I?"

A small smile tipped up Noah's lips, and he nodded.

"My mom and your grandma were so mad. Walker and I were grounded for two whole weeks in the middle of summer."

Noah's smile grew wider. "And Grampa made you guys muck out the whole barn, right?"

I ruffled Noah's hair. "He did. And let me tell you, mucking stalls in the dead of summer is a smelly job."

Noah giggled. "I bet."

"All right. Ready to keep trying?"

"Ready."

I pointed towards the forest floor. While most of it was riddled with pine needles, there was a small patch of soft soil showing through.

Noah's head snapped back to me. "Tracks!"

I rose, helping Noah up as I went. "Let's go see if it will show us where they're headed."

We made our way over to the patch of ground, and Noah crouched low, studying the hoof prints. "I think…" He paused, nibbling on his bottom lip. "I think they're going that way." Noah pointed off to the east.

"I think you're right."

Noah's face brightened, and he rose.

"What do you know that's in that direction that the deer might be interested in?"

His thinking-face scrunch was back. Noah looked like a cross between Yoda and an adorable Pug. I fought the chuckle that wanted to escape. His face brightened. "The creek! Maybe they're thirsty."

"That's exactly what I was thinking. Let's head over there and see what we can find."

Noah grinned but faltered. "I don't know exactly where I'm going, can you lead the way?"

"Of course." I stepped over a fallen log. "The more you come out here, the easier it will be to remember exactly how to get where you want to go."

"I just have to keep a lookout for landmarks, right?"

I couldn't help the massive smile. Noah was so eager to learn. "That's right. But no coming out here alone, remember?"

"Oh, I won't. I don't want to shovel horse poop for two weeks like you and Uncle Walker."

I chuckled. "Smart man."

Noah grabbed my hand. "Look!" The single word came out on a whisper-shout. I froze. "There's babies."

My gaze shot to the creek where a herd of about eight deer, including three fawns, drank. "You did it. You found them."

Noah looked up at me, wonder filling his expression. "I did, didn't I?"

"I'd say you're on your way to becoming a tracker."

He didn't let go of my hand. "Thanks for teaching me, Tuck."

Warmth flooded me at his words. "Anytime, little man."

"I can't wait to tell Mom."

My chest tightened. Yet another reason I needed to keep Jensen filed away in the sister category. I didn't want to lose this with Noah. I already had one family in shambles, I couldn't risk the one I had built for myself.

I pulled my truck up to the fence line at Jensen's property. She'd been busy this afternoon. Two smaller paddock areas had been set up next to her small barn. I turned off the engine, my gaze searching for that flowing, brunette mane.

I pushed my door gently closed as my eyes caught on her form. Jensen stood forehead to forehead with Phoenix in the pasture. My steps halted. Watching Jensen with her horses was always a sight to behold. The connection. The trust. It was simply breathtaking.

Phoenix must've caught my scent because she broke the hold first, her head turning towards me. Jensen followed, raising a hand as she headed my way. "Hey. Where's Noah?"

I ducked between the rails in the fence. "We stopped by the ranch house on the way up here, and he opted to stay with Irma so they could practice their karate moves."

Jensen laughed as the wind whipped her hair around her face in a wild dance. God, she was beautiful.

I swallowed hard and looked towards the newly erected paddocks. "I take it you've found at least one new member for your herd."

Jensen took a step closer, and I could see hints of that old wildfire dancing in her eyes. "She's beautiful, Tuck. Beaten down, but so beautiful. We're gonna give her a safe place to rest."

"She couldn't land anywhere better."

Jensen gazed out at the horizon. "Except back with her family."

I couldn't ignore the flicker of pain in Jensen's eyes. I pulled her to me, wrapping an arm around her and resting my chin on top of her head. "You're going to give her a new family."

"I hope it's enough." She whispered the words against my chest.

"Enough what?"

J pulled back so that she could meet my gaze. "Right now? She's just surviving. I want her to *live*."

I wondered if Jensen was aware just how much she had in common with the horse she was going to be taking in. Maybe they could bring each other back to life. "When are you—?"

My words were cut off by the sound of tires on gravel, and I recognized Walker's truck. I instinctively took another step away from Jensen as if Walker would be able to sense the thoughts I was fighting so hard against, the ones I was certain he'd deck me for if he knew I was having them. He'd probably ban me from ever entering the Cole property again, too.

My hands tightened to fists, but I forced a grin. "Hey, Walk." He didn't look happy. Had he seen us hugging?

Walker ducked between the fence rails. "Hey, guys."

"Hey, big bro, what are you doing up here?" Jensen grinned up at him.

"Mom said you're adopting another horse. A senior one."

Jensen's mask, the one I fucking hated, slipped into place at her brother's tone. "I am."

Walker eyed her carefully and gentled his voice. "Are you sure that's a good idea?"

"Why wouldn't it be?" There was the slightest flicker of doubt in Jensen's voice, and the hint of fire in her eyes was now long gone.

I had a sudden urge to deck my best friend.

Walker took a step towards his sister. "You've had so much going lately. You're overworked. You're not sleeping. Are you really sure adding another horse is really a good idea?"

Annoyance flitted across Jensen's face. "I know what I can handle."

Walker sighed. "Are you sure about that?"

"Walker." My single word was a warning.

Of course, Walker didn't heed it. "Come on, you can't think this is a good idea. The last thing she needs is another responsibility on her plate."

A muscle in my cheek ticked. "Actually, I think it's a great idea."

"Hey, jackasses." Both Walker and I started at Jensen's interjection. "Thanks for fighting over what's in *my* best interest. But, guess what? I don't need permission or approval from either of you. And now that you've completely ruined the happy buzz I had going, I'm going to leave. You two can stay out here all night and argue about what's best for me, it won't change a damn thing." Jensen started for the fence line.

"J," Walker called. But she didn't even slow.

"Fuck." I rubbed at my temples.

Walker whirled on me. "You really think this is a good idea?"

I watched as Jensen got into her SUV and took off. "She has a point. It doesn't matter what we think. But, Walk,"—I turned to face him—"when she talked about that mare, it was the most life I'd seen in her eyes in months."

"Really?" He looked towards J's vehicle, disappearing in a cloud of dust.

"Really." And I would do anything to keep that spark of life in Jensen's eyes.

CHAPTER
Twelve

Jensen

I SUCKED IN A DEEP BREATH, LETTING THE COOL, PINE scent soothe every tired muscle in my body. It had been a long week. I'd brought Willow home on Monday—*Willow*, that's what I'd named the mare with the haunted eyes. For the trees that were known to withstand the highest winds so well they would bend but never break.

She was adjusting to her new home perfectly, but I'd been spending extra time with my herd just to make sure. There was karate and family dinners and prepping lunches and work. I was exhausted, but I'd come into the Kettle extra early the past three days so I could mix extra dough to get ahead on the baking schedule and steal away for a couple of quiet hours today.

I needed this time. I had to reclaim one of my favorite places in the world. If I didn't, it would forever have a darkness to it. And this place, as well as the meadow and forests surrounding it, should always be bathed in light.

I tightened the straps on my pack. No one could accuse me of not taking precautions now. I'd told my mom exactly where

I would be. Heck, I'd even borrowed one of the satellite phones my dad kept on hand.

I would've asked Tuck to go with me, but I knew he was working, and he probably would've tried to talk me out of it. Not to mention, I was still a little pissed at him. Him and my brother. Their overprotectiveness and desire to make all my decisions for me was stifling.

I took another deep breath. This was why I needed horses. Mine and the ones who still ran free. With them, I could just be. I couldn't explain it exactly, but they eased my soul somehow.

I began the hike up the familiar path, but this time, I rounded the ridge and headed straight for the meadow. I wasn't quite ready to revisit the site where I'd found the fallen mare. I'd take the more popular trail.

I hiked for an hour before I saw them. Tension seeped from my muscles as I recognized the stallion. I counted at least ten mares. Four foals. Everyone was safe. They all looked healthy. I let out a long breath. My sleep had been restless for the past couple of weeks, but not for the usual reasons. Instead of being filled with Bryce, my nightmares had been filled with fallen horses.

I needed this. Had to know they were okay. And now I could tell Lee the same. I found a spot to settle in. I set down my pack and pulled out my bottle of water and a sandwich. I sat and watched and ate. I let the horses' peaceful energy flow over me. Soaked up each precious moment as the family interacted, coaxing their young ones along, searching out grass to eat. This glimpse of life was the perfect remedy to the heartache of the lost mare.

"What are you thinking coming out here?"

I jolted at the sound of Tuck's voice. "What are you doing here?"

He glowered at me. "I'm working a case. You know the one where you found a horse shot to death?"

My mouth fell open. Tuck was overprotective, but this felt extreme. "You think the hunter's going to come back to the same place?" Tuck's jaw worked, but he said nothing. Pieces began to slide into place. I shot to my feet. "You don't think this was an accident."

A muscle ticked in Tuck's cheek. That flicker of movement I was so very familiar with. "I don't have evidence either way, and there haven't been any other incidents."

My eyes narrowed. "But your gut's telling you it wasn't an accident."

He ran a hand through his hair. "It doesn't matter what my gut says, you shouldn't be tromping around where a crime was committed."

My hands fisted. "I'm not. I didn't take that unmarked trail. I took the official, marked path. I didn't see any signs that said it was closed. Has the Forest Service closed this trail, Tuck?"

That muscle in his cheek was dancing to a staccato beat now. "I need you to trust me to handle this."

I let out an exasperated sigh. "I do trust you to handle it. I'm not poking around, looking for evidence or anything. I just wanted some time with the mustangs. It's been a long week, and I needed—"

"You needed to catch your breath." Tuck's gaze held me captive, his ice-blue eyes burning into mine.

How did he see me better than anyone? "With them, with my herd, it's the only place I breathe easily."

Tuck stepped closer. "I don't want you to get hurt."

"I won't." I gestured towards my pile of stuff. "I've got a stocked pack, a sat phone. I'm covered."

Tuck pulled me against him. "It's not enough. Please. Don't come out here alone again. Call me."

His body was all rigid muscle. I spoke into his pec. "Okay."

"Promise?"

I fisted my hands in his shirt. "I promise."

Tuck's lips pressed against the top of my head, and I fought the urge to let my hands wander.

"Thank you." He released me.

My hands seemed to tingle where I'd touched him. I swallowed hard, hating how much I felt the loss of those strong arms around me. "I brought an extra sandwich. Want to have lunch with me?"

Tuck grinned. "Have I ever turned down any food you made?"

I tapped a finger against my lips. "I don't think so."

We settled down into my spot in the grass, and I handed him my second sandwich. He dug into it with gusto. "This bread with the rosemary," he said around a full mouth, "it's the best."

"Nina from the bakery and Tessa came up with the recipe." I took a sip of water.

Tuck motioned for my bottle, and I handed it over. He took a swig. "Those two come up with the most unlikely but delicious concoctions."

"That they do." I stared out at the grazing herd.

"I need to get some of this for my mom."

I stole a peek at Tuck from the corner of my eye. "How is she?" Knowing when I could ask about his parents and when it wasn't okay was a delicate balance. People thought that Tuck and his dad just didn't get along that well. I knew the truth. Craig Harris had broken his son's heart.

Tuck turned his gaze to the horses. "She says she's fine. But he's slowly stealing her life one day at a time. She just doesn't seem to see that."

I knew a little something about hoping a man would change even when he had given you all the signs in the world that he never would. After I'd gotten pregnant with Noah, and Cody had run off to who knows where, I'd hoped and prayed for months that he'd realize what he was missing and come back. That first night in the hospital after Noah had been born and I finally came to terms with the fact that I was going to raise him alone, I'd bawled so hard a nurse had come running.

"Give her time. Everyone has to find his or her own way to what makes them happy."

Tuck turned to me. "And what about you? Are you happy?"

I plucked a blade of grass and twisted it around my finger. "I'm happy enough."

An angry scowl took over Tuck's face.

I chuckled and reached over to pinch his cheek. "Oh, come on, don't be such a grumpy butt."

"I'll show you grumpy." Tuck dove for me, going straight for my most ticklish spots, my sides just above my hip bones.

I shrieked, laughing and twisting, trying anything to escape his hold. "Okay, okay, you're not grumpy."

Tuck stilled his assault but stayed hovering over me as I lay in the grass. The heat of his body seemed to pour into mine. My belly tightened. His eyes tracked over my face. "I want you to be so happy, so full of joy it seeps out of your skin."

My breath hitched. "Maybe one day."

"Yeah, one day."

CHAPTER
Thirteen

Tuck

M Y EYES TRACKED THE MOVEMENT OF JENSEN'S HIPS as they swayed on the dance floor. She wore jeans that might as well have been a second skin, and a top that dipped down low enough in the back for me to know there was no bra underneath. My back molars ground together.

One last get-together before Liam and Tessa left on his tour. It had seemed like a good idea at the time. Good friends, cold drinks. What could go wrong? Just me having to live through the nine circles of Hell in the form of the temptation on the dance floor.

Jensen threw her head back, letting out a cackling laugh I could hear over the country music that spilled out of the speakers. She spun in circles with Taylor and Tessa. They were all three sheets to the wind, but I was happy that she was letting loose. Even if it meant my jeans felt two sizes tighter.

There was heat at my side, but I kept my gaze on the dance floor. Firm breasts pressed into my arm.

"Hey, Tucker."

I turned to take in Lucy Bigsby. My gaze traveled the length of her. She had certainly grown up over the past few years. I'd heard she was off getting her masters somewhere, but she must have been home for an end-of-year break. "Hey, Lucy."

"How you been?" She blinked up at me, her long lashes fluttering.

"Been good, darlin'. How about you?" I tried to stay focused on Lucy, but my gaze kept being pulled towards the dance floor. A flash of mahogany hair in the lights caught my eye as Jensen did some sort of twirl that almost landed her on her ass.

There was a tug on my collar. "I've been good. I was hoping I'd see you when I came home. I was thinking maybe we could hang out later. Or...now. We could call it an early night..."

I should've taken Lucy up on her offer. She was exactly what I probably needed to get my mind off the brown-haired beauty trying to execute some sort of ballerina move on the dance floor. But the thought of Lucy's hands on me made me cringe. "Sorry, Lucy. I'm here with some friends. Kind of a going-away deal."

I watched as Liam swooped in to pull Tessa to him as the music changed to something a little slower. He swept the hair away from her face and pressed his lips to her temple, his embrace staying there for a few beats.

The gesture was so tender, I had to look away. My gaze flicked to Walker, who held Taylor in his arms, nuzzling her neck. She giggled and grabbed his butt. I chuckled to myself.

Then my vision zeroed in on Jensen. Some rancher I knew by sight only had yanked her into his arms, even though she was barely staying upright. His hands inched lower. *Oh, hell no.*

I pushed off my stool so abruptly, Lucy staggered backwards. "Sorry," I called as I charged towards Jensen and Mr. Handsy. He took one look at me striding towards them and released J with a start. She stumbled back, almost falling, but I caught her. "Get lost."

"Whatever, dude." Mr. Handsy went off to sulk.

"Tuck." Jensen curled into me as if seeking comfort and heat. "Dance with me."

I wrapped my arms around her as she began to sway. "I don't know if that's such a good idea."

"Mmmkay." She kept swaying. Her lean, athletic curves pressed up against me, and her cheek rested on my chest over my heart. Suddenly, her swaying slowed. "I don't feel so good."

Oh, shit. "Come on, Little J, let's get you home."

Her face scrunched up. "I'm not little."

"No, you're certainly not," I muttered. I flagged down Walker. "I'm gonna take her home. I think she's about to be down for the count."

Walker eyed Jensen's drooping form. "She's gonna be hurting tomorrow." His gaze flicked to me. "You sure you don't mind?"

I shook my head. "You guys stay, have fun."

I jerked up my chin at Liam, who returned the gesture. Then I headed for the exit. As I pushed open the doors, Jensen leaned harder into my side. She was officially done for.

"Can I take a nap here?" Her words slurred slightly together as she started to slide down my body towards the sidewalk.

"Not quite yet, darlin'." I swung her up into my arms. This would be far easier.

Jensen's face scrunched. "Don't call me darlin'."

I headed towards my truck in the back lot. "Why not?"

"You call your roving band of bed buddies darlin'."

I let out a bark of laughter. How she'd managed to string those words together in her state was beyond me. "Roving band of bed buddies, huh?"

Jensen yanked on my shirt, forcing my ear closer to her lips. "You're kind of a slut," she said in a stage whisper.

I chuckled, but something foreign burned in my gut. "What can I say? I like women." I usually did, anyway. Lately, I'd been having the same reaction to most as I had with Lucy earlier.

Jensen leaned her head against my shoulder. "You could use a little more discerning taste."

"I'll take that under advisement."

"Good." Her eyes fluttered closed. "But you probably shouldn't listen to me."

"And why's that?" I lowered Jensen's feet to the ground and leaned her against myself and the truck, beeping the locks.

She tipped her head back against my truck, eyes still closed. "Because I haven't had sex in so long, I've probably forgotten how."

I nearly choked on my tongue. Instead, I let out a spluttering cough.

Jensen's eyes fluttered open, and she stared up at the stars. "I need to get laid."

Words I definitely did not need to hear from Jensen. *Little J*, I reminded myself. Someone I should be looking at as a little sister, not as a grown woman with curves for days and eyes I could lose myself in as I took her hard and fast.

I shook my head. *Get ahold of yourself, man.* "Let's get you home."

Jensen nodded. "That sounds good."

I pulled open the truck door and helped Jensen in. Leaning over her to buckle her seat belt, I caught that scent of jasmine. The one that always undid me. My jeans got tighter. I snapped the belt in place and got the hell out of there.

Rounding the vehicle, I took a moment to inhale deeply, using the cold night air to clear away the remnants of jasmine. *Just get her home, get her in bed, and get out.* I could do this.

The drive back to the Cole Ranch was quiet, Jensen dozing in the seat next to mine. I reminded myself over and over that she wasn't for me. There were so many reasons I should stay away. It would be a betrayal of my friendship, no... my brotherhood with Walker. Not to mention that I wasn't sure I was equipped to be the man Jensen and Noah needed. But, most of all, if I fucked things up with Jensen, I'd lose the only family I had left.

I pulled to a stop outside the guest house. The best thing I could do for her—and for myself—was to be her friend. And when the right guy came along, I'd step aside and let her be happy. It would kill something inside of me, but it was the right thing to do.

I got out and rounded the truck, pulling open the passenger-side door. I held my breath, reaching over to unbuckle Jensen's seat belt. I slipped an arm under her legs and another behind her back, lifting her from the seat. I leaned against the door to close it. "J, where's your key?"

"Let me sleep," she grumbled into my neck.

I chuckled. "I need your key before you can sleep."

"Back pocket," she mumbled, aggravation clear in her tone.

I carried her up to the door, then set her feet on the ground as I held her up with one arm. I slipped my free hand into her back pocket. Jensen had always been in incredible shape. From the day that she could walk, she had tried to run. She'd chased Walker and me around from the moment she got her sea legs. She played every sport possible from the minute they were offered to her. Now, she hauled hay and feed to her horses. She mucked stalls and chased her son around. Her body was strong and muscled, which created curves that would make any man drool.

I squeezed my eyes closed as my hand rounded her tight ass, searching for that damn key in the pocket of jeans so tight, I thought my hand might actually get stuck there. My fingertips touched metal. I clasped the edge of the key with two fingers and slowly pulled it out. I unlocked the door and pushed it open. "Come on, champ. Let's go."

Jensen muttered something unintelligible and tried to get through the door on her own steam. Instead, she ran smack into the entryway table, sending it toppling and her teetering. Thankfully, Noah was at his weekly slumber party with his grandparents, so at least we weren't going to wake anyone up.

I grasped her arm. "Whoa there. Why don't I just help you get upstairs?"

Her head bobbed. "'Kay."

I closed the door, locking it behind me as I swung Jensen up into my arms once again. I headed up the stairs, being careful not to let her head bang into a wall or something.

When we reached the second floor, Jensen's eyes flew open. "I'm gonna puke."

"Oh, shit." I jogged to the bathroom, set her down on the floor, and opened the lid of the toilet just in time for her to empty the contents of her stomach. I pulled her hair away from her face and rubbed a hand up and down her back as she retched. It took some time, but finally, her body quieted. "You think you're done?"

She nodded slowly, and I lifted her up, setting her on the counter. I wet a washcloth and carefully cleaned her face, including the makeup she rarely wore. I liked her better without it, as if I could see the truth in her face better or something. I ran her toothbrush under the water and placed some toothpaste on it.

I wrapped her fingers around the brush. "Here, this will make you feel better."

Jensen nodded again and began to brush her teeth. The movements were awkward and jerky at first, but she got there. She spit into the sink, and I handed her a cup of water to rinse.

When she was done, I lifted her down from the counter. "Think you can walk?"

"Yup."

I kept an arm around her waist just in case.

We made our way inside her bedroom. I hadn't been in here in years. Maybe since Walker, Andrew, and I had painted it when

Jensen moved in. The space was totally her. Earthy, jewel-toned colors. A cozy comforter and a worn quilt covered the bed, along with so many pillows I couldn't count them all.

Jensen plopped down on the bed and started pulling off her shirt.

I spun around to face the wall. "What are you doing?"

"Can't sleep in these clothes, Tuck."

"Well, you shouldn't be doing a striptease either."

Jensen laughed. "It's not like you've never seen boobs before."

I coughed. "I haven't seen yours." *And that's how it's going to stay.*

"They're covered now, oh innocent one."

I slowly turned around, wondering if it might be some trick, but Jensen was, in fact, wearing a worn t-shirt.

Her jeans were halfway down her thighs, and she glared at them. "I need your help with these. They're too damn tight."

No shit, those things were too damn form-fitting. They should be illegal. In fact, I was going to take them with me and burn them so Jensen and her swaying hips could never tempt me again. I crossed to the bed and crouched to help her. Slowly, I peeled the denim from her long, tanned legs. My knuckles grazed skin that was so soft I had to bite back a curse. After what felt like both an eternity and a second, the jeans fell to the floor.

"Thank you," Jensen breathed, collapsing back onto the mattress.

"Come on, let's get you under the covers." I threw pillow after decorative pillow to the floor. "Why do you have all these fucking pillows?" I growled.

Jensen giggled. "My bed is my nest. I like lots of cozy things."

"I think you've got cozy covered."

She grinned up at me as she slipped those never-ending legs beneath the sheets and wiggled down. "My bed's the best."

I was sure it was, but that fact had nothing to do with five hundred pillows and a stack of blankets a foot high. "Get some rest."

Jensen's hand shot out and grasped mine. "Will you stay till I fall asleep?" My brow furrowed. "I get nightmares," she whispered. "If I know you're here, I won't be so scared to fall asleep."

In that moment, I wanted nothing more than to resurrect Bryce Elkins so I could be the one to end his life. I schooled my features and squeezed Jensen's hand. "Close your eyes. I'll be right here."

Jensen's gaze held mine for a fraction longer, and then she let her eyes close. Slowly, her breathing evened out and deepened. Her hand relaxed in mine. But still, I sat there, as though I could guard against the things in her nightmares.

I wasn't sure how much time passed, but eventually, I forced myself to stand. I leaned over Jensen and kissed one temple and then the other before my lips rested on her forehead. I kept them pressed there for longer than I should have, soaking up the feel of her skin. When I released her, I leaned down and whispered in her ear. "You're safe now. I won't let anyone hurt you ever again."

CHAPTER
Fourteen

Jensen

A LITTLE DRUMMER BOY PLAYED A STACCATO BEAT IN MY brain. I cracked open one eyelid and moaned. It was too bright, way too damn bright to do anything that involved eyes being open. I would just have to keep my eyes shut until after sunset.

A buzzing noise came from the nightstand, and I opened one eye a sliver. Just enough to spot my cell phone and reach for it.

Mom: *I hope you don't mind but we told Noah we'd take him to brunch and to see a movie today. Is that all right?*

There was a God in Heaven. I loved my little boy, but if there was one thing I couldn't handle with the hangover from hell, it was Noah and his buckets full of energy.

Me: *That's great. Thanks so much. Give him a hug for me.*

Mom: *Will do. Hope you had fun last night.*

Last night… I bolted straight up in bed as a slew of memories slammed into me. Dancing with the girls. Tequila shots. A handsy dance partner. Tuck. Me telling Tuck I probably didn't remember how to have sex. Almost barfing all over Tuck. Doing some sort of awkward strip down in front of Tuck.

My face flamed. I was going to die one thousand deaths from embarrassment. I covered my face with my hands and groaned. Why had I drunk that much? I knew I didn't have a high tolerance anymore.

I let my hands drop and looked around the room as if Tuck himself might jump out and start laughing in my face. On my bedside table sat a large glass of water, a ginger ale, a banana, a sleeve of crackers, and a couple of Tylenol. There was a note beside them in Tuck's rough scrawl. *This should help.* It was the exact combination of things I'd eaten when I had horrible morning sickness during my first trimester. And Tuck had remembered.

Warmth filled my belly. Then I remembered peeling off my shirt in front of him. I groaned, shoving my head back against my pillows. "Kill me now."

After inhaling some of the crackers and ginger ale and soaking under a steaming-hot shower, the majority of my hangover had abated. Now, I sat at my kitchen table, staring at my cell phone. Waiting would only make things worse.

I tapped Tuck's contact on the screen and blinked. I was a big girl. I could own up to my idiocy and apologize.

"How ya feelin', Little J?" Tuck didn't sound angry. He didn't even seem annoyed.

I twisted the cloth napkin on the table. "Better than I have a right to."

He chuckled. "Glad to hear it."

I cleared my throat. "Listen, I just wanted to thank you for taking care of me. And, um, apologize for the puke and the stripping and, uh, the—"

Tuck let out a bark of laughter. "No apology needed. You gave me a hell of an interesting night."

My face heated. "I'm sure it wasn't at the top of your list of dream nights, so, I'm sorry."

"J, you don't have to apologize. Hanging with you is always a good time. Even if you are puking up your guts."

My fingers toying with the napkin stilled. "Well, I'm glad you aren't plotting your revenge." I paused for a moment, remembering the last time I'd gotten sick on Tuck's watch. I had been in high school, and he and Walker had been home on break from college. I'd taken one too many shots of Fireball at a field party. I puked in the back of Tuck's truck. He and Walker had repaid me by placing twenty cinnamon air fresheners in my bedroom. To this day, the scent made me nauseous.

I grinned down at the table. "What are you up to today?"

"Not much. I was just going to watch a little basketball. You?"

I traced the design on the napkin's fabric. "Well, my parents took Noah for the day. Would you maybe want to go out to Pine Meadow, visit the horses before we're snowed out for the season?" During the worst of the winter months, there was enough snow up there that visiting the horses became nearly impossible.

"They're calling for our first snow today." Tuck paused. "But I think we should be able to get there and back before things get too bad. Sure. I'll pick you up in thirty?"

I pushed up from my chair. "That's perfect."

"Make sure you dress warm."

I rolled my eyes. "I'm not seven. I know how to dress for cold weather."

"Yeah, yeah. See you in a few."

I hit end on the call and jogged up the stairs to layer up. After I grabbed my coat, hat, and gloves, I went outside to wait for Tuck. He was right, it smelled like snow. But the scent and the cold air were precisely what the doctor ordered, chasing away the last remnants of my hangover.

I stood as I saw Tuck's truck round the bend in the gravel road.

Before he even had a chance to turn off the engine, I was pulling open the passenger-side door and hoisting myself up.

He scowled in my direction. "I would've gotten your door."

I grinned. Nothing pissed off guys like my brother and Tuck more than stealing their chance to be chivalrous. "I've got working limbs, I can open a door. I can even get in a vehicle all by myself."

Tuck turned his annoyed stare to the road as he reversed. "That's not the point."

I couldn't hold in my laugh. "You and Walker are too easy to annoy."

Tuck shook his head. "You always were an expert at it."

I settled back into my seat. "There are few things in life that give me greater pleasure."

"Brat."

"Behemoth."

I tapped my fingers against my denim-clad thighs. "So, did you go back to the bar after you put me to bed?"

Tuck glanced at me from the corner of his eye. "No. Why?"

I gave a one-shouldered shrug. "My evening is a little hazy, but I'm pretty sure I remember Lucy Bigsby giving you some pretty strong signals."

Tuck grinned. "Can't blame a girl for trying. But, nope. I went home alone."

I made a humming noise. "Not interested?"

Tuck headed out of town towards the old highway that led up the mountain road to Pine Meadow. "I guess she's just not my type."

I snorted. "You don't have a type."

Tuck's scowl returned. "How would you know?"

"Because I've seen you pick up your share of women. And I've heard half the women over the age of twenty-one and under the age of fifty in this town talk about their encounters with you in far too much detail."

Tuck shifted in his seat. "So, my tastes are varied. I'm a lover of women in all shapes and sizes. That's not a crime."

It was true. I'd seen Tuck with long and lean, short and curvy, plump and petite. He didn't seem to see color or creed. He just saw female. "I actually think that's nice. But it also means you don't have a type."

Tuck's grip on the wheel tightened. "Maybe that's changing." His gaze flicked to me for the briefest of moments. "I've had a pretty specific type on my mind lately," he muttered under his breath.

I glanced at Tuck out of the corner of my eye, something flickering in my chest. Hope, maybe? I needed to shove that down. Tuck was not for me. No one was.

By the time Tuck and I reached the meadow, fat flakes of snow were falling in earnest. He glanced up at the sky. "I think we should head back to the truck."

I looked from him to the meadow and then back again. "I just want to get one quick peek. To make sure they're okay."

"Fifteen minutes. If we don't find them by then, we're heading back."

"Deal."

Of course, fifteen minutes turned into thirty, and by then, our boots were cutting through at least an inch of snow.

Tuck caught my elbow. "We have to turn back. If we don't, we'll never make it home, and I have zero desire to freeze to death in my truck on the side of the road."

I studied the quickly accumulating snow. "You're right. Can we come back when the weather's better?"

"Of course. Whenever you want." Tuck began leading us back the way we had come. I hadn't thought about how much fast-falling snow would hamper our progress, but man, did it ever. Luckily, Tuck was so familiar with the area that we didn't have to worry about finding the exact path. But we did have to worry about where we stepped.

After I'd rolled my ankle approximately five times, I tugged on Tuck's coat. "You need to slow down, or I'm going to bite it."

When Tuck turned, I saw little worry lines creasing his brow. "I'll slow down."

"Is everything okay?"

Tuck studied the sky and then the path ahead. "I'm worried about us making it back in this."

Shit. I shouldn't have pushed him to hike that extra thirty minutes. "I'll go as fast as I can."

"Don't hurt yourself. Because if I have to carry you, that will only slow us down even more."

I nodded and concentrated on exactly where I was putting my feet.

"I'll shorten my stride. Just try to step where I do."

I nodded and set my sights on the large boot prints his feet left behind. It took us at least three times as long to make it back to the truck than it usually did, and by the time we got there, at least eight inches of fresh powder covered the ground. I was soaking wet from my knees down, and I was freezing.

Tuck beeped his locks and helped me up into the truck. He rounded the vehicle with an agility that seemed otherworldly. Turning over the engine, he looked over at me. "I think we need to look for a place to stay up here. I don't feel good about trying to tackle the mountain roads in this."

I nodded, teeth chattering. "I just need to call my parents so they can keep Noah."

Tuck pulled onto what I hoped was the gravel drive, but who could really tell in this mess of white. "There's a bed and breakfast at the base of this road. Hopefully, they'll have rooms open."

Tuck made his way down the mountain road at a painfully

slow pace I was grateful for as I held my hands up to one of the heater vents and rubbed them together. "Sorry I made you stay out longer."

"It's not your fault. It doesn't usually come down this heavy this early in the season." Tuck's shoulders seemed to ease a fraction when we pulled into a parking lot outside what looked like a large log cabin. "Come on."

I grabbed my pack and hopped down, wading through the snow until I reached Tuck's side. We made our way towards the cabin, pausing to knock powder off our boots by the front door. Tuck pushed it open, and a curvy woman with red, curly hair wearing an apron greeted us. "Oh, you poor things. Come in, come in. Get out of that dreadful snow."

Tuck pulled off his hat. "Good evening, ma'am. Would you happen to have any vacancies? We don't feel good about driving on these roads."

"Well, you shouldn't. I just heard they closed the pass because there was an avalanche."

I blanched. Geez, this was worse than I'd thought.

The woman ushered us forward. "You lucked out because I have one room left."

Tuck eyed me.

"It's fine," I whispered. I was a grown-up. I could handle sharing a bed with Tuck for a night without jumping him or performing another striptease. At least, I hoped.

"That would be great, ma'am."

The woman started down the hall. "Follow me. My name's Trudy, by the way. This is my place. Usually, we just serve breakfast. But given the storm, I've put sandwiches and drinks in everyone's mini-fridge and a whole lot of snacks. There'll be something warm in the morning."

I hurried to keep up with her and Tuck. "Thank you so much, Trudy. I'm Jensen, and this is Tuck. You wouldn't happen to have a gift shop, would you? Somewhere I could get some fresh clothes? Something to sleep in?"

"No gift shop, honey, but I've got robes in the rooms, and if you leave your clothes in a bag outside your door, I'll have them freshly laundered by morning."

I paused next to Trudy as she stopped in front of a door. "That would be amazing."

"Of course, dear." She unlocked the door. "Here you go, home sweet home. I'll see you both tomorrow morning. Just give me a holler if you need anything else."

Trudy was already headed back down the hall before I had a chance to make it through the doorway. When I did, I gasped.

Tuck let out a snorted chuckle. "Think she likes flowers?"

I'd never seen anything like it. Some form of flower adorned every surface in the room. The wallpaper, the bedding, hell, even the mini-fridge was covered. "At least it looks clean."

"Can't have her shrine to flowers getting dirty." He opened the mini-fridge. "Fridge's stocked. You want to hop in the shower?"

I glanced at a phone by the queen-sized bed. "I need to call my parents. You can go first."

Tuck nodded and headed for the bathroom. I picked up the phone and began to dial. By the time the water shut off, I had assured my parents that we were fine and would keep them updated when we could.

The bathroom door opened, and steam billowed out. "It's all yours." Tuck emerged wearing a fluffy white robe. "There's a bag on the floor for clothes."

I swallowed. Hard. "Okay." My voice cracked on the second syllable.

"Noah okay?"

"He's fine. My parents are worried but glad we found somewhere safe to stay."

Tuck gestured towards the fireplace in the corner with wood

stocked beside it. "Even if the power gets knocked out, we'll be fine."

I nodded. "I'm going to get clean." I darted past him and into the safety of the bathroom. A wet and naked Tuck was not what my sex-deprived self needed. He was my friend. Probably the best one I had. I needed to keep him in that box. It was safe. I quickly shed my clothes, stuffing them into the laundry bag, and then stepped under the spray. The hot water was everything I needed in this world.

I took my time washing up and even gave my hair a cursory blow-dry before steeling myself to step back into the room. *Get ahold of yourself, Jensen. He's just a good-looking man. You've re-sisted making a total fool of yourself in front of him for most of your life.*

I pulled open the door and made a beeline for the hall to set our laundry outside. I could sense that Tuck was on the bed, but I couldn't get myself to look quite yet. I dropped the laundry on the floor and retreated back inside the room. Turning, I took in Tuck. He was sprawled cozily as could be across the mattress, a beer on his nightstand, and a paperback in hand.

My gaze caught on the book. My brows rose. A shirtless man in a kilt graced the cover. "Interesting reading material you've got there."

"There weren't a lot of options, but at least with this one, I know I'll get sex." He patted the bed next to him. I crossed the room and settled myself against the pillows. He handed me the book. "Want to read aloud to me?"

I took the paperback from his hand and smacked him with it.

"Oh, you've done it now. You've insulted Kiernan and Marion's love, prepare to go down." Tuck went straight for my ticklish sides. I let out a peal of laughter but did my best to bite it back since I knew the other rooms were occupied. I wiggled and squirmed, trying to escape until Tuck stilled.

His body was pressed flush against mine, his lips a breath away, and I suddenly became aware of something long and hard pressed against my inner thigh. I sucked in air. Before I had a chance to tell myself it was a monumentally stupid idea, I closed the distance between us.

My mouth met his in a bruising kiss. It wasn't pretty or graceful. It was pure need. Tongues dueled. Teeth caught on lips. I pressed myself into him, my thighs clenching.

Tuck pulled back on a gasp. "I can't." He stared down into my eyes, his hand coming up to cup my face, not looking away. My heart hammered against my ribs. "Oh, fuck it." He slammed his mouth down on mine. His tongue darted in, massaging my own. His teeth caught my lower lip with a tug, and I groaned.

Tuck's hand darted to the tie on my robe, pulling it free. The air seemed to almost sting my overly sensitized skin, my nipples puckering even tighter. "Fuck, you're so damn beautiful." Tuck's words caught me off guard as he palmed a breast in one hand before ducking down to suck my nipple into his mouth.

I bowed off the bed. It was as if there were a direct line from my nipple to my clit, and I had to squeeze my legs together to try and get some relief. "Tuck, I need you inside me. Now."

He came off my breast with a pop. "Now?"

I nodded furiously. "Now."

"Shit. Condoms." He pulled open the flowered nightstand drawers and came back with a strip of condoms. "Apparently, Trudy is passionate about two things. Flowers and safe sex."

I pulled the strip of condoms out of his hand and tore one off. "They're good things to be passionate about."

"Can't argue with you there."

I tore at the little metallic square as Tuck unbelted his robe. As he shucked it, I gasped. I'd been with all of two men in my life, so it wasn't like I had a lot to compare Tuck to, but he was huge. Massive and beautiful. I swear I could've stared at him all night if I hadn't been dying to get him inside me.

His bronzed skin seemed to shimmer in the low light of the room, stretched tautly over broad shoulders and lean, sculpted muscles. And that V... I'd sworn those things were fake. But, nope. Here was one—live, and in person. I wanted to trace it with my tongue.

Tuck's dick twitched, and I startled. He chuckled. "You stare at it like that, there's only going to be one reaction."

I nodded, fumbling with the condom. Tuck stilled my shaking fingers, helping me roll it on. "Are you sure, J? We can stop."

Our gazes locked. It might end up being yet another thing that I added to my list of colossal mistakes, but I was sure of one thing. "I need this."

Tuck nodded, taking my mouth in a slow kiss, ratcheting up the heat that seemed to flow through my veins. My legs encircled his hips, and his tip bumped my opening. Tuck eased in. So damn slowly, I wanted to cry. I sucked in a breath as he fully seated himself in me.

Tuck brushed the hair away from my face. "You okay?"

I nodded but kept my eyes squeezed closed. "Just. Give me. A minute."

"Got all the time in the world." Tuck's hand found my breast and began to play. Teasing, rolling, pinching my nipple in an ever-changing pattern of caresses. My body started to melt, my muscles easing. Any hint of pain I felt turned to molten heat.

"Move. You can move."

Tuck pressed his lips to my temple. "You sure?"

"Yes, dear God, please just move."

He chuckled as he began to ease in and out of me. Small movements at first. I urged him on, my heels digging into his muscled ass, my fingertips gripping onto those incredible shoulders.

Tuck picked up speed, his thrusts becoming faster, deeper. I arched back into the bed, letting out a cross between a moan and a plea, the cord inside me tightening. Tuck reached between our bodies and gave my clit a single strum. That was all it took. That rough fingertip against that tight bundle of nerves sent me right over the edge.

CHAPTER
Fifteen

Tuck

I AWOKE TO A DELICIOUS BACKSIDE PRESSED UP AGAINST ME, my cock nestled perfectly between those cheeks. My hand palmed a breast so soft and malleable, I wanted to weep. The creature next to me arched back, letting out a little moan. My eyes fluttered open.

Fuck. No, *fuck* was not a strong enough word. The perfection I was wrapped around. The best sex of my life. It was a girl I should've looked at as a little sister. Fuck.

Jensen tilted her head to face me and gave a sleepy blink. It was fucking adorable. "Morning."

I released her breast and rolled to my back, my dick protesting the motion. "Morning."

Jensen maneuvered to her side, pulling the sheets up to her chin, the most adorable blush staining her cheeks. "So..."

I studied her face, trying to read what she might be thinking. I got nothing. "So."

Jensen nibbled on her bottom lip. "You regret this, don't you?"

"What? No." I sat up. "That was the best sex of my life. It

would be damn difficult for me to regret it." I just had no idea what it meant for us going forward. It was impossible to erase chemistry like that. Now that I'd tasted her skin...how the hell was I going to walk away?

Jensen gave a slow nod. "Okay..."

I watched as her mind seemed to go in circles as she reasoned through something. "Just tell me what you're thinking."

Jensen raised herself up on one arm, the sheets slipping down and revealing those perky little nipples that had my mouth watering. "I think we should keep doing this."

My head jerked. "What?"

She gestured between the two of us. "We should keep doing this." She waited, seeming to check to see if I was going to freak out on her. I said nothing. "I've never had sex that explosive." Her teeth rolled her bottom lip. "I want to keep having it."

Jensen sat up farther, the sheet dipping just a bit lower. "We have great chemistry. We respect each other. You're one of my best friends. There's no reason we can't have a sort of friends-with-benefits thing going on."

"J, I don't know..." The second the words left my lips, I wanted to steal them back. Experiencing the silk of her skin, the curve of her hips, how it felt to be buried deep inside her. How could I walk away, knowing I'd never feel that again?

Jensen broke in before I could say another word. "It'll be our secret. No judgement. No prying eyes. No pressure. Just two friends enjoying each other. Neither of us is looking for a relationship, so there's no risk."

She made it sound so simple. Maybe, just maybe I could work her out of my system. I couldn't have her forever, but I could have her for this brief moment in time. "It might work..."

Jensen smiled. "There's just one thing..."

I arched a brow in question.

"You can't sleep with anyone else while we're sleeping

together." Jensen's gaze held mine, challenging. "Do you think you can handle that?"

A wicked grin spread across my face. "Oh, I can handle it. But I'm going to need you often." If I had any prayer of getting my fill of this woman, I'd need to keep her locked in my bedroom twenty-three hours a day.

Jensen let the sheet fall all the way off her body. "I think that can be arranged…"

I was going to Hell. And I was going there after Walker murdered me when he found out what I was doing with his sister. But it would be worth it.

I watched as Jensen pulled on freshly-laundered jeans over her pert little ass. Oh, it would totally be worth it. "You about ready to go?"

The roads had been cleared enough that we'd be able to make the hour trek home. I just wasn't sure what life would look like when we got there. How would I be able to keep my hands off Jensen in front of everyone? Would they look at us and immediately know? An image of Walker socking me in the jaw as soon as we walked in the door flashed in my mind.

Jensen tugged on my shirt, pulling me flush against her. "What's with the grimace?"

I brushed my lips over hers. I would never get enough of her taste. "I'm imagining what your brother would do if he found out."

Now it was Jensen grimacing. "That's not going to happen. We'll be careful."

I let my hands trail down her body, squeezing her ass. "Super-secret sex. I like it."

Jensen rose up on her tiptoes and tugged on my lip with her teeth. "It makes things that much more exciting."

I brushed the hair back from her face, giving a stray strand a couple of light tugs. "That it does, Little J."

Jensen shoved at my chest, forcing me to release my hold on her. "If we are doing the dirty, you have to stop calling me *Little J.*"

I chuckled. "Doing the dirty?"

Her hands went to her hips. "You know what I mean. Having sex, bumping uglies, assault with a friendly weapon, boinking, buttering the biscuit, *fucking.*"

I let out a bark of laughter and pulled Jensen to me. "You've certainly got a wide and varied vocabulary, Miss Cole." I bent my head, running my tongue along the column of her neck. "But I think the word I like coming out of your mouth most is *fucking.*"

Jensen seemed to melt just a bit in my arms, and her words came out with a bit of a breathless quality to them. "Well, then. If we're fucking. You can't call me Little J."

I gave her pulse point a quick nip. "Then what should I call you?"

Jensen's hands fisted in my hair. "How about my name?"

I tugged on her earlobe with my teeth. "Nope. Everyone calls you Jensen. I want something just for me."

Her hands trailed down my back. "Fine, but you're going to have to think it up. And nothing dirty."

I chuckled. "Hmm…" I took her mouth in a slow kiss that soon turned hot. I pulled back, and her eyes blazed with that fire I'd been missing, the one that reminded me that she'd always have that bit of wildness to her. "I've got it."

She blinked up at me, annoyance filling her expression. "What?"

"Wilder."

Jensen's brow furrowed. "Wilder?"

"Yup." I pulled her back to me, wanting to soak up every second of her body pressed against mine before we had to reenter the real world. "You've always had a wildness to you. It's been missing for a while, but it's coming back. And when I light that match, your eyes burn with it."

Jensen's cheeks heated. I brushed the hair out of her face, kissing each temple and then her forehead. "Don't get embarrassed. It's the hottest thing I've ever seen."

"Wilder…" She let the word trail off her lips. "I like it. I think it's about time I had some wild back in my life."

CHAPTER
Sixteen

Jensen

THIRTY MORE MINUTES, AND MY DAY WOULD BE DONE. I could flip the sign in the window to *Closed*, clean and pack up, and go home. I really hoped no more customers came in tracking snow everywhere and creating more messes for me to clear. I wanted to feed my horses and cuddle my son and call it a night.

The bell above the door sounded, and I fought a grimace. As I lifted my head, my forced smile turned genuine. "I wasn't expecting to see you today."

"Couldn't stay away, Wilder. You're like a drug." Tuck swaggered towards me, those lean hips and muscular shoulders of his causing saliva to pool in my mouth.

We'd been stealing time everywhere we could these past two weeks. As the holidays approached, I knew those moments would get rarer, so I was thrilled to see him today. I chose to ignore the little flip my stomach did every time he walked into a room. It had to be a side effect of the amazing chemistry that sparked between us, nothing more.

Tuck rounded the counter and tugged me into the kitchen.

As soon as we were out of the line of sight from the front of the shop, his mouth was on mine, hot and demanding. That was the thing about Tuck, he never settled for less than my all.

His tongue delved into my mouth, stroking mine. His hands cupped my ass and lifted. I wrapped my legs around his hips, searching for just a bit more. The friction of him pressing against the seam of my jeans had me letting out a little moan.

The bell over the door sounded, and we froze. Two deer caught in a pair of headlights. I shook myself from the stupor Tuck's kisses seemed to put me in and smacked his back. "Let me down."

Tuck snapped into action, carefully lowering me to the floor. I started out to the front room, but he caught my arm. "Hold on, you're a little—" He reached up and smoothed down my hair.

I let out a startled laugh. *Whoops.* "Be right with you," I called. "Do I look presentable now?"

Tuck leaned forward and nipped my bottom lip. "You look too damn sexy for your own good."

I grinned and headed for the front. The smile fell from my face, and my steps faltered. *No. No. No.* This could not be happening. I blinked several times, hoping the person standing at the counter of my tea shop was not who I thought it was.

"Hey, J."

I felt Tuck's heat at my back, but not even that was a comfort. Because standing before me was the man who had torn my heart to smithereens and then spat on it. And there was only one reason he would be here. *Noah.*

"What are you doing here, Cody?"

I felt Tuck stiffen at my back. While he'd never met Cody, he certainly knew the name.

Cody gave me a gentle smile, the same one he'd given me so many times before. The smile that was a lie, but one I'd believed hook, line, and sinker. "Can we talk in private?"

"No."

Cody's eyes widened a fraction. "No?"

"No." That's right. I wasn't the same naïve girl he'd manipulated all those years ago, and it was best he learned that now. "Whatever you have to say to me, you can say it here and now. And then leave."

A flicker of annoyance flashed in his expression. "I don't even know this guy." He gestured to Tuck.

"Not my problem."

Cody let the hurt show, but I was better at spotting his lies these days and knew the emotion wasn't genuine. "You've changed."

I raised a single shoulder and then let it drop. "That's what happens when someone tells you they love you, that they can't wait to marry you, then knocks you up and takes off. Leaving nothing behind but the realization that the person you fell in love with never existed."

Cody took a step closer, and I felt Tuck move to my side. "That's not fair, J. I was a dumb kid. I made the worst mistake of my life, and I'm here to make it up to you. You and my son."

A roaring sound filled my ears, and the blood in my veins turned to fire. I was going to commit murder on the floor of my tea shop, and then Tuck would have to arrest me. "Guess what? I was a kid, too. *Four years* younger than you. And you left me all alone to deal with everything. And never once looked back." Tuck wrapped an arm around my shoulders, squeezing a few times.

Cody's gaze flicked to the movement and then traveled to Tuck. "Who are you?"

Tuck let out a menacing chuckle. "Not that it's any of your fucking business, but I'm a friend."

Cody let out a scoff. "Yeah, a friend trying to get in her pants."

My body went rigid. Tuck strode towards Cody. "It's time for you to leave, buddy."

Cody looked at me. "Are you seriously going to let him kick me out? We need to talk."

"There's nothing for us to talk about." I kept my shoulders squared and my spine straight, even though all I wanted to do was curl in on myself. Cody Ailes would never see me brought weak by his actions again.

Cody pinned me with a stare. "I'll be back. We're going to talk. I want to see my son."

CHAPTER
Seventeen

Tuck

RAGE FLOWED THROUGH ME, CAUSING MY BLOOD TO pulse in my veins in a staccato beat. That rage was accompanied by something foreign. Uncertainty. I turned to face Jensen. She gripped the counter behind the register, the wildfire in her eyes slowly dimming.

I strode towards her, pulling her into my arms and resting my chin on the top of her head. "You okay?"

She nodded against my chest. Her silence had my gut twisting.

I brushed my lips against her hair. "What can I do?"

"You're doing it." We stood there for I don't know how long before Jensen spoke again. "I'm scared."

Her words ripped at my skin. God, I wanted to drop-kick that guy into the next county. "We're gonna figure this out."

Jensen pulled back so she could look at me. "I have no idea what rights he has. What if he takes me to court?"

"No judge in their right mind would let that jackass have custody or even visitation rights for Noah." I ran a hand down the ridges of her spine. "But you need to see a lawyer now, as a preventative measure. And I'll go talk to Walker, see what we can dig up on Cody."

"Thank you." Jensen let her head fall against my chest. "I hate that, yet again, I'm bringing trouble into all of our lives."

I tipped up her chin so Jensen had to meet my eyes. "This is not your fault."

She pulled back and began to pace. "I fell for Cody's bullshit. Believed every lie and pretty story he told me. Same with Bryce. What is wrong with me that I can't see the truth?"

I caught Jensen's arm to still her movements. "You were involved with master manipulators. That has *nothing* to do with you. None of us saw Bryce for what he was. And you didn't bring him into our lives. He was already here." I let my gaze bore into hers. I needed her to hear the truth of my words.

Jensen met my stare. "You never liked Bryce."

I chuckled. "That had nothing to do with thinking he was a psychopath. I just didn't like that he always had eyes for you."

Jensen's eyes flared. "That's why?"

I brushed the hair out of her face. "That's why." I wasn't saying any more. This thing was temporary. Just until Jensen realized she could reach for more. A husband, a family. Things I wasn't equipped to give her. But I would soak up every damn moment I could get in the meantime.

I pressed my lips to one temple, then the other, and lastly her forehead, lingering there. "I'm going to go find Walker. I think he's still at the station. I want to get some basic information on Cody."

Jensen swallowed hard. "Okay. Walker's going to be pissed."

"He is. But not at you."

Jensen shrugged. "There are times I'm pretty sure he thinks I'm an idiot."

"Wilder, your brother has done so much stupid shit in his life, he'd be in no place to judge." I brushed my lips against hers.

"We're all just doing the best we can with the hand we've been dealt. He knows that."

Jensen let out a sigh. "Okay. I'm going to clean up here and then I have to go meet my mom and Noah."

I gave a strand of her hair a little tug. "You gonna be okay?"

She nodded. "You think you could come up with a reason to stop by later?"

An invisible fist tightened around my chest, the sensation toeing the line between pleasure and pain. "I think I can do that."

"Thank you."

I brushed my lips against hers quickly and then headed for the door. "I'll call you after I talk with Walker."

I took off down the street, not stopping to engage in conversation with anyone. I made the five-block trek to the police station in record time. Jogging up the steps, I pushed open the door. A young officer named Greg greeted me.

"Walker in?"

Greg must've read the seriousness in my tone because he just pointed to Walker's office. I strode in that direction, giving Walker's door two quick raps.

"Come in."

I pushed open the door to find Walker at his desk, bent over paperwork. "Walk, we've got a problem."

The paperwork was immediately forgotten. "What's going on?"

I shut the door behind me. "Cody showed up at the Tea Kettle today."

Walker shot up from his chair. "What? Why didn't Jensen call me?"

I raised a hand. "Calm down. She didn't call you because he just showed. I happened to be there, which is why I just dragged my ass over here to tell you in person."

Walker's jaw worked. "What did that asshole want?"

My hands fisted. "He said he came to make amends. He wants to see Noah."

"Like hell! He's not getting within twenty feet of my nephew."

I sank into one of the chairs in front of Walker's desk. "J pretty much said the same thing, but she's freaked. We need to get her a lawyer, and we need to look into Cody."

Walker pulled his chair back and sat, waking up his computer. "You're right. She should've had his rights terminated a long time ago." He began typing on his keyboard.

"We need to get the best lawyer we can on this now."

Walker nodded. "I know someone. I'll call him after I finish this search."

My brow rose. "You abusing police resources, Deputy Chief Cole?"

"Oh, fuck off. Like you wouldn't do the same."

Walker was right. I'd do anything for Jensen. I didn't care who stood in my way. I would keep her and Noah safe and happy.

Walker began typing. "I never liked that asshole. From the first moment I met him, I knew he'd be trouble."

My hands tightened around the armrests of the chair. "What vibe did you get off him back in the day?" I needed to know if we were dealing with someone who was simply a prick, or if this was more than that. Darker.

Walker paused in his typing and looked up to meet my eyes. "He was slimy. Everything about him was too smooth. Too perfect. And he had J so far under his spell, it was scary."

The chair creaked as my hands fisted even tighter. Walker went back to typing. My gut roiled. What if Cody could get Jensen under his spell again?

"This is interesting." Walker's eyes scanned the computer screen.

I leaned forward in my chair. "What?"

Walker hit a couple of keys. "Cody Ailes has had a house

foreclosed and two vehicles repossessed, all in the last three months."

My gut churned. "He know J comes from money?"

Walker looked up from the computer. "You know how my parents are, they keep that pretty close to the vest and never spoiled us growing up. I don't think he would've known in college."

My grip on the chair tightened. "But he could've found out since."

"Yes, he could."

CHAPTER
Eighteen

Jensen

"Mooooooooom, stop hugging me so much." Noah squirmed free of my hold to bring his plate to the sink.

I watched as he stepped up on the stool we'd painted together so that he could rinse off his plate before putting it in the dishwasher. The top of the step had the crest from Captain America's shield. I'd wanted to curse when Noah had said that was how he wanted to decorate it. I had been thinking more along the lines of paint splatters and handprints.

I'd spent an entire evening studying the dang design and tracing it onto the stool so that Noah and I could paint it the next day. I'd thought it would be something fun that would get him excited about chores, washing his dishes, helping me prep meals. I fought the tears that wanted to fill my eyes when I realized he wouldn't need the step much longer. My boy was growing like a weed.

I twisted a kitchen towel in my hands. Part of me wondered if I should say something to Noah about Cody being in town. To warn him. Images flashed in my mind of Cody approaching us on the street before I'd had a chance to tell Noah anything.

No. I would sort this out first. Figure out what Cody was after before I told Noah anything. If Cody stayed around and really did want a relationship with Noah, *maybe* I would consider supervised visits. Guilt swamped me. Every time I thought I'd figured out what the right thing to do was, my mind flip-flopped. Cody may have been a first-class asshole to me, but what if he truly was here to make amends and build a relationship with his son?

I had absolutely no perspective when it came to Cody Ailes. So, I planned to take the advice my dad had always given me: *Hope for the best but prepare for the worst.* And preparing for the worst meant talking to the lawyer Walker had sent me the name of as soon as possible.

The front door opened, and Walker appeared, followed closely by Tuck. I hated that all I wanted to do was run to Tuck and have him wrap his arms around me and tell me that everything would be okay. I detested that weakness I felt within me. I loathed that Cody's return had me questioning every move I made, especially when it came to Tuck.

"Uncle Walker! Tuck! I gotta show you what we learned in karate yesterday. It's so cool!" Noah abandoned his dishes and went running for the guys.

Walker hung up his coat on a hook with one hand and caught Noah in a hug with the other. "I'd love to see it. Why don't you show me while Tuck talks to your mom about some stuff, and then you can show us both."

Noah's little brows pulled together as if he were unsure, but then he nodded. "We can practice a demonstration for Mom and Tuck."

"Sounds like a plan, little man."

Tuck ruffled Noah's hair as he ran past, and soon Tuck and I were alone. "Hey, Wilder." He crossed to me, reaching up to give my neck a few gentle squeezes.

I stepped back out of his grasp, picking up a towel from the counter, and drying a dish.

Tuck edged closer. "What's wrong?"

I rubbed an invisible spot on the plate. "Oh, I don't know, maybe my douchebag ex showing up out of the blue, and me being terrified that he's going to try and take my kid away from me?"

Tuck was silent for a moment as I put the dish in a cabinet. "J, it's going to be okay. We'll figure this out." He reached out, trying to pull me to him, but I stepped out of his hold again. "What the hell, Wilder?"

Tears burned the backs of my eyes. "I can't."

That muscle in Tuck's cheek ticked. "Want to tell me why not?"

My eyes began to fill. "I don't trust myself."

Tuck's brow furrowed. "What do you mean?"

"I've only ever made horrible decisions when it comes to men. What if you're just one more in a line of bad choices?"

Tuck's expression gentled. "I probably am."

"Are you serious?"

He eased forward, slowly reaching out and giving me all the time in the world to stop him, but I didn't. Tuck wrapped his arms around me. "We might end up regretting this. It might be the *wrong* choice, whatever that means. But if we stop taking risks, we stop living. I don't want that for you. And I sure as hell don't want that for myself."

My body seemed to deflate at his words. "I hate this. I feel like my mind is playing tricks on me, and I don't know how to stop it."

Tuck brushed his lips against my hair. "It's just going to take time. You'll start to hear that voice inside again, but you're the only one who can take the steps needed to act on whatever it's telling you."

I started to nod, but a peal of laughter from the living room had us jumping apart. Walker and Noah were just fifteen feet away. Tuck and I had to be more careful.

Tuck gave me a sheepish smile. "You got any coffee? We can sit while we talk."

I nodded and poured him a cup while I made a chamomile tea for myself. We sat, and Tuck stirred his coffee. I let out an exasperated sigh. "Just tell me already. You sitting there in silence is just making things worse."

Tuck stopped stirring. "There's not a ton to tell just yet. What we do know is that Cody won't be paying child support anytime soon. He's leveraged up to his eyeballs."

The hand on my teacup tightened. "I wouldn't take his money even if he offered it."

Tuck took a sip of his coffee. "You should ask your lawyer what the best course of action is if he offers. I think the fact that he's never paid a dime over the last nine years of Noah's life will play in your favor if this ends up in court."

My hand began to shake, rattling the teacup on its saucer. I set it down on the table. "Maybe I'll get lucky, and he'll get bored and leave. Or meet some bimbo tourist and follow her out of town."

Tuck reached under the table and gave my thigh a squeeze. "I'll hope for that, but in the meantime, I want you to be cautious."

I nodded. "I already planned to fill in Noah's school tomorrow just in case. And I had Walker tell my parents and Grams."

A small grin tipped Tuck's lips. "And how'd ol' Irma take things?"

I let out a snort of laughter. "She called me up and asked when we were going huntin' for assholes. Said she's got a spot on her wall picked for his head. And I got the impression she was talking about the head down south."

Tuck spewed coffee across the table. I handed him napkins

and rose for paper towels. Tuck mopped up the mess. "Hell, remind me not to cross that woman."

I smiled at the thought of what might happen if my grandmother found Cody. It was a good thing she no longer had a driver's license. The smile slipped from my face. "My stomach's in knots over all this."

Tuck pulled me back down into the seat next to him. "That's understandable. But you're not alone."

I let my fingers twine with Tuck's under the table. "I know I'm not." I paused, just taking a moment to soak up the easy affection in his gaze. "I wish you could stay tonight," I whispered.

"I wish I could, too. Fuck, do I wish that."

I rubbed at my eyes as I lifted my cup off the counter and took another sip of my green tea. This shift felt like it would never end. My nightmares were back, and my sleep was paying the price. It wasn't until the dreams returned that I realized they'd left in the first place. Since Tuck and I had gotten together, my night terrors had been nearly nonexistent. Until last night.

The dream had started innocently enough. Noah and I playing tag in the field behind our guest house. As he ran, escaping my grasp, Cody showed up. He threw Noah over his shoulder and ran for his car. I chased after them, but the harder I pushed my muscles, the slower I went. And just as I reached the fence, Bryce appeared, long, gleaming knife in hand.

I'd woken in a cold sweat. After taking a shower so long the hot water had run out, I didn't chance sleep a second time.

I jolted at the jingling of the bell over the door. It was a miracle I could even hear it over the sound of the old men bickering with each other over their bridge game. I forced a smile as I lifted my gaze to greet the customer. The grin fell from my lips, as did my desire to issue a greeting.

Cody stood across from me with a bouquet of flowers and a gift bag in his hand. "Just hear me out before you kick me to the curb."

I ground my teeth together. "You have sixty seconds."

"I'm sorry about yesterday. I mean, I'm sorry for a lot more than that, but let's start with yesterday." He set the bag and the flowers down on the counter. "I don't always handle it well when other people know what a mess I've made of my life, and I didn't know that guy who was here, and things just spiraled."

I said nothing. I understood where Cody was coming from, but there was so much more water covering that bridge.

"The flowers are an apology to you for yesterday. And the bag is stuff for Noah. You don't even have to tell him it's from me."

"I won't." The comment slipped from my lips before I could curtail my inner bitch. I took a deep breath. "I'm not saying that because I'm evil. I'm saying it because I have no idea how long you're planning to stick around, and I won't subject my son to having someone in his life who's just going to abandon him all over again."

Cody's jaw clenched. "I'm here for as long as it takes."

I threw my hands up. "And then what? You go back to wherever it is you live now?"

"Well, I was thinking about maybe moving to Sutter Lake. See if I could find work here."

My brow arched. "Really?"

"Really. I'm serious about being a part of Noah's life." His eyes locked with mine, a familiar look in them. "And yours."

My blood began to boil. "Oh, no, you don't. The only way I factor into this equation is as Noah's mother. Other than that, I don't exist for you."

A muscle ticked in Cody's jaw. The one that meant he was two seconds away from losing his shit. "Don't you think Noah deserves a chance to have a two-parent home? Most single moms would kill for that opportunity."

"You need to leave. Listening to the bullshit falling out of your mouth is pissing me off."

"Everything okay over here, Jensen?" I hadn't even noticed that the bridge game had stopped and that Arthur now stood, holding the cane he used for stability in snowy weather like he might use it as a weapon.

"Everything's fine, Arthur. This gentleman was just leaving." I gave Cody a pointed look.

His shoulders slumped. "I'm sorry. That didn't come out right. But I'll call you, and we can talk at a more appropriate time."

I shook my head as Cody left. The *appropriate time* would be a quarter till never.

Arthur shuffled closer to the counter. "Who was that guy?"

I rubbed my temples. "One of my many mistakes come back to haunt me."

CHAPTER
Nineteen

Tuck

"THANKS FOR LETTING ME KNOW." I TAPPED END ON my phone's screen and opened the door of my truck. A ranger had found another dead mustang. I gripped the phone tighter. Between some psycho hunting down these peaceful creatures for no good reason, and Jensen's ex showing up out of the blue and putting her through the wringer, I was about to snap.

I took a deep breath, letting the cold air ease my temper. I wasn't going to let anything ruin this day. I was taking Noah and my girl sledding. But…Jensen wasn't mine. Not really. I was only stealing her for this brief moment in time. But when Cody had shown up at the Kettle the other day, I'd wanted to claim her as mine. In every way possible.

I shook those thoughts from my head as the front door opened, and Noah shot through it, going as fast as his little snow-suit-covered legs would allow.

"Tuck! I've got the two-seater sled. Will you go on it with me?"

I lifted him high in the air as he reached me. "You got it, little man."

Jensen shut the door, locking it behind her. "We'll need to take my SUV. Do you want to drive? Or do you want me to?"

I inclined my head towards my vehicle. "We can take my truck."

Jensen shook her head. "Noah still needs his booster seat—" Her words cut off as she took in the backseat of the cab of my truck. "You got a booster seat?" Was it just the glare of the sun, or were her eyes a little bit misty?

I shrugged. "I've been meaning to get one so it's easier for me and the little man to have our hang sessions."

"Yes!" Noah cheered, shooting his little fist into the air.

I pulled open the back door, and Noah hopped up.

Jensen crossed to me, getting close but not touching. "Thank you."

I fisted my hands, wanting so badly to reach out and brush the hair back from her face. "It's no big thing. I really have been meaning to get one." Jensen nodded. "So, where's this infamous sled Noah's talking about?"

Jensen gestured to her SUV, and I jogged over to grab the inflatable sled. The thing was as tall as I was. Thankfully, I had the cover on my truck, and there was plenty of room in the bed.

As we drove to the hill on the border between my family's ranch and the Coles', the same one Jensen, Walker, and I had spent countless winter days on, Noah chattered nonstop. He told me about all the moves he was learning in karate, the practice book of guitar lessons Liam had given him before leaving on tour, hell, the kid even detailed what he'd eaten for breakfast.

I looked over at Jensen, who was trying to stifle a laugh with a cough. I reached over and gave her thigh a squeeze. I wanted so badly to touch more of her. *All* of her. There was something about losing myself in Jensen that was unlike anything else I'd ever experienced.

I pulled to a stop at the bottom of the most perfect sledding hill to ever exist. And two seconds after I'd shut off the vehicle, Noah was out of his booster seat and climbing out of the truck.

I turned to Jensen. "Think he's excited?"

Jensen grinned. "He's been talking about nothing else for days. He adores you."

Warmth flooded my chest, followed quickly by a trickle of dread. I didn't want to lose this, what I had with Jensen and Noah, but this was all so very temporary. What happened when there was another man ready to take my place? My hands fisted as I tried to push the thoughts from my mind. "Can't leave the little man waiting." I slid out of the truck and circled around to pull out the sled.

"Hurry up! Let's go!" Noah tugged on my sleeve.

"You get a head start. I'll catch up."

That was all Noah needed to hear. He took off up the hill, going so fast he fell every few steps. Jensen's laugh sounded beside me. "Do you remember what it felt like for life to be that simple?"

I reached up and tucked a strand of hair behind her ear. "You've built a wonderful life for him, Wilder. The thing he worries about most right now is how quickly he can get to the top of that hill."

Jensen stamped her foot down a little harder than necessary in the snow. "I'm glad someone thinks so."

I grabbed J's arm to halt her progress. "What do you mean?"

"Ugh, nothing. It's just freaking Cody." She threw her arms wide, dislodging my hold. "He had the nerve to show up at my shop yesterday and insinuated that I was a bad mother if I didn't give him a shot. That Noah deserved to grow up in a home with both his parents. Well, that's what I had in mind for Noah, too, but Cody wanted no part of that. Now, it's too late."

My entire body locked. "Cody showed up at the Kettle yesterday?"

"Yup." Jensen chuckled. "I thought Arthur was going to smack him with his cane."

I clenched and flexed my fists. "And why didn't you call to tell me?"

Jensen's brow furrowed. "Why would I? I had it handled."

That familiar muscle in my cheek ticked. "Sure, why would you tell me anything?" I started back up the hill. She didn't owe me anything, we weren't together, we were simply bed buddies. For the first time in my life, I hated that. I wanted more. I wanted the right to call her mine. But that wasn't in the cards. Maybe we needed to end this thing now while we could still be friends.

"Tuck, wait." Jensen hurried behind me, but her shorter strides couldn't compete with mine. "Would you slow down, you giant behemoth?"

I wouldn't let her adorableness melt my resolve. I kept right on climbing.

"Seriously? Oh, shit!"

I turned just in time to see Jensen's arms wind-milling as she teetered backward. I dropped the sled and ran towards her, but I wasn't fast enough. She fell back and began rolling down the hill.

"Awesome! I'm gonna do that!" Noah shouted from the hilltop.

I jogged after Jensen, doing my best not to bite it myself. By the time I reached the bottom of the hill, Jensen was a human snow cone. She spluttered and coughed as she wiped snow away from her face.

"Are you okay?"

"I think so." She extended a hand. "Will you help me up?"

"Of course." I reached out to pull her to her feet when she gave my hand a swift, hard tug. I always forgot how strong Jensen was, but that lean frame packed a punch. Soon, I was lying face-first in a snow bank. "What the hell was that for?"

"That," she said, pelting more snow at me, "was for being a jackass and not stopping to explain what I did to piss you off."

My teeth ground together, but I said nothing.

Jensen let out an exasperated sigh. "I'm going to tell you the same thing that I tell Noah. Use your words."

I grunted.

"Well, that was a sound, so it's closer."

I tossed a pile of snow at her. "I wanted you to call me."

Jensen's forehead furrowed. "You wanted me to call you?"

"When some jackass shows up at your shop and gives you trouble? I want you to call me. Even if you have it handled, I still want you to call. I know we're just friends who are fooling around, but I want you to call."

Jensen's expression gentled. "Next time, I'll call."

My jaw dropped. "That's it? You just agree?"

A smile stretched over her face. "That's what happens when you're a big boy and use your words."

"That's it. You're going down." I dove for Jensen, heaping as much snow on her as I could. "Come on, Noah, we gotta get her."

Noah charged over from where he'd landed at the bottom of the hill and leapt on us both. As I held them both in my arms, this woman and her son, both giggling and shrieking, I knew one thing with absolute certainty. No matter how this thing ended...I was totally and completely fucked.

CHAPTER
Twenty

Jensen

I STUDIED THE GIRL WHO SAT ACROSS FROM ME AT ONE OF the tables near the front windows of the Kettle. She wasn't at all what I'd expected. She was young, maybe in her early twenties. While her clothes were just the slightest bit worn, there was an elegance to her that I couldn't quite explain.

I took a sip of my tea. "So, Kennedy, what brings you to Sutter Lake?"

Kennedy set down her cup. The movement came with practiced ease, her back remaining straight, and the cup not giving even the slightest rattle in the saucer. "To be honest, I needed a fresh start."

My brows rose. "There trouble that's going to try and follow you to this fresh start?"

A shadow passed over Kennedy's eyes, but she shook her head. "No, nothing like that. I had some family issues, and it was just time for me to stand on my own two feet."

I so understood the desire for that. "Do you have any experience working in a restaurant environment?"

Kennedy straightened the napkin in her lap, picking at a thread on the corner. "No. The only long-term work experience I have is interning at a law firm and some volunteer work. I served food at one of my volunteer jobs, but I've never prepared it. I promise I'm a hard worker and a quick learner."

I fought the sigh that wanted to surface. Teaching someone from the ground up would be a pain in the ass, but there was just something about this young woman that made me want to help her. It was the same tingle I'd gotten when Tessa had shown up looking for a job, and hiring her had been the best decision I'd ever made. "You found a place to live?"

Kennedy shook her head. "I'm staying at the motel for now until I'm sure I found a job. Then I'll start looking for somewhere to rent."

My face scrunched up. "That place is awful. You can't keep staying there."

Kennedy let out a light laugh. "It's not so bad."

"You should be scared of catching something incurable from those rooms."

Kennedy took another sip of her tea. "I did do a pretty thorough cleaning after I checked in."

I shook my head. "Well, at least there's that. How many hours a week are you looking to work?"

Her face brightened. "I'll take as many as you're willing to give."

"We start early here. Six a.m. to four p.m., usually. I'll pay you an hourly rate, and I've got a studio apartment upstairs that you can stay in if you'll help me with inventory each month." I freaking despised inventory.

Kennedy straightened even further in her seat. "Could I see the apartment?"

I stood from my chair. "Of course, come on."

I motioned to my mom, who was helping out behind the counter, telling her with gestures that I was taking Kennedy upstairs. She smiled. I led the way down the hall and up the back steps. Unclipping a keyring from my belt loop, I unlocked the door. When I pushed it open, Kennedy gasped.

"Oh my God. This is perfect."

I watched as she glided through the space, running a hand across the worn quilt at the end of the bed, peeking in the bathroom, checking out the kitchen.

"All utilities included. There's internet, but no TV."

Kennedy beamed at me. "That's amazing." Her smile faltered a bit. "There might be one problem."

Uh-oh. "What's that?"

She nibbled on her lip. "I have a dog. He's small," she rushed on. "Around twenty pounds. And very well behaved."

"Does he bark?" I loved dogs, but I couldn't have one barking all day when customers came into the shop to relax.

Kennedy shook her head. "He's deaf as a doornail so he wouldn't even know when there was something to bark at."

I chuckled. "Then he's welcome."

Kennedy jumped up, clapping her hands together and doing a little squeal. Then she threw her arms around me. "Thank you so much. This is amazing. I promise I will be the best employee you've ever had." She pulled back as if suddenly realizing that she was hugging someone who was basically a stranger. "Sorry, I'm just so damn excited." Her cheeks heated. "Eeeek, and I'm sorry for cursing."

I laughed harder. "Believe me, cursing around here is just fine. Just try not to do it in front of any customers. Or my nine-year-old."

Kennedy sobered. "Of course."

"Let's go downstairs and get your paperwork all filled out, and a copy of your driver's license made." I braced to see if she balked at that. I wasn't totally convinced that Kennedy wasn't running from *something*. But she just nodded and followed me down the stairs.

When the paperwork was done, I looked across the desk. "Do you need someone to help cart all your stuff over here?" Kennedy had arrived on a bicycle, and riding that thing in the snow and ice did not give me the warm and fuzzies for her.

"That would actually be great. I can get around fine walking or on my bike, but with my suitcase and Chuck, a car might be the safer bet."

My pen paused. "Chuck?"

Kennedy grinned. "My dog."

"Ahh. Well, I can come over with my SUV tomorrow afternoon, would that work?"

"That's perfect. And thank you again for the opportunity. I promise I won't let you down."

I walked Kennedy out, little worry lines creasing my forehead as I watched her get on her bike and head down Main Street.

"Is that girl riding a bike in this weather?" my mom asked from behind me.

I turned and crossed to the counter. "I don't think she has a car."

Worry lines that mirrored my own appeared on my mom's forehead. "You gave her the job, didn't you?"

I grinned. My mom and I were two peas in a pod on this subject. When someone needed a hand up, and we could help, there was just no way we could say no. "Of course, I did."

"Thank goodness."

I rounded the counter and wrapped an arm around my mom. "You might not be saying that for long. She's never worked in a restaurant setting before, I'm going to have to train her from the ground up."

My mom gave my waist a squeeze. "I'll help out as much as you need. It'll be worth it."

The bell over the door jingled, and Arthur pushed his way in, cane in hand. "It's as slippery as a buttery nipple out there."

"Arthur!" my mom chided.

I chuckled. "Come on in and get warm, old man."

Arthur crossed to the counter. "Who you callin' old, missy? I could take you any day of the week."

I grinned. "I know you could. So, you want your usual?"

"Yes, please." His face sobered. "How you holding up with the news?"

My brows pulled together. "What news?" My stomach flipped. Had someone found out that Cody was Noah's dad and that he was back in town?

Arthur's eyes widened a fraction. "I thought Tuck would've told you already. They found another horse dead yesterday morning."

My mind flashed back to the day with Tuck. He had to have known. Why hadn't he told me? My blood started to heat. He didn't want me knowing, that's why. "Thanks for letting me know. Do you have any idea where they found the mustang?"

Arthur's eyes grew sad. "Near Clintock's spot."

I nodded and turned to my mom. "I need to go check on something. Can you handle the shop for a few hours?"

"Sure, honey. But be careful."

"I will." I held up my cell. "I've got my phone if you need me. I'll be back by three."

I grabbed my coat and headed towards the feed store. It was just after lunch, and there was usually an influx of ranchers around that time. If Tuck wasn't going to keep me in the loop, I'd just have to find the information another way.

I pushed open the door to the feed store, a bell ringing as I did. A handful of men standing at the counter turned at the sound. The welcome was not the warmest. The feed store owner, Ken, and Bill were the only ones to give me polite smiles.

My gaze caught on a figure in the corner. There was something familiar in his form, his shoulders, the set of his jaw. Tuck's father. He grinned down at a woman who worked at the store before reaching out and giving her braid a teasing tug. My stomach pitched. He was certainly getting more brazen. *Poor Mrs. Harris.*

Ken cleared his throat as he set down the papers in his hand. "Miss Jensen, what can I help you with today?"

I straightened my shoulders and focused on the task at hand. "I'm actually just looking for a little information."

Ken's brow furrowed. "I'll help if I can."

I turned to the rest of the men at the counter. "I thought you might be able to help me. Do you know what happened to the mustang up by Clintock's spread?"

Tom, the man who had come into the Kettle with Bill a few weeks ago, snickered. "It got what it deserved."

My blood began to heat. But before I could say anything, Ken stepped in. "I won't have that kind of talk in my shop."

Tom made a rude sound. The rest of the men stayed silent.

Bill stepped forward. "Jensen, why don't I walk you to your car?"

I eyed him. "Sure." My SUV wasn't even here, but it didn't matter.

We headed back out the door. When we made it to the end of the block, Bill tugged lightly on my elbow to stop my progress. "I know you care about those horses, but you can't come into the feed store asking those kinds of questions. Those men,"—he looked back to the store—"they aren't going to respond well. And there's already enough tension."

I gritted my teeth. "I just want to know what's going on. And I'm not up there every day, you guys are."

Bill held up his hands. "I get that you're concerned. But see it from our perspective. Those horses hurt our ability to put food on the table for our families. And I'm sorry some of them have been killed, but I'm always going to prioritize my family over some four-legged creatures."

My shoulders slumped. I'd find no help or information here. "I'm sorry I put you in a bad position."

Bill gave me a gentle smile. "It's okay. And just so you know, I haven't seen anything suspicious going on up there. It truly might just be a couple of accidents."

I wished I could believe him. "Thanks anyway, Bill." I gave him a wave as I headed back towards the Kettle. Instead of heading inside like I should've, I made my way to the parking lot in the back. I hopped into my SUV and headed for the ranch.

I needed a few stolen minutes with my mustangs. Something to ease the pain in my chest. My vehicle bumped over the gravel road, but as I caught sight of my herd, a little of that pain eased.

I slipped from my SUV and walked to the fence line. Phoenix was the first to greet me. "Hey, girl." I pressed my forehead to hers, breathing in her scent and letting her spirit soothe me. "Just needed to see you guys."

I looked out at the pasture. The twenty or so mustangs huddled in groupings, some ran and played, others snacked on hay, and some just soaked up the bright sun on this cool winter day. I spotted Willow with two other mares, doing some sunbathing.

"You taking care of our new girl?"

Phoenix let out a little huff of air as if to say, "*of course.*"

I sighed, stroking Phoenix's neck. "I'm glad you're safe." I might not be able to protect my wild friends, but at least this herd was protected.

I slumped onto my bed. I was so tired, I could barely convince myself that crawling under the covers was vital, even on a winter night. I'd spent the rest of the afternoon catching up on baking tasks since I'd taken that unexpected hour off during the middle of the day. Then I'd spent all evening chasing Noah around. From karate to ice cream to dinner with my family and too many bedtime stories to count. I was exhausted.

My phone buzzed on my nightstand. I slapped the surface until I found it.

Tuck: *You up for a midnight rendezvous, Wilder? I could climb in your bedroom window.*

I was too tired to still be angry with Tuck. But it had melted into a pouting sort of hurt.

Me: *I'm spent. Already in bed actually and about to crash.*

It wasn't a lie. But it wasn't the whole truth either. I was aware that I was being a total hypocrite when I'd given Tuck so much shit the other day for not telling me what he was so upset about. But I needed time to process and figure out what I had a right to be pissed about and what I needed to give him the benefit of the doubt on.

Tuck: *Get some rest. Maybe you should ask your mom to open for you tomorrow so you can sleep in.*

My lips pressed together. This was part of the problem. Tuck was always so dang overprotective, in every sense of the word. There was one part of me that loved it, the feeling of being precious to someone. The other half of me hated it. That wilder part of me that was determined to stand on my own and not have anyone even dare to try and fence me in.

Me: *I'm fine. I just need a few hours' sleep.*

Tuck: *Stop being grouchy. I just don't want you to get so run down you get sick. Then I won't be able to kiss you all over.*

A little of my frustration melted.

Me: *It's about time you put your mouth to good use.*

Tuck: *Throw down the gauntlet like that, and I'll be over there in a flash, not giving a fuck if you don't get any sleep.*

My belly clenched. *No, Jensen. Not tonight. You need to figure out just what you're doing with this man.*

Me: *Go away. I'm trying to sleep like a good girl.*

Tuck: *You wouldn't know good if it bit you in the ass. And just to be clear, I like it that way...*

I chuckled and set my phone on the nightstand and turned out the light. It was mere minutes before sleep took me under, but it wasn't long before the dreams found me. This time, it wasn't just Bryce trying to kill me, it was a shadowy figure who was trying to kill me *and* the mustangs. And when I called out for Tuck, he never came...

CHAPTER
Twenty-One

Tuck

I POURED ANOTHER CUP OF CRAPPY BREAK-ROOM COFFEE. I'D slept for shit last night, and this afternoon was dragging. I couldn't put my finger on why exactly, but it seemed like Jensen had been blowing me off. That familiar muscle in my cheek ticked. It'd better not be because she was giving that fucker, Cody, a second shot. I would step aside if Jensen found a good man, but I wasn't stepping aside for some dipshit.

"Tuck, there you are. I've been looking everywhere for you." David appeared in the doorway to the break room, looking annoyed.

"Just grabbing some coffee, sir." I lifted my cup.

David crossed to the counter and picked through the assortment of pastries, getting his grubby fingers on all of them. "Well, I need to talk to you."

David's brother appeared in the doorway after him, giving me a sympathetic smile and a shake of his head. Bill was a local rancher, and nothing like his prickly sibling. I had no clue how the two had been raised in the same home. Bill was always helping other ranchers who were struggling and had a kind word for just about everyone.

I gave him a chin jerk and turned back to David. "What did you want to talk about?"

David picked up a donut, sniffed it, and then put it back on the platter. "That friend of yours has been nosing around our case."

My brow furrowed. "What friend, and what case?"

"You know, that girl. And the wild horse case, what other case would I be talking about?"

David could've been talking about one of a dozen, but I resisted the urge to say as much. However, there was only one girl he could mean. My jaw flexed.

Bill sighed and poured himself a cup of coffee. "David, she wasn't nosing around. I shouldn't have said anything. Jensen is just concerned."

David began spluttering. "Of course, you should have said something. We can't have civilians nosing around in Forest Service business."

I focused in on Bill. "What was Jensen doing?"

He ripped open a sugar packet, dumped it into the black coffee, and stirred. "She just stopped by the feed store, asking what we knew about the wild horse that had been killed. I wouldn't have said anything, but I was worried she might get herself into trouble. Most of the ranchers around here don't take too kindly to wild horse supporters getting in their business."

Bill cringed. "But looking at your face right now, maybe I should've worried about getting her into trouble with you." He set his mug down on the counter. "Don't be too hard on Jensen. Like I said, her heart's in the right place. Maybe just encourage her to leave the investigating up to you all."

I began to rub my temples. "I'll talk to her."

David huffed. "You better. Because if you don't, I'm arresting her for interfering with an investigation."

I gave a quick nod, dumped my mug in the sink, and headed for my truck. An arrest was the least of Jensen's worries.

I pushed open the door to the Kettle a little more forcefully than necessary, sending the bell over the door into a disjointed jangle. I strode towards the counter, not giving one shit that Jensen seemed to be teaching some willowy girl how to use the cash register. "We need to talk."

Jensen straightened. "Well, now, who's the grouchy one?"

"Kitchen. Now," I gritted out.

Jensen's hands went to her hips. "I don't take orders from you, mister."

I let out a growl of frustration.

Willowy girl's eyes jumped between Jensen and me like our exchange was a ping-pong match.

I didn't have time for this. I rounded the counter, bent, and threw Jensen over my shoulder.

She slapped at my back. "What the hell, Tuck?"

"Uh, Jensen, should I call the police?"

I shot a narrow-eyed stare at the woman who was now holding a cell phone in her hand. "Lady, I am the police." Or at least close enough.

I walked through the kitchen and out the back door into the parking lot and alley, Jensen hissing and spitting the whole way. I set her down with a thud, but she was lucky I didn't toss her into the snow bank. "What the hell were you thinking?"

"What the hell was *I* thinking? What about you? Have you lost your mind? This is my place of business." She shoved at my chest.

I didn't move an inch. "What the fuck were you thinking talking to those ranchers?"

Jensen blanched but recovered quickly. "I don't see what

business that is of yours. It's not like we share what we've found out about the mustangs with each other."

I ground my back teeth together. "I didn't want to ruin a perfectly nice day together."

"You wanted to shield me."

I ran a hand through my hair, tugging on the ends of the strands. "And so what if I did? Is it so awful that I want to protect you from horrible things?"

Jensen threw her arms wide. "Life is full of horrible things, Tuck. Are you going to protect me from all of them? Then I'll barely be living. Newsflash, bucko, you have to experience the bad so you appreciate the good. I don't want you to shield me. I want you to stand next to me."

All the wind went right out of my sails. For as long as I could remember, I'd always wanted to protect Jensen. And now that she was grown, standing on her own two feet, this wild warrior, I didn't know how to let her own that power and keep her safe at the same time.

She sucked in a breath. "God. I need to listen to my own advice."

My brow furrowed. "What do you mean?"

Jensen looked out at the fields and forest behind the shop. "I've been living this half-life. Too afraid to act for fear of screwing up again. I'm not doing it anymore." Her gaze met mine, the fire in her eyes burning bright. "I need you to help me live life to the fullest, not keep me from it."

I edged closer to Jensen. "I'm sorry."

A small smile pulled at her lips. "What was that?"

I grimaced. "I'm sorry. It's instinct. I want to stop anything that might cause you pain from ever reaching you."

She stepped forward, hands dipping into my coat pockets. "That's a sweet thought, but totally and completely unrealistic."

I grinned down at her. "Are you doubting my manly skills in protecting you against all things that go bump in the night?"

A shadow flickered across her face, but it was gone so fast, I wondered if I'd really seen it. "If anyone can do that, it'd be you." Her gaze met mine. "But I don't want you to."

I sighed, wrapping my arms around her and pulling her to me. "I can't promise I'll stop trying to protect you, that's just an impossibility. But I promise not to hide things from you that you deserve to know."

A bit of the rigidness went out of Jensen's muscles, and she burrowed into me. "That seems like a fair compromise for now." She tipped her head back so her chin rested on my chest. "Now, can we go back inside so you can apologize to my new employee for being so rude?"

I grinned. "Want to make out first?"

Jensen shoved at my chest. "Men! Always a one-track mind."

But I didn't think she minded too much because her lips met mine in a kiss that stayed with me for days.

CHAPTER
Twenty-Two

Jensen

A S I PULLED UP TO THE PASTURE, I SAW THAT THE HORSES were pacing, their movements almost agitated. When Phoenix spotted me as I slipped from my SUV, she let out a whinny and ran for the fence line.

I hurried over. "What's got everyone so upset?" I rubbed her neck as I scanned the fields and surrounding forests for any signs of predators. Wolves were rare but not unheard of now that their numbers were rising again. I didn't see a thing out of place.

Phoenix whinnied again. "It's all right, girl." I turned to scan where my property met up with the Harris ranch and froze. Scrawled on my storage barn was hideous graffiti. *You can't save them all.*

My stomach roiled. Some asshole had dirtied the safe place I had created for these mustangs, and myself. My gaze darted back to the herd, and I counted quickly. They were all there and unharmed. I jogged back to my SUV, unlocked my vehicle's gun safe, and pulled out my rifle. I walked through the snow towards the barn. As I got closer, I saw that the paint was dry. The person responsible was likely long gone.

I blew out a breath and pulled out my phone, tapping Tuck's name.

"What's up, Wilder?"

I clenched my phone a little tighter. "Someone vandalized my barn. I'm pretty sure it's the same person who's been killing the mustangs."

All levity left Tuck's voice. "I'm on my way. Get in your vehicle and lock the doors."

I scanned the area, still nothing. "Whoever did this is long gone. And I've got my rifle."

An engine turning over sounded across the line. "For once in your life, will you just do as I ask without being stubborn?"

I rolled my eyes heavenward. "Fine. But don't get used to it." I hit end and stomped back over to my SUV, climbing inside. I rested the rifle across my lap and waited. I kept scanning the area, hoping to catch a glimpse of something, but there was nothing to see.

It wasn't long before Tuck showed, his tires spitting gravel everywhere as he sped up the road. I rested the rifle back in the gun safe and slid out of my vehicle just as he pulled in. He jumped from his truck, fury barely contained on his face and came towards me in strides that ate up the distance.

Tuck pulled me into his arms with a ferocity that pushed all the air from my lungs. "Are you okay?"

"I'm fine. The only thing that isn't fine is my barn." I attempted to look over my shoulder to scowl at the offending scrawl, but Tuck held me firmly in place.

"Just give me a minute."

I'd give him eternity. Standing there safe in his arms, there was nowhere else I'd rather be.

Finally, Tuck released his hold. "Show me."

I led Tuck over to the barn and showed him the graffiti.

That little muscle in his cheek ticked, the one that told me he was really freaking pissed. "I have to call Walker. This is technically his jurisdiction. Which means, we'll probably end up working the case together." Tuck pulled out his phone, tapped a few keys, and was filling my brother in within seconds.

On one level, I was glad that the case would be getting some additional attention. On the other, my brother was going to freak. If there was one thing Tuck and Walker brought out in each other, it was their overprotectiveness for the women in their lives. I sighed.

Tuck slipped his phone into his back pocket. "You know why this happened, don't you?"

My brow furrowed. "What do you mean?"

Tuck's jaw flexed. "It happened because you've been nosing around. Obviously, whoever's doing this heard you were talking to ranchers, and that did not make them happy."

"That's a good thing, isn't it? It gives us more clues as to who it could be. It would have to be someone who works on one of those ranches or who's friends with someone who does..." My voice trailed off.

"Which is basically every person in Sutter Lake. Anyone could've heard about you asking questions."

My shoulders slumped. *Dammit.* I'd thought we had our first break.

Tuck must have seen the defeat in my expression because he pulled me to him, wrapping his arms around me and resting his chin on my head.

"Well, what is my son doing behind the barn with pretty little Miss Jensen?"

We startled apart, and I regained my composure a little quicker than Tuck. "Hi, Mr. Harris. I was just upset, and Tuck was comforting me."

Tuck's dad gave me a grin that looked like he'd meant for it to be charming, but it came across smarmy. "Comforting you, huh? Is that what they're calling it these days?"

Anger came off Tuck in waves, I could almost feel the heat of it. "Don't be a jackass. Look at her fucking barn."

Craig turned to check out the building, and his eyes widened. "Shit. When did this happen?"

Tuck cracked his knuckles. "Sometime last night. What are you doing out here?"

Craig gestured to his truck. "Riding the fence line. That's not breaking the law, is it?"

Tuck ignored his father's barb. "You see or hear anything suspicious last night?"

"No, officer, I did not."

Craig had always belittled Tuck's choice to go into law enforcement, and at this very moment, I wanted to sock him in the face for it. I stepped closer to Tuck, placing my hand on his back, trying to give him a show of silent support. Craig's gaze caught the movement, and he shot Tuck a shit-eating grin. He opened his mouth to speak, but the sound of tires squealing had him looking in another direction.

Walker's truck tore up the hill, gravel flying everywhere. I held up a hand for him to slow the hell down, and he did. The last thing I needed was my horses being freaked out more than they already were.

Walker jumped out of his truck and strode towards us. "Show me." The order was directed at Tuck, but I led the way around the barn. "Fucking hell." Walker turned to Craig. "You see or hear anything last night?"

Craig shook his head. "Not a thing."

Walker turned to me, pinning me with his best big-brother stare. "Why did you call Tuck and not me?"

I groaned and let my head tip back. "Maybe because this was his case?"

Walker scowled. "It might be his case, it might not, but I'm your damn brother and the deputy chief of police."

Tuck stepped between us. "Now, children, can't we all just get along?"

Craig chuckled. "Yeah, I'm sure Jensen had a *real* good reason for calling Tuck and not you."

I was going to murder Tuck's father right here and now. I wondered how that would impact the future of whatever it was that Tuck and I had going on. I also wondered if my brother would arrest me or help me try to cover up the crime. Either way, Craig Harris was getting my boot up his ass at the very least.

CHAPTER
Twenty-Three

Tuck

I WAS GOING TO MURDER MY FATHER. OR AT LEAST, DECK him. Why it had become his mission to try and ruin every good thing that came my way, I'd never know. But by now, the *why* didn't even matter.

I glanced in Walker's direction. He didn't seem to have picked up on the insinuation. He was still railing on Jensen about not calling him.

I moved my gaze back to my father. I hated that his blood flowed through my veins. That his DNA and guidance had a role in who I was as a man. My stare hardened. "I think it's time for you to get back to the ranch. This is a crime scene, and the techs will be here soon."

A muscle in his cheek ticked. The same one that flickered in mine when I was pissed. "Remember who your elders are, boy."

"I'm well aware. But on this playing field, I'm the one in charge. Why don't you go spend some time with Mom." It was a dig designed to piss him off, and it was successful.

My dad's face reddened, and he stormed off back to the pickup on the other side of the fence. Good riddance.

"Where's he going?" Walker asked.

I turned back to the siblings. "Said he had some work to do."

Walker nodded, but little worry lines appeared in Jensen's brow. "*You okay*?" she mouthed.

I gave a small nod. I wasn't, but there was nothing to do about that. "Walk, your guys on their way?"

He crouched by the barn, studying the footprints in the snow. "Yup. They should be here any minute."

I wrapped an arm around Jensen. She stiffened at first, but then relaxed against me, realizing this was something we'd always done. I gave her shoulder a few reassuring squeezes.

She sighed. "Nothing says 'Merry Christmas' like a spray-painted barn."

With Christmas and more snow only a few days away, it was unlikely that this would get remedied before the spring snow-melt. "I'm sorry, Wilder."

Walker pushed to his feet. "We'll get it fixed as soon as we can. But for now, I don't want you coming up here alone. Grab one of the hands to come with you."

Jensen stiffened. "I'm not going to let this creep change the way I do things."

Walker cursed under his breath. "Either you agree to bring someone, or I'll tell Dad to just assign someone to be up here waiting for you."

She glared at her brother. "You always were a little tattletale. You know snitches get stitches, right?"

Walker chuckled. "I could always throw you in lockup, that'd keep you safe."

I couldn't hold in my laugh.

Jensen turned her glare on me, as well as the end of her elbow. "You two deserve each other." She threw up her hands. "I'm going to work. Do me a favor and feed my horses while you're up here, would you?"

I nodded through my laughter but sobered when I caught sight of the angry letters on the side of the barn. "This guy could be fixated on her now, you know that?"

Walker ran a hand through his hair. "I know. I'm hoping it's just some pissed-off rancher and not the same person shooting the horses." He met my gaze, and his look said we both knew that was unlikely. "I don't want to freak her out, but I want her to be careful."

My hands fisted. "We'll just have to keep a closer eye. I'm gonna start doing a drive through the property at night. Maybe I'll catch sight of someone. Or, if they're watching, they'll see that someone's keeping an eye out."

Walker nodded. "I'll do the same. Between the two of us, we'll keep J safe."

I rolled to a stop outside Jensen's guest house. I knew Walker had told everyone that we'd both be doing drive-bys, so I wasn't going to get my ass accidentally shot. But he didn't know that I might be lingering.

Guilt filled my gut. Walker would lose it if he knew. My truck continued idling as I stared up at the bedroom windows. Noah's room was dark, but there was still a light on in Jensen's. I pulled my phone out of the cupholder.

Me: *Can I come in?*

Two minutes passed with no response. I put my truck in reverse when my phone buzzed.

Wilder: *You're here?*

Me: *Should I throw some pebbles at your window?*

Wilder: *Only if you're okay with me throwing some at your truck.*

I grinned down at my phone, starting to type out a reply when the front door opened. Light spilled out around Jensen, silhouetting her form in the doorway. A body clad in only a short robe. I jumped out of my truck and strode for the door. "What are you doing? You'll catch your death," I whispered.

Jensen straightened the towel turban on her head that I hadn't even noticed—her damn legs had been too much of a distraction. "Well, hello to you, too." Jensen did not whisper.

"Shh." I made a pointing motion to where Noah's room was overhead.

She laughed. "He's next door. He and Irma had a viewing of *The Karate Kid* so they could get ideas for the fight they're choreographing, and he fell asleep mid-movie. They figured they'd just keep him over there for the night."

I let out a chuckle. "Irma's doing a fight with Noah?"

"She's surprisingly limber for someone her age." Jensen studied my face. "How are you doing?"

As always, Jensen saw right through any facades I had in place. "I'm fine. I just needed to see you." I pulled her to me, resting my chin on her towel-covered head. I wasn't fine. Someone was killing the horses I loved, that crazy person now had their eyes on Jensen, and the run-ins with my dad were only getting worse.

Jensen placed a kiss on my pec. "I haven't seen your dad in a long time. Why didn't you tell me things had gotten worse?"

I sighed. "I don't have to deal with him often. I just feel bad for my mom."

Jensen wrapped her arms tighter around my waist. "I hate what he puts you both through. You know, I was mentally plotting his murder this morning."

I let out a bark of laughter. "I was, too."

I felt her grin against my chest. "What can I do?"

"You're doing it. Just being with you eases something in me."

Jensen stepped out of my hold. "Let's see if we can't do one better." Her fingers tugged at her robe's sash. It came loose. And without a word, she let the terrycloth fall to the floor.

CHAPTER
Twenty-Four

Jensen

COOL AIR RUSHED OVER MY BODY, THE HEAT HAVING been turned down for the night. My nipples beaded, the tightening causing a mirrored action in my core. But Tuck's eyes were molten heat as he glanced down the length of me. Each place his gaze touched seeming to spark.

Then he was on me. Lifting me, my legs wrapping around him. Tuck took the stairs two at a time as though I weighed nothing. He tossed me on the bed, and I landed with an "oomph," the towel coming free from my damp hair.

I scowled up at him. "Well, that wasn't very nice."

Tuck grinned at me, and the only word to describe the expression was *wicked*. He toed off his boots and began unbuttoning his shirt. "There's no time for nice. Not when you drop a robe like that."

I lay back against my array of pillows. "Then show me what's not nice."

That was all it took. Tuck shucked his pants so fast, I'd barely blinked before his body covered mine. His hands were in my hair, and his lips took mine in a bruising kiss. The movements were desperate, starving, as though the only thing that could ground him to this Earth was my body.

Tuck's lips trailed down my neck. The juxtaposition of the softness of his mouth and the sandpaper of his scruff sent a riot of sensations over my skin. My hands began to explore, relishing the feel of smooth flesh over tight muscle, the broadness of his shoulders, the way his silky hair slipped through my fingers.

I'd never get enough of him. That should've terrified me, but somehow, it didn't. I simply lost myself to the feeling of... everything.

Tuck's lips closed around my nipple. He played a symphony with the sensations he caused. First sucking gently, then pulling the bud deep into his mouth. His teeth giving a quick nip and then his tongue laving away the sting.

Everything inside me wound tighter as I began to pant. "Need you."

His head came away from my breast. "Now?"

"Now."

Tuck reached for a foil packet I hadn't even seen him toss on the bed. I watched in fascination as he rolled the condom over his tip and then down his length. God, he was beautiful.

Tuck settled himself between my legs, his gaze holding mine. Something unnamed passed between us. He held still for a moment, his tip just bumping my opening as he stared. It was as if he were trying to commit everything to memory. Burning it so deeply in his mind that it would never get out.

Something about that had me fighting the urge to cry. I reached up to cup his cheek, and he leaned into my hand. "Let me feel you," I whispered.

Tuck pressed his lips to my palm as he slowly pushed inside. My legs wrapped around him as I let out a little gasp. I still needed a moment to adjust. Tuck brushed his lips against mine as he gave me that time. His tongue swept in, caressing mine. A hand came to my breast, fingers toyed with my nipple. Soon, all I felt was heat.

My hips rose to meet his, encouraging without words. It was all he needed. Tuck began to move. Slowly at first, and then faster. Deeper. More. My back arched as I met his thrusts, my body seeming to move of its own accord. The rhythms, while different, complemented each other perfectly.

Everything inside me wound so tight, it was almost painful. I strained for what was just out of reach. Tuck's thrusts grew more frenzied. Almost animalistic. My nails dug into his back as I stretched to the breaking point.

My head dug back into the pillows, my spine arched, and the world came apart at the seams. Light danced behind my lids as my walls clamped down on Tuck. He cursed as he thrust one more time.

Tuck collapsed on me and then quickly rolled so that I was now on top. He twitched inside me, and I involuntarily clenched around him. Tuck grunted. "You're going to kill me, Wilder."

I grinned against his chest, damp with sweat. "It'd be a hell of a way to go, though."

Tuck chuckled, sending all sorts of sparks through my body. "Damn straight." He swept my hair back from my face. "I didn't hurt you, did I?"

Always worrying about me. "That was the best sex of my life."

Tuck's brow quirked. "Is that a no?"

"That's most definitely a no." I'd be tender for a day or two, but it was so worth it.

He kissed one temple, and then the other, and lastly, my forehead. God, I loved when he did that. "I gotta get rid of this condom."

I nodded and lifted myself off him, feeling a slight sting at the loss of him. I rolled to my back, watching him rise, muscles bunching and flexing, tanned skin that seemed to glow in the low light of the room. He turned for the bathroom, and I gasped.

Tuck spun around. "What's wrong?"

My hand covered my mouth. "Your back. I murdered your back."

Tuck smirked. "You murdered my back?"

I jumped off the bed, urging him into the bathroom. "Look!" I turned his body so that his back faced the mirror and pointed.

Instead of the horror I expected to see, Tuck grinned like a cat who got the canary. "You marked me."

On his back were deep, red scratches. I'd even broken the skin in a couple of places. "What the hell is wrong with me?"

Tuck's head snapped back around. "Not a goddamned thing." He pulled me to him and then cupped my face. "You lost yourself with me. I fucking love that. I did the same. I was so deep in that with you that I never wanted to come out. Not a thing you did hurt me. All it did was drive me higher." A small smile curved his mouth. "My Wilder." He brushed his lips against mine. "I like you just as you were meant to be. Wild and free."

I slumped into him. "You're sure?"

Tuck swept the hair out of my face. "Never been more sure about anything in my life."

"Can I at least clean those scrapes?"

"Oh, you can clean them, all right." He reached in and turned on the shower. "As long as I can return the favor." His gaze traveled over my body. "And let me tell you. I am very thorough."

"Merry Christmas Eve Eve," I called to Arthur as he headed out the door of the Kettle.

"You guys really get into Christmas around here, don't you?" Kennedy asked.

I grinned, looking around at the festively decorated space. I really didn't think much about it because we went all out every year. As soon as Thanksgiving passed, we were in full-on Christmas mode. Winter-themed cookies in the display case, little white lights hanging everywhere they could, and an array of vintage Santas decorating each table.

"My mom is big into pretty much every holiday, so I don't even think about it anymore. I just let her go to town and enjoy the end result. But I have to put it all away after New Year's."

Kennedy laughed. "I guess that's fair."

I paused in wiping down the counter. "Hey, do you have plans for Christmas Eve? Want to come over for dinner? We always have a big, crazy group, and it's super low-key."

Kennedy straightened from rearranging the bakery case. "I actually have plans, but thank you for inviting me. That is really kind of you."

I wondered what Kennedy could be doing since she'd just arrived in town a couple of weeks ago and didn't seem to know anyone yet. My nosy self couldn't resist asking. "What are you up to?"

Kennedy smoothed out invisible wrinkles on her apron. "I, um, I'm volunteering at the shelter."

Well, I was a shitty human. Here I was, planning to gorge myself on my mom's epic feast, and Kennedy would be spending her time helping others. "That's really kind of you."

She waved me off. "It's nothing, really. I wish I could do more."

"You know,"—I started wiping down the counters again—"we do those early morning orders tomorrow before we close at ten, and we always have leftovers. Why don't you take the extras with you to the shelter?"

Kennedy's expression brightened. "That would be amazing. I'd offer to help bake some extra, but I don't know if that's a good idea yet."

I chuckled. So far, Kennedy hadn't quite gotten the hang of the baking side of the business. Making drinks, serving tables, helping customers, in those, she was a rock star. But every time she had tried to bake something on her own, it had turned to disaster. "I think that's probably a good idea. I'll come in a little early and see if I can't add on a few more dozen cookies."

Kennedy shut the case and turned to face me. "You have a really good heart, Jensen."

Heat rose to my cheeks. "It's nothing. And I'm glad to help."

Kennedy was about to say something else when the bell over the door sounded. I bit my lip to fight the scowl that wanted to surface at the new arrival. Cody. And his arms were laden with presents. Had he not heard a word I'd said the last time he was here? Presents would not erase nine years of Noah without a father.

Cody wore a bright smile. "Hey, J. It's good to see you."

I said nothing. What could I say? It wasn't good to see him.

His smile faltered a little, but he pressed on. "I brought some presents for you and Noah."

I turned to Kennedy. "Can you man the register for a bit?"

Her gaze jumped from me to Cody and back again, trying to put the pieces together. "Of course."

I motioned for Cody to follow me to a back table. "We need to talk."

Cody eased himself into a chair. "I'm glad you think so, too."

I wasn't so sure he'd like what I had to say. "I filed to have your parental rights revoked." Cody's face reddened, but I held up a hand before he could speak. "Just hear me out. I need to protect Noah. I haven't seen you in a decade. I have no idea who you are now, and the man I knew all those years ago, I didn't end up respecting."

I grasped my knees and squeezed, hoping I was doing the right thing. "I'm willing to give you a shot. Supervised visitation.

If you prove that you're in this for the long haul. I'm sure you think I'm being a bitch, but the truth is, I don't give a damn. All I care about is protecting my son. And that means making sure you truly have his best interests at heart."

I was taking that step out in faith and trusting my gut. My intuition that said Cody had no real plans to stick around. I'd just have to wait him out. And if he proved me wrong, I'd gladly eat those words. But for now, I was doing all I could to protect Noah.

Cody's jaw worked. He didn't speak for a long moment. "I have his best interests at heart." His gaze met mine. "I want my family back."

I fought the urge to throw something at him. "You never had that family to begin with. You threw us away before we even had a chance to get started. But if you're serious, you can have a relationship with your son."

Cody held my stare. "I'm here for the long haul. And I'm not afraid of a fight." He rose from his chair. "You'll see."

I let my head tip back and bang into the wall. The man needed to catch a clue. I pulled out my phone, not wanting Tuck to somehow hear about this before I had the chance to tell him. I just hoped my sharing Cody's little visit didn't end with Tuck in lock-up for Christmas.

CHAPTER
Twenty-Five

Tuck

M Y MUSCLES WERE STRUNG SO TIGHTLY, ANY ONE OF them felt like they might snap at any moment. Each hour that passed seemed to string them tighter. Cody's stopping by the Kettle yet again had not put me in a good headspace, and then I'd had to face Christmas with my family. Each moment seemed to ratchet up the tension in the room another degree. I pushed back from the table.

"Are you sure you can't stay for lunch?" My mom asked the question with so much hope in her eyes, it almost killed me. But after a Christmas Eve and Christmas morning with my parents, I'd had about all I could take.

"I told the Coles I'd come by their place, so I need to get going. Thank you for an amazing breakfast." I rose from my chair and kissed her cheek.

My dad let out a snort of derision and took another sip of his bloody Mary. "Of course, he's heading over to the Coles. Can you say 'desperate,' son? Don't you know another family doesn't want you around on Christmas?"

"Craig," my mom pleaded.

I continued ignoring my dad. "Mom, you're welcome to come with me. I know Sarah would love to see you."

"She's staying here with me."

My gut twisted. "Why? So you can leave her alone when you go to the bar later? Nothing says Christmas like sleeping alone while your husband ties one on."

The sarcastic bite of my words had my dad charging to his feet, tipping over his chair and sending his bloody Mary spilling across the white tablecloth. "Goddammit! Now look what you've done. You always were more trouble than you were worth."

My mom started mopping up the spilled drink with her napkin. "Both of you, stop it right now!"

I did what I thought was best for everyone. I left.

Starting up my truck, I took off for the Cole Ranch. I was there in a matter of minutes but was in no state to go inside. So, I just sat there, clenching and unclenching my fists, trying to slow my breathing. *How had we gotten here?* My dad had always had some asshole in him, but today was a whole new level.

The entire scene had me searching through memories, wondering when things had taken a turn into irreparable. The cheating, the berating, it all seemed to get exponentially worse the more he drank. I had memories of when I was a child of him being a good father, but they just came farther and farther apart the older I got. Until they stopped altogether.

I couldn't be around him anymore. I couldn't even set foot in that house if there was a chance he would be there. It killed a little something inside me. Our family ranch held so many special memories for me. My grandfather teaching me to ride. Working the vegetable patch with my mom. Playing hide and seek with Walker and Jensen. Now, it was this dark and ominous place.

I let my head tip back against the headrest. I had to tell my mom the truth. Something in my gut told me it wouldn't make a difference, that it would only add to the pain she lived with daily, but I had to try. I just had to hope she could forgive me for keeping the secret for so long.

I hadn't meant to, but it had started when I was young. That muscle in my cheek ticked as I remembered my dad's words. *You keep this between us, son. If you don't, your mom will leave, and we'll be all alone.*

Who said that to their kid? A shitty human being, that's who. The years of keeping that secret as a child had turned into a weight I just couldn't seem to shed. So much fucking guilt.

I jerked as my passenger door opened, and Jensen slid inside. "You almost gave me a heart attack."

Worry etched her face. "You looked like you were thinking pretty hard there. Everything okay?"

"What do you think?"

Jensen reached over and linked her fingers with mine. "I think you've had to spend the past two days with your asshole of a dad and you're about ready to break some shit."

Her words brought a small smile to my face, but it didn't linger. "Will you go for a drive with me?"

"Of course." There was no hesitation. Just easy agreement. Anything she could do to ease my pain. She pulled out her phone and sent a text. "I told them we'd be back in a bit. Let's go."

I put the truck in reverse and then took off down the gravel drive. In minutes, we were off ranch property and out on winding country roads. Snowy fields flew by as we drove. No music, no chit-chat, just silence and that peace that comes from being with someone who knows all of you. The good and the bad.

I flashed back to the drives Jensen and I used to take after I got my license and she just needed to get away. When girls at school were pulling petty shit, or she'd gotten in a fight with her mom. She'd call, begging for me to get her out for an hour. We'd sit in silence like this until she was ready to talk.

The same went for me. Jensen had been the one to pick up on

what was going on with my dad first. She'd always had that little bit of extra perception about people. Animals, too. Irma would say that she'd passed her "psychic gift" on to Jensen, but Jensen was in denial about it. Whatever the reason, Jensen could always tell when I needed to get away from it all.

We would drive up to the horses, out to the lake, or sometimes, like now, just crisscross the county in circles until we worked out what we needed to. There was something about J's fingers interwoven with mine that added a whole new level of peace to the scenario. I traced circles on the back of her hand with my thumb. "He's getting worse."

Jensen said nothing, just let me go at my own pace.

"I don't think I can go back there. At some point, it's going to escalate to something neither of us can take back." I gripped the wheel a bit harder. "It almost did today."

"Do you have to? Go back, I mean. Can't your mom come to your place? She has to know this isn't a good situation for you to be in."

I let out a sound of frustration. "I don't know what she thinks." I hated that as time went on, I lost more and more respect for my mother. Because no matter what Dad did, it never seemed to warrant her leaving. It didn't change that I loved her, but I didn't like her all that much anymore. And that made me feel guilty as hell. Even more guilty because I hadn't told her the one thing that might push her over the edge to leaving.

Jensen squeezed my hand. "You're angry at her."

I released Jensen's hand and used mine to run through my hair. "Damn straight. And then I feel like a garbage human for being mad. I'm just losing patience with them both. They make each other miserable, so why the hell stay together? If they broke up, they'd at least have a shot at finding some happy, even if that happy was alone. Though for my dad, it would probably be with a harem of women."

Jensen twisted a strand of hair around her finger. "I think when you're used to life a certain way, even if that way is miserable, it takes a lot to break free of that. But they might be closer than you think."

We'd circled around Sutter Lake and were headed back through downtown. I pulled my truck into a park. "Do you think I should tell her?"

Jensen's hand squeezed mine. "I hate that you've been carrying the weight of that for so long." She stared up at me. "I would want to know. I'd also want to know that my husband had forced my son to keep that secret for so long. But I also think there's going to be fallout, and I hate that you might be the casualty."

I blew out a loud breath. "Fuck."

Jensen reached up and ran a hand through my hair. She began massaging my scalp, easing the tension away. "You'll know when the time is right."

My eyes slowly opened. "I hope you're right." I glanced around. The place was dead. I cupped Jensen's face in my hands and took her mouth in a long, slow kiss. I could've lost myself forever in her lips and died a happy man.

Reluctantly, I pulled back. "I've got a little something for you."

Jensen's face lit up. "What is it?"

I chuckled, reaching into my backseat and handing her a small box. "You'll have to open it to find out."

Jensen quickly untied the ribbon and opened the box. Her brow furrowed. "You got me a paintbrush?"

My chuckle deepened. "Well, I couldn't exactly wrap the present." I slipped my hand beneath the fall of her hair, giving her neck a few squeezes. "I know how much that graffiti on your barn has been pissing you off, so I painted over it yesterday."

She blinked rapidly. "You painted my barn?"

I nodded.

"You would've had to shovel snow away from the exterior walls. And it was ten degrees yesterday."

I shrugged.

Jensen launched herself at me. Her fingers dove into my hair, and her lips crashed down on mine.

When her hands slipped under my shirt, I had to pull back. "Jensen, we have to stop."

She nodded, breathing hard. "That is the most thoughtful gift anyone has ever given me."

I grinned. "I'll definitely be painting more things for you in the future."

Jensen smiled. "I have something for you, too. But it wasn't exactly something I could give you in front of my family..." She let her words trail off. "There's lace involved."

My dick jerked. Never in my life had a woman affected me the way Jensen did. "Wilder, you really are going to kill me one of these days."

Jensen laughed, but it cut off. "Shit."

"What?" I turned to see a figure walking away.

"I'm pretty sure that was Cody and that he just got an eyeful of us making out."

My head swung back around. "Fuck."

Jensen nibbled on her bottom lip. "I don't think that's going to make him very happy."

My hands itched to haul Jensen to me. "Tough shit."

One corner of her mouth quirked up. "Tough shit?"

I threaded my fingers through the hair at the base of her scalp, pulling her to me until her mouth was just a breath away from mine. "He can throw a hissy fit for all I care. This mouth." I swept my lips against hers. "It only belongs on one body."

Jensen's breath hitched. She closed the distance between us in a swift, hard movement, that fire in her flaring to life. Her hands fisted in my hair as she half hauled herself over the console.

I forced myself to pull away. "Jensen." Her name came out on a pant.

She sank back in her seat. "I know, I know. It would be a real bummer end to Christmas if my brother got a call that his sister and best friend had been arrested for indecent exposure."

I chuckled, but that niggling guilt settled in my gut. "So very true."

Jensen began worrying her lower lip again, her gaze traveling to where Cody had disappeared.

I linked my fingers with hers. "You think he's going to make trouble for us?"

"I'm not sure…"

CHAPTER
Twenty-six

Jensen

"**H**OW ARE YOU DOING?"

For once, the question didn't frustrate me like it normally did. Usually, I would've interpreted it as pity. But now, I could hear it for what it truly was, care and concern. I looked up at Taylor as I handed her the change for her tea and scone. "I'm actually doing pretty well."

It was true. Considering that I was waiting for the other shoe to drop when it came to Cody, I had a surprisingly cheery outlook on it all. Maybe it was the shift in the weather. The two days of sixty-degree temperatures had the sun shining and the snow melting. The horses all had an extra burst of energy, along with room to run and play.

Or maybe it was Tuck. I couldn't help the little smile that came to my lips. He made me happy. And instead of letting that freak me the hell out, I was just going to roll with it.

Taylor took her change. "What's that look about?"

My body gave a little jolt. "What look?"

Taylor grinned, pointing to my face and drawing a little circle in the air. "The one that makes you look like the cat that got the cream. Do you have a man in your life, Jensen?"

This was the thing about good friends, they paid attention. I pressed my lips together.

Kennedy leaned on the counter. "This I have to hear."

My palms started to sweat. Kennedy had seen Tuck in here more than a few times. "There's no one. I just think I'm finally starting to get out of my funk."

Taylor tapped the top of her to-go cup. "I'm not so sure I believe that. But I'll let you have that play for now." She headed for the door, but it opened before she could reach it. "Tuck, what're you doing here?"

He grinned at Taylor. "Good morning, gorgeous. Just getting myself some snacks." He patted his stomach. "And I might see if I can get that friend of yours to play hooky with me today."

Taylor looked from Tuck to me and back again, her eyes dancing. "I think that's a great idea. Don't take no for an answer."

I let out a breath I hadn't realized I'd been holding when Taylor finally headed out. The last thing I needed was her chatting away to Walker about Tuck and me.

Tuck sauntered up to the counter. "Wilder, run away with me."

I laughed. "Apparently, the warm weather is getting to everyone."

He placed his hand on the counter, his fingertips just touching mine. "I have the day off, and there's somewhere I want to take you."

Kennedy bumped my hip. "Go."

I looked up at her. "Are you sure? I haven't left you alone yet."

"The baking is done. Taylor was the last of the morning rush. Your mom's coming in at two." Kennedy ticked each point off on her fingers. "I'll be fine. *Go.*" She eyed Tuck up and down. "I would."

Tuck chuckled. "The girl has a point."

My stomach gave a little flip. "Okay. Thank you. My cell

number and my mom's are on the board. If you get slammed, call her, and she can come in early."

Kennedy grinned hugely. "Have fun, you two."

I rounded the counter. "What do I need for where you're taking me?"

Tuck looked me up and down, not in a sexual way, more assessing. "Can you hike in that?"

That was one of the perks of working in such a casual environment. I was wearing jeans, boots that would support a ten-mile trek, and a long-sleeved gray tee. "Yup."

"It's sunny, but it's still cold. You got a coat?"

The overprotectiveness would never end. I smiled and pointed to my puffy jacket hanging by the door. "Good to go."

Tuck grabbed the coat and slipped it over my shoulders. "Don't want you catching a cold." He leaned in closer, his lips brushing the shell of my ear. "I need to be able to kiss you whenever I want."

"Tuck." The single word was meant to be a warning, but it came out way too breathily for that.

"Yes?" His tone was playful with an edge that hinted at mocking.

I shoved at his chest. "You don't fight fair."

"Never said I would."

The drive was quiet, like so many of our drives were. Just the easy peace of being together. It soothed my frayed edges in a way nothing else could.

It didn't take long for me to figure out where we were headed. As we drove up the mountain pass, I was relieved to see that the snow from the blizzard a few weeks ago had melted, and though more snow would come, for now, the bitter cold had given us and the mustangs a break.

Tuck pulled to the side of the road. We'd stopped at a spot I hadn't been to before. It was easy to forget just how vast the forest was. So many unexplored nooks and crannies, so many wondrous sights to take in.

Tuck reached over and gave a strand of my hair a few gentle tugs. "You ready to go?"

I leaned across the console. "I don't know where we're going, so how can I know if I'm ready or not?"

Tuck gave me one of his signature grins that made my insides flip. "You're ready."

I shook my head. "Okay, then. What about you?"

Tuck gestured to the back of the cab. "I've got my pack in the back, so we should be covered."

Tuck was always prepared for an adventure. Or an emergency. Since he and Walker were on both the SWAT and Search and Rescue teams, they never knew when they'd need to head into the wilderness.

I slipped out of the truck. Closing my eyes, I inhaled deeply. The air was so fresh, so clean, so…pure. It held the dampness of recently melted snow. The unique scent of a specific type of pine tree only found in this part of the world. The smell, the feel—it was home.

Tuck tugged on my hand. "Come on. There's something I've been wanting to show you."

He led me through the forest, following a path only he could see. Yet again, we walked in silence, the familiar peace sliding over my skin. I loved these moments with him.

I wasn't sure how long we hiked. I let my mind wander, soaking in the sights and sounds around me. Tuck stopped suddenly, and I almost ran into his back. "Geez, behemoth, watch where—" My words cut off as I gasped.

In front of us was the most beautiful waterfall I'd ever seen. The water was so crystal-clear it almost had a turquoise hue to it. A massive tree had fallen by a pool at the base and was now covered with the most vibrant green moss I'd ever seen. It was the most breathtaking place I'd ever been. I could only get one word out. "How?"

Tuck wrapped an arm around me and pulled me into his side. "I was tracking the herd one day, and they led me here. I've never told anyone about it. Never brought anyone here. There's just something about it that's so pure. I didn't want to sully it with other people."

I looked up at him. "Thank you for sharing it with me."

Tuck brushed his lips against mine. "Look." He gestured down the stream that led out of the pool at the base of the waterfall.

I turned, and my heart clenched. There were our mustangs. A family band of about twelve getting a drink at the stream. We stood watching, saying nothing, just soaking up the experience of this magical place together. I closed my eyes, wanting to commit this moment to memory forever.

Tuck brushed a hand over my face, and my eyelids rose. He opened his mouth to say something but was cut off by a loud crack. The color drained from Tuck's face and, suddenly, we were falling.

CHAPTER
Twenty-Seven

Tuck

M Y BODY DROPPED, COVERING JENSEN. THE BAND OF horses at the stream took off at a gallop. The crack of another bullet filled the air. *Fuck!* Where was the shooter? I tracked the sound the best I could, trying to determine the trajectory.

Jensen grabbed at my shirt, tearing at it with a frenzy that I'd never seen from her before. "Where? Where are you hit?"

"Wilder, calm down." I needed her quiet and, more importantly, still. "Steady. I'm fine. I wasn't hit."

She froze, her beautiful face marred with dirt looking up at me. "But you dropped like a ton of bricks," she whispered.

"Yeah, because I wasn't looking to get shot." I attempted to glance over my shoulder without raising my head. I couldn't get a good look. "J, on the count of three, I'm going to roll us, okay?" She nodded. "One, two, three." I rolled us until we rested up against the protection of that massive fallen tree. At least now, we had cover. I pulled my Glock from its holster. "Stay down."

Jensen gripped my shirt. "Don't. We don't know where he is."

I rolled onto my side. "I got a location when he shot the second time. But I need to see if he's taken off."

Jensen's lips pressed together in a tight line. "Okay. Please be careful."

"Always." I crept up the side of the fallen tree until I had a sightline to where I knew the shooter was. Nothing. I steadied my breathing and cleared my mind. Listening. Truly listening for any sounds that shouldn't have been there.

The rushing water of the falls behind us didn't make things easy. At first, there was nothing I could place. And then, finally, I heard something that didn't belong. An engine. An all-terrain vehicle if I had to guess. I scanned the forest around us. He was gone.

I sank back to the ground. "He took off."

Jensen stayed where she was. "You're sure?"

I nodded and reached out a hand to help her sit up. She winced as she did. "What's wrong?" I was instantly on alert. Could she have been hit and I hadn't realized it? I immediately began scanning her legs, I started to lift up her shirt, and she batted my hands away.

"I'm fine. I just got a little banged up when you tackled me. You're not exactly a lightweight."

I winced. "Let me see. I've got a first-aid kit in my pack." Jensen nodded, and I lifted up her shirt and jacket to examine her back. I hissed. *Shit.* She had a deep cut running on a diagonal across her lower back. I didn't think it needed stitches, but it had to hurt. "I'm going to call this in, and then I'll get started on your back."

Jensen looked at me over her shoulder. "You'll have to tell them where we are."

My brow furrowed. "Yes…"

"They'll know where your special place is."

I shook my head. "That's the last thing I care about right now.

We need to get you out of here safely and then see if there's any forensic evidence we can find."

Her expression grew stormy. "This creep is ruining everything."

"You aren't wrong." I pulled my sat phone out of my pack and called Dominguez. He and Mackey were on today. The call only took a few minutes, and I asked Dominguez to call Walker so he could pick up Jensen. I shoved the phone back into my pack. "They should be here in about an hour. In the meantime, let me deal with your back."

Jensen nodded and lifted her shirt. "Did you have to ask them to call Walker?"

I grinned and pulled out the first-aid kit. "How else were you going to get home?"

"I could've just waited for you to be done."

I pulled on a pair of gloves, not wanting my dirt-covered hands anywhere near Jensen's open wound. "It's going to take me hours to finish up here. You need to go home and soak in a hot bath. Your muscles are going to be killing you tomorrow." I ripped open an alcohol swab.

Jensen hissed as the pad touched her raw flesh. "Fuckity freaking fracking fuck! That stings."

I blew on the wound. "Sorry. That better?" She nodded. I worked as quickly as possible. Wiping an antibiotic salve across the cut and covering it with gauze. I eased her shirt and jacket down. "I'm pretty sure that shirt is done for."

Jensen shrugged and leaned back against the log, careful to avoid her wound. "It's just a shirt."

I wrapped an arm around her and pressed my lips to her hair. "I shouldn't have brought you up here."

Jensen tensed. "Don't put this overprotective guilt trip on yourself. There's been no sign of any other injured horses, right? Or the shooter."

"No…"

She smacked my stomach with the back of her hand. "Then quit this crap." Jensen was silent for a moment. "All the horses are okay?"

I reached over and squeezed her thigh as I looked to where the horses had taken off. "They're fine—" I caught sight of a small form at least one hundred yards out. "Fuck." I grabbed my pack and took off running.

"Tuck—oh, God."

I could hear Jensen behind me, but I didn't slow. I pushed my muscles harder. It was one of the foals. She jerked at the sound of my approach, trying to stand but unable to. I slowed, holding a hand up to Jensen to do the same. "It's okay, girl. I'm not going to hurt you. I just want to help."

It was her right front leg from the looks of it. I scanned the rest of the foal's body. I didn't see any blood. No sign of other injury.

Jensen pressed into my back. "It's her leg."

"I know."

She grabbed hold of my arm, squeezing hard. "What do we do?"

The foal was still trying to rise. "I'll have to tranquilize her. She's going to hurt herself more if she keeps trying to get up."

Jensen released me, immediately moving into action mode. "Tell me what to do."

"Nothing just yet." I set my pack down, working quickly to set up my tranq gun and adjust the dosage for the foal's smaller form. I hated that I'd have to cause her more trauma before I could help.

I inhaled deeply and aimed for her hindquarters and fired. The foal reared slightly at the sting. I closed my eyes.

Jensen's arms encircled me. "You did what you had to do so we can help her. She'll forgive you."

I pulled Jensen to me. She understood me without words. How I'd never been able to hunt unless the animal would be eaten, and even then, I honestly hated the whole ordeal. She knew how I hated to see any living creature suffer. While people like my father saw it as a weakness, Jensen saw it as a strength.

"Thank you." I whispered the words into her hair. "I have to call Mackey again, let her know we're going to need transport." Thank God, there was a Forest Service road not too far from here, we'd be able to get this little girl some help.

I placed the call, and within minutes, the foal was slipping under. I edged forward. "Okay, now I can examine her."

Jensen immediately eased down to the forest floor, stroking the horse's cheek. I made quick work of assessing the foal's injuries and checking her vitals as best I could. It seemed to just be her leg, but I was pretty sure it was bad.

"It's broken, isn't it?"

I looked up to meet Jensen's gaze. "If I had to guess."

Tears glittered in Jensen's eyes, but she kept stroking the horse's cheek. "It's okay. We're gonna do everything we can to fix you up."

I scooted closer to Jensen, pressing my lips to her temple. "Mackey was already bringing some extra guys, so we'll be able to evac her. There will be a trailer waiting on the Forest Service road."

Jensen nodded and opened her mouth to speak, but hurried steps in the underbrush stopped her.

"Boss?" It was Dominguez.

"Over here." I stood and waved them over. I breathed a sigh of relief when I saw the four other guys trailing my team members.

We worked quickly, the only words spoken the most necessary ones. As soon as the foal was strapped in, the four guys Dominguez and Mackey had brought with them took off for where the trailer would meet them.

"Where are they taking her?" Jensen stood off to the side, not wanting to get in the way, her arms wrapped tightly around herself.

I strode over, pulling her to me, not giving a single fuck that there were others around. "The equine center outside Cleary."

Jensen nodded against my chest. "That's good. I'll call Dr. Neill when I get home. Tell her I'll cover the costs of whatever she needs done."

"You've got the best heart of anyone I've ever known, Wilder." I whispered the words against her hair.

Jensen fisted my shirt and straightened to meet my gaze. "I want to kill this asshole, Tuck."

I pushed the hair back from her face. "I know you do. And I'm not far behind you."

"Tuck! Jensen!" The voice that broke through the forest was almost as familiar as my own.

Jensen sighed. "Oh, goody, brother bear is here."

I stood and pulled Jensen to her feet. "Cut him some slack. He's been worried about you lately. And with everything going on, you're liable to give him a heart attack."

Jensen blushed. "I know. You're right. I'm just pissed off."

Walker broke through the trees. "Are you guys okay?"

I held up a hand. "We're totally fine."

As soon as he knew we were all right his face began to redden. "What the hell were you thinking coming up here with all this going on?"

Jensen stepped in front of me. "Oh, no, you don't, brother dearest. There hasn't been an incident in a month. And just because something bad happened up here, doesn't mean I'm going to avoid it for the rest of my life. These horses mean the world to me."

Walker's face approached the shade of a tomato. "That's, that's—"

I gripped his shoulder. "What Jensen meant to say was, now that we're aware of the depth of the danger, she will be staying away from Pine Meadow until this asshole is apprehended. Once he is, she'll be back up here with her horses on the regular. Isn't that right, Jensen?"

Jensen stuck her tongue out at me. The action seemed to take some of the wind out of Walker's sails. "I was just worried."

Jensen gave her brother a hug. "I'm sorry. I didn't mean to worry you."

"I know." He squeezed her harder, and she winced. "What? What's wrong?" He looked at me. "I thought you said she was fine."

Jensen smacked at Walker to release her. "I *am* fine. I just got a little banged up when Tuck threw me to the ground." She narrowed her eyes on her brother. "You know, when he shielded me from bullets with his own body. You might say 'thanks for trying to save my sister's life.'"

Walker looked from Jensen to me and back again. "Why would I want to do that when you're so damn annoying?"

Jensen gave him a shove. "Guess I'm walking home."

Walker reached out a hand and pulled me into a half-hug, whispering in my ear. "Thank you, man."

"I'd do anything for her." My voice cracked on the last word, the emotion of the day finally hitting me.

Walker released me. "I know you would. Are you guys good here? I think I'm going to get her home."

I nodded. "I'll give you a call when we're done and update you."

"Appreciate it. Jensen, let's go."

Jensen and I stood a few feet apart. The call of her was so strong, it almost brought me to my knees. I was dying to pull her into my arms. Kiss her. Never let her go. But I couldn't. Because that wasn't what we were. That invisible fist clamped down around my chest. "I'll call you later to check in."

J nodded. "I'm going to try and convince Walker to make a stop at the equine center on the way home, but I'll have my cell." She glanced around the surrounding forest. "Be careful."

"I will." I watched until the two of them had disappeared into the forest before I turned to my team. "Anyone else coming?"

Mackey grimaced. "The boss should be here any second. He said he'd be right behind us."

I was hoping that was a good sign. An indication that David was going to take this case more seriously. The sound of twigs snapping had me turning around, and there he was.

He pulled out a water bottle and took a swig. "Fill me in."

I brought everyone up to speed on what had gone down.

David grimaced. "You should've never brought that girl off the trail. You both could've been killed."

I sighed. "I know my way around here better than my own backyard. But if it eases your mind, I won't be bringing her back until we catch this bastard."

David nodded, somewhat appeased.

I gave Dominguez and Mackey their assignments and then turned back to David. "Have you gotten the ballistics report back on the bullet yet?"

David scowled. "Those idiots at the lab accidentally damaged the bullet during testing. All the results would be useless at this point."

I swiped a hand through my hair. "Fuck."

"You got that right."

We had officially lost our only lead.

CHAPTER
Twenty-Eight

Jensen

I SWEPT THE BROOM EVER SO SLOWLY ACROSS THE FLOOR OF the Kettle. It probably looked like a zombie was doing clean-up. But this time, it wasn't because nightmares were keeping me up at night, those had started to come more infrequently once again.

Kennedy straightened from where she was wiping down tables. "Uh, Jensen, are you okay?"

I paused in my sweeping. "I'm fine. I got up early this morning to go and visit the foal again." I had been visiting her before work a few days a week and was paying the price, but my girl was worth it. She was a fighter, and the vet had given me every hope that I'd be able to take her home in a few weeks. But she'd need special care and rehabilitation for the next six months or so.

A smile tipped Kennedy's lips. "How's she doing? You name her yet?"

I leaned against the broom, using the handle to hold myself up. Kennedy was as bad as my mom, giving me a hard time about picking out names. "She's doing great. And, as a matter of fact, I have."

"Well, give it to me already."

I laughed. "Ember. She's kept the fire within herself burning through all she's been through, so it seemed fitting."

"Oh, Jensen. It's perfect."

I started sweeping again. "I think so. I can't wait to get her home." Ember had already begun to acclimate to having people around her, but it would be a good while before anyone fully had her trust again.

The bell over the front door tinkled, and I turned. My stomach twisted. Cody. Gone was his attempt at a charming smile. In its place was cold calculation.

"Jensen. We need to talk."

Kennedy took the broom from my hands. "I can finish this." She eyed Cody. "If you're okay."

I gave her arm a squeeze. "I'm fine." I crossed to Cody. "Yes?"

"I want to cut a deal."

My stomach roiled. *A deal?* "What do you mean?"

Cody eyed Kennedy and then dropped his voice to a whisper. "You give me five hundred grand or I'm taking your ass to court and filing for full custody."

I burst out laughing. I couldn't help it. "What in the world makes you think I have five hundred grand just lying around?"

Cody's eyes narrowed. "I know you've got it. Just collecting dust in that nice fat trust of yours."

My blood turned cold. I did my best to hide my family's wealth. Mostly because I viewed it as exactly that. My family's, and not mine. I'd used some of the money to start my business and to pay for the costs of supporting my rescued horses, but other than that, I didn't touch it. I supported myself and Noah with what I made at the tea shop. It wasn't diamonds and caviar, but it was a good life, and I was proud of it.

The fact that Cody knew anything about my trust meant he'd been looking into me. I took a slow, steadying breath. "I'm not going to pay you anything. My lawyer has already informed me that no judge would award custody to a father who abandoned his child for nine years."

A sneer stretched across Cody's face. "But what would a judge say if I made the case that you never told me I had a son?"

My heart began beating faster. "But I did tell you."

"You got any proof of that?"

My mind circled back to those dark days when I had felt so alone. As soon as I had told Cody that I was pregnant and wanted to keep the baby, he'd taken off like a shot. He'd already had enough credits to graduate, so he'd left college a semester early. I'd called and emailed, but his phone had been disconnected, and the emails bounced back. "Th-there's a record of me trying to contact you." I hated that my voice shook.

"But what if I make a case that you knew I was changing my contact information. You know, real world, new number and email. That's what lots of kids do."

My mouth opened, but no words came out.

Cody chuckled. "And imagine what the judge will think when he learns you brought a serial killer into my son's life."

My body jerked. "What?"

Cody widened his eyes. "Oh, what? You didn't think I'd do my research? I really should thank you. You've made this so damn easy." He leaned in closer to me. "I wanted to go about this the right way. Give you a chance to be a family. But, oh no, Jensen Cole thinks she's too good for me now."

A sneer stretched across his face. "Instead, she's slutting it up with some trail guide. You made the wrong choice going for him, Jensen. And now, this is the way it has to be. Five hundred grand. You have two weeks."

My vision went unfocused. I stood frozen to the spot, only slightly aware of the tinkling of the bell, meaning that Cody had left. I began to shake.

"Jensen." There was a voice from far away. "Jensen, are you okay?" A hand on my arm. "Let's sit you down." Movement. A chair. "I'm going to get you some water."

Moments passed. "Do you want me to call someone?"

The bell sounded again, and I jolted, blinking furiously, trying to clear my vision to see if Cody had returned. Someone was in front of me.

"Wilder, what's wrong?"

I couldn't seem to get the words out of my throat.

The voice sounded just a bit farther away. "What the hell happened?"

I reached out, fisting Tuck's coat. "Cody's going to take Noah. He's going to take Noah, and it's all my fault."

Tuck plucked me from the chair, then turned and sat, settling me in his lap. "Cody is not going to take Noah. Tell me what happened."

Slowly, voice shaking, I recounted everything that Cody had said. Tuck's body grew tighter with each passing word. "I'm going to *kill* him."

I tightened my grip on Tuck's coat. "I have to get him the money. But I can't just pull five hundred grand from my trust. It doesn't work that way. I'll have to ask my parents. They'll help me, right?" My words came faster and faster.

Tuck cupped my face. "Breathe. Just breathe." He mimicked slow and steady breaths for me to follow. "Please trust me to handle this for you. I'm going to take care of it."

My gaze locked on Tuck's. "Are you going to slit his throat and drop him off a ravine?"

Tuck let out a bark of laughter. "As much as I'd love to, no, I'm not."

I burrowed into his chest. "I trust you." I nibbled on my bottom lip. "Do you think you could not tell Walker? I don't want him to lose it and do something that could cost him his job."

Tuck tipped my head back and brushed the hair away from my face. "I won't tell Walker yet if you promise to call Taylor and your mom right now and fill them in." I opened my mouth to protest, but Tuck silenced me with a quick kiss. "You need support right now. They're it."

I nodded and pulled out my phone.

Tuck ran his hand under the fall of my hair. "I need to get some things in play to deal with Cody. Are you going to be okay if I leave?"

I straightened. "I'll be fine. I just need to find my mad and hold onto that for a little while."

"That's my girl." Tuck swept his lips across each temple and then my forehead.

I rose, and Tuck followed. "Be careful." A feeling of dread settled in my stomach, and I couldn't put my finger on why.

"Always." And with that, he was gone.

CHAPTER
Twenty-Nine

Tuck

I KEPT MY COOL UNTIL I REACHED MY TRUCK. WHEN I GOT inside, I slammed my fist down on the steering wheel so hard it was a miracle I didn't crack the thing in two. "Fuck!"

Cody had escalated things because I'd been careless. Making out with Jensen in a parked car like we were high schoolers. What had I been thinking? My gut burned. Just another reminder that Jensen deserved so much more. But I wasn't sure I could walk away.

I blew out a long breath. I needed to focus on the task at hand. I'd made it sound to Jensen like I'd have this whole thing figured out no problem, but I wasn't so sure that would be the case. The thing I hadn't wanted to tell her was that she *could not* give this guy money. Could her family afford the payoff? Sure. But if she did that, he would keep crawling back for more. One payoff would never be enough for him.

I drummed my fingers against the steering wheel. I needed a plan. And for that to happen, I needed more information. I grabbed my phone and started scrolling through my contacts, looking for a specific name.

Cain Hale. He was a friend of mine and Walker's from college. He'd taken his law enforcement and programming degrees and created a tech empire that could rival just about anyone else in the world. But I needed him for his hobby. Hacking.

I hit Cain's contact and waited as the phone rang. He'd come through in a clutch when Tessa had been kidnapped a few months ago, and I hoped he would again. If there was anything that pissed Cain off, it was men trying to harm women in any way.

"Tuck."

That was all I got. I rolled my eyes. Always so serious. "Hey, Cain. I need your help with something."

I heard a door close. "Anything. You know that."

Walker and I had seen Cain through some dark days, and he'd always made it clear that if there was anything he could do to return the favor, he would see it done. "It's about Jensen."

There was silence for a moment. "Then why are you calling me instead of Walker?"

I swallowed hard. The three of us were brothers. No, not by blood, but by choice. And asking him to keep something from Walker flickered close to the edge of betraying that brotherhood. But Jensen had been right. If Walker knew that Cody had threatened her, he would lose his mind. "He's not aware of the latest developments on the issue."

"And why is that?"

I grunted. "Because Jensen and I don't want him to lose his job. Or worse, end up in prison."

A chair creaked. "Jensen and you, huh?"

I wanted to curse. Cain had always been too damn observant for his own good. "We're friends. You know that."

"I haven't heard you mention her name much lately. That's all."

My hand clenched around the steering wheel. "We've been spending more time together."

More silence. "Tuck. Are you sure that's a good idea? You're not exactly built for commitment."

It sounded so similar to the things my dad used to say. *Men aren't designed to be monogamous, especially Harris men.* I gritted my teeth. "We're just friends."

Cain, of course, read my subtext, which was something to the effect of "*fuck off.*"

"I didn't mean anything by it. If you told me you were ready for a serious commitment and you were pursuing J, I'd be over the moon for both of you. But you weren't exactly looking for that in the past. And I don't think Walker would be too pleased about you going after his sister for your usual fix."

My hand squeezed even tighter around the wheel, the knuckles going white. "We're just friends. But none of that matters right now because her douchebag ex is in town trying to extort money out of her with the threat that he's going to take her to court to get full custody of Noah. So, if you could stop your gossipy girl shit for two minutes, I'd really like for us to focus on that for a bit."

"Fuck." A chair squeaked again, and soon, I heard typing. "What's his full name?"

My shoulders relaxed a fraction. "Cody Ailes."

"You got a date of birth?"

"Hold on." I put Cain on speaker, opened the notes app on my phone, and read off Cody's birthday.

"This is my first priority. Give me a few hours for a preliminary, and a couple of days or a week for a deeper dive depending on what I find."

I let out a long breath. "Thank you."

"I've always got your back." Cain paused. "And, Tuck?"

My jaw clenched, and I braced for more shit about Jensen. "Yeah?"

"If you want more, you should reach for more."

My back molars ground together. "She deserves better than me. My family. My history. I'm not sure I'm capable of being what she needs." I hated each and every word that came out of my mouth.

"Tuck. I've known you since we were eighteen. We've both done some stupid shit. But there is nothing in you that isn't good." Cain paused for a moment. "And it sounds like you're already what she needs."

I wanted so badly for that to be the truth. Because I knew deep down that things were changing. That hope that I could burn out this fire between us, so all that was left was easy affection and friendship was a distant memory.

I wanted more. I wanted everything. And that scared the hell out of me.

CHAPTER
Thirty

Jensen

"I CAN'T BELIEVE YOU GUYS WERE GOING TO KEEP THIS from me." Walker picked up his drink but his gaze stayed focused on me.

I sighed and took another sip of my beer. My brother was never going to let me hear the end of it. After I'd told my mom everything that had happened with Cody, she'd told my dad, who then spilled the beans to Walker. "I just didn't want you to lose it and do something stupid."

Walker scowled at his whiskey. "You think I have no self-control or something?"

Tuck grunted. "Not when it comes to your sister."

Walk took a sip of his drink. "Like you're any better."

Taylor reached over and placed a hand over Walker's. "This is not helping Jensen get her mind off things." She gave me a sympathetic smile across the table.

After Walker had calmed down from losing his shit over Cody's actions, Taylor had suggested that we all go out to get our mind off things. At first, I'd resisted, not wanting to leave Noah's side, but he was asleep with my parents standing guard downstairs, and I'd been outvoted.

I'd called my lawyer, who was doing everything he could to move along my filing for the termination of Cody's rights. Tuck promised that he was working an angle, too. So, there was nothing else I could do. I took another swig of beer. There was nothing else I could do unless you considered murder. And that was the backup plan playing on a steady repeat in my brain.

A hand reached over and squeezed my thigh. I glanced to my left, my gaze catching on Tuck. His silent support was always what I needed. I hated that we couldn't be more careless with our displays of affection. I hated that it made that jealousy spike inside me when I looked at Taylor and my brother.

That's not what this is. Friends with benefits, I reminded myself. But something told me my traitorous heart had forgotten those rules.

"Jensen?"

I jolted at the sound of Taylor's voice. "Sorry, what did you say?"

Taylor laughed, but her gaze danced between Tuck and me. "I asked how things were going with your new hire? She seems super nice."

I took another sip of beer, trying to get my emotions and nerve-endings under control. "Kennedy's great." I paused. "Well, other than the fact that she's a disaster in the kitchen. She's great with the drinks, the customers, the register. But when it comes to baking, she gives you a run for your money."

Walker chuckled, and Taylor smacked him in the chest. "I'm not that bad." Walker just stared at her. "Okay, fine, but I'm getting better."

Walker wrapped his hand around the nape of her neck. "Short-stack, you almost burned down the kitchen yesterday."

I covered my mouth in an attempt to conceal my giggle, but it wasn't long before the entire table had given in to the laughter. I felt the energy beside me shift before I saw anything. An unidentified tension floated through the air. I looked at Tuck, who had gone stone-still, his jaw hard, his eyes blazing.

I followed his gaze. Sitting on a stool at the bar was Tuck's father. But that wasn't what had Tuck boiling. Craig stood with his arm wrapped around a woman who was not Tuck's mother. He bent, whispered in her ear, and then pressed his lips to her neck. I sucked in a breath.

Tuck began to rise up out of his chair, but I clamped a hand on his thigh. "Don't. He's not worth it."

Tuck's gaze landed on me, and the raw pain I saw there stole all the air from my lungs. "I have to. He can't do this to Mom."

Tuck shook off my hold and headed towards his father.

"Shit," I muttered and began to stand.

Walker reached out and grabbed my arm, a look of confused concern on his face. "What's going on?"

I met my brother's gaze. Every now and then, he could be so damn oblivious. "Tuck's dad is a cheating asshole."

Walker's eyes flared, shooting to Craig at the bar. I pulled my arm out of his grasp and headed over.

Tuck's fists were clenched, and that muscle in his cheek ticked. "This is a whole new level of low even for you, old man."

Craig took another sip of his beer and pulled his companion a bit closer. "Oh, the high and mighty Tucker is going to tell me how to live my life, huh? Too good to work on the ranch with me. Had to go out into the forest like some sort of fucking hippie. Just because you aren't a real man, doesn't mean I ain't."

What Tuck's father was saying didn't even make sense. I watched as Craig wobbled a bit. He was shitfaced.

Tuck flexed his hands. "You're not doing this to Mom. I'm calling you a cab. You need to go home."

Craig pushed off his stool, upending the woman who was half in his lap. "You always were a fucking mama's boy. Go on. Tattle on me. See if I give a fuck."

"How about I have you arrested for public intoxication? See how a night in the drunk tank treats you."

Craig's face reddened, and he charged. He tried to clip Tuck in the jaw with his fist but missed, hitting his son's shoulder instead. Tuck retaliated with two blows to his dad's side, sending Craig crumpling to the ground.

The entire bar was dead silent. I'd never heard it so quiet in my life. Tuck's gaze swung around the space, almost a feral quality to his gaze, and then it landed on me. "I have to get out of here."

"Go. I'll have Walker deal with your dad."

And with that, he took off, but not before I saw the look of true hopelessness on his face.

CHAPTER
Thirty-One

Tuck

I JOGGED THE TWELVE BLOCKS TO MY HOUSE, THE BITTER winter wind stinging my skin the whole way. I had hoped temperatures hovering around zero would cool my temper. It didn't work.

I slipped my key into the lock and pulled open the door. I hated this house. Loathed that it was in town and not on my family's property. From the time I was young, the plan had always been for me to build on a piece of the acreage on Harris Ranch. But when things really shifted, I couldn't handle being in such close proximity to my father. So, I'd bought this modern craftsman in town.

I didn't like that my neighbors were close. That there was no open space or view. I could've bought another ranch, but that sort of felt like giving up. I hated that my father had enough power over my life to ruin even more. Keeping me from my birthright, the place my soul used to feel the most settled, my *home*.

"Goddammit!" I spun, crashing my fist through the wall, sending plaster flying everywhere. I pulled my hand from the drywall, blood dripping from my knuckles. "Fuck."

I headed for the kitchen. Turning the water on as cold as it would go, I stuck my hand under the spray and hissed.

"Tuck?" Jensen's voice called out tentatively from the entryway.

I was silent for a minute. I should've stayed far away from her in that moment. Far away from anyone. "In here." My selfish desire for her was too strong.

Her boots sounded on the hardwood floor. "Doing some redecorating?"

I kept my gaze focused on the stream of water, my back to Jensen. "You shouldn't be here."

Her heat was at my back. "Shit. Where's your first-aid kit?"

"It'll be fine in a minute or two."

Jensen's heat was gone as she muttered something about macho alpha males and infections that would kill them. She was back in under two minutes, holding the first-aid kit my mother had stocked in one of the bathrooms. It had never been opened. Jensen took the roll of paper towels from the counter and tore off a few. "Give me your hand."

I removed it from the spray, then turned off the water and placed my palm on the bed of paper towels she held. I stared at my hand as Jensen tenderly dried it with short, patting motions, nothing that would catch on the torn skin. They were the movements of a caring mother. Something in my chest twisted.

Jensen laid my hand and the bed of paper towels on the counter. "Don't move."

I obeyed, eyes still locked on my hand. I couldn't bear to look her in the face, to have her see the depth of my weakness.

Jensen's movements were both quick and careful. She washed her hands, dried them, then opened the first-aid kit, taking a moment to assess her options before removing a tube of antibacterial ointment and a roll of gauze. She dabbed the gel on my torn knuckles and then slowly wound the bandage around them.

The dressing was secure but not too tight. She taped it off. "Sit," she said, inclining her head toward the kitchen table.

I followed her instructions, still not meeting her gaze.

Jensen moved around my kitchen with comfortable ease. I often forgot how well she fit into my life. Because she had always been there. For almost as long as I could remember, she'd always been a part of me.

Jensen filled a plastic bag with ice and grabbed a towel from a drawer, wrapping it around the homemade ice pack. She slid into the chair next to me, gently laying the ice across my knuckles. It felt like heaven.

We sat in silence. That comforting quiet I always had with Jensen. She waited until I was ready.

"I hate him. I hate him because of the secrets I've kept for his sorry ass. I hate that he's torn our entire family apart." I sucked in air, each word seeming to catch on invisible barbed wire in my throat. "I hate him because I'm just like him."

Jensen went stock-still. Then she moved, grabbing my face in her hands and forcing me to meet her eyes. "You. Are. *Nothing*. Like. Him."

Our gazes locked, twining with each other, imprinting the words we'd never say aloud onto each other's souls.

I stood, my chair rocking back, the ice pack falling to the table. I grabbed Jensen around the waist and lifted. Her legs wound around me. I'd never needed her more than I did in that moment. I strode towards my bedroom, my dick hardening with each step, straining to get to her. The pressure against my zipper was painful, but I relished the pain.

When we reached my room, Jensen slid down my body, and I let out a pained groan. She tore off her shirt, her breasts bouncing with the action. Then her bra was gone. We both toed off our boots. I used her belt loops to yank her to me. My fingers unbuttoned her jeans.

I couldn't wait. I needed a taste of her heat. I slipped a hand into her panties. Already wet. *Fuck.* I plunged a finger inside.

"Tuck." The single word was uttered on a breathy moan.

"Gonna make you come just like this." I swirled that single finger around inside her and added another. My palm rubbed against her clit, and she sucked in a breath. I worked her higher and higher, relishing the feel of the tiny convulsions around my fingers.

I pumped deeper, starting a come-hither motion, searching for that spot I knew would make her detonate. Jensen's legs began to tremble. I bent my head, taking her tight nipple into my mouth and sucked deep. Jensen let out a garbled noise.

I rolled the bud between my teeth as my fingers inside her stroked deeper. As she began to tighten around me, I pressed my palm hard into that bundle of nerves and let my teeth sink lightly into her nipple. Jensen's head fell back, and she clamped down around me so tightly, I was sure it cut off circulation to my fingers.

Jensen began to crumple, and I laid her back on the bed, slipping my hand from her jeans. She stared at me intently as I brought my fingers to my mouth and sucked them clean. Her eyes blazed. "Take me. Now."

CHAPTER
Thirty-Two

Jensen

I EASED MY JEANS DOWN MY LEGS, MY GAZE STAYING LOCKED with Tuck's as he unbuttoned his shirt. Stepping out of my pants, my hands went to Tuck's jeans, but my eyes never strayed from his. There was something different about this time. Something unnamed that I couldn't quite put my finger on.

Tuck pulled his wallet from his back pocket, removing a condom and tossing the billfold onto the pile of clothes. I helped Tuck roll the latex on, relishing the feel of him beneath our joined hands. His dick pulsed, and something tightened deep inside of me. "Now, please," I whispered.

Tuck laid me back on the bed, hovering over me for a moment, his gaze tracing my face. His lips grazed one temple, then the other before lingering on my forehead. My eyes closed as I tried to soak up every sensation of his lips on my skin.

He settled between my legs, entering me so slowly and tenderly, tears gathered in my eyes. The pace Tuck set was deliberate as if he wanted this to last as long as possible. His strokes were long and deep and delicious.

My hips rose to meet his, finding the rhythm that was ours

and ours alone. A dance that said more than either of us had the guts to voice. Beads of sweat began to pepper my skin. My heels dug into his ass, spurring him on.

We both picked up our pace, our rhythm becoming more frenzied. My nails dug into Tuck's back. His thrusts bottomed out inside me, hitting that spot that caused sparks to dance across my vision.

Deeper. Faster. More. Everything. Sensations flickered through my body in a cascade. Pleasure. Pain. Strain. Need. I'd never experienced so much at one time.

My walls began to tremble. Tuck thrust deeper than he ever had before. We came apart together. Our worlds shattering. And I knew I'd never be the same.

Tuck's fingers traced the ridges in my spine.

I let out a long breath. "I should probably go." His fingers stilled. "It's the last thing I want to do, but if I don't, there will be questions."

Tuck pressed his lips to my hair. "I'll walk you out."

We dressed in silence. Something inside me yearned to ask, *"is this more?"* My bad track record when it came to men kept me silent. What if I said something, and it ruined the thing between us? I couldn't name what it was we shared. All I knew was that it was beautiful. And so very fragile.

Tuck walked me to my car, pulling open my door. His lips grazed my temples, and then my forehead. "Drive safe. Text me when you're home."

I brushed my lips against his. "I will. Put some more ice on that hand."

Tuck grinned. "I'm fine."

I rolled my eyes. "Stubborn behemoth."

"Takes one to know one."

I shook my head as I climbed into my SUV. The drive home was silent with only the clear, starry sky to keep me company. The farther away I got from Tuck, the more the phantom pain in my chest flared to life. Tears gathered in my eyes, soon spilling over and tracking down my cheeks. What was I doing, letting my heart latch onto a man who had never once been in a relationship? Who'd never once made a promise to me beyond the here and now. When Tuck needed his freedom—and at some point, he would—I was going to be crushed.

As I pulled up to my guest house, the front porch lamp illuminated my grandmother. I wiped at my face before turning off the car, hoping the low light would disguise any signs of crying. I slipped from my vehicle and made my way to the house. "Where are Mom and Dad?"

My grandma tipped her rocker back and forth. "Those two lovebirds? Couldn't keep their hands off each other, so I sent them back to the ranch house so they could get busy without worrying about me being underfoot."

I grimaced. "Did you really have to share those details?"

She shrugged. "You asked. Have a seat." She inclined her head to the rocker next to her.

I sat and began to rock, letting the cold night air soothe me.

"Want to tell me why you've been crying?" Grandma kept staring straight ahead, still rocking.

Of course, she would know I'd been crying. Grams would likely say it was because she was psychic, but I knew it was because she had such strong empathy for those she loved. I let out a long breath. "I did something stupid again."

Her rocking stopped. "You stop talking about my granddaughter like that or I'll take you over my knee." My brows rose. "I've held my tongue, but I can see now that was a mistake. None of what has happened around here recently is your fault. Just like falling for the wrong guy in college wasn't your fault. Is Noah a mistake?"

"No. Never."

Grandma started rocking again. "Of course, he's not. Jensen, awful things happen—betrayal, death. Our world is full of it, but that doesn't mean there can't be some good that comes from it. Always look for the good, baby girl. Noah is that good. Taylor and Walker finding each other is that good."

"I think I'm in love with Tuck." The words just tumbled out of me as if they had a mind of their own.

Grandma kept right on rocking. "Of course, you are."

"Excuse me?"

"You and Tucker have loved each other since before you knew what that meant."

My hands gripped the arms of the rocker. "Tuck is not in love with me."

My grandma stilled and turned to face me. "Of course, he is. But it terrifies him, and he doesn't know what to do with it."

Something that felt a lot like hope flared to life in my chest. I shoved it down. "He cares about me. Maybe even loves me in his own way. But I don't think he'll ever want to commit to a single woman for the rest of his life." I stared out at the starry night sky. "If I let him all the way in…I'm not sure I'll recover when he leaves."

Grams reached over and patted my hand. "Love is always a risk. There's no way around it. He'll hurt you. You'll hurt him. One of you might lose the other. But it will also be so beautiful, the light of it so bright, it'll outshine all of the dark."

Tears pricked at my eyes. A longing burned deep in my chest. "I want that." It was the first time I'd been able to truly admit that to myself since Cody had smashed my heart to smithereens. Bryce had seemed like a safe choice at the time, but he'd never made my heart take flight, my blood sing, my soul feel at peace. There was only one man who did that.

Grams smiled, the tip of her lips barely visible in the low

light. "You're going to have to hold on tight to that one because it's going to be a bumpy ride." Her gaze bore into mine. "But I promise you, it'll be worth it."

I just had to hold on.

CHAPTER
Thirty-Three

Tuck

I GROANED AS MY DOORBELL RANG FOR A SECOND TIME. I glanced at my phone. I had thirty minutes before my alarm was due to sound. Seeing as I'd tossed and turned for hours last night, I needed those extra thirty minutes. The bell rang again.

"Fuck." I pushed out of bed, grabbing my tee from the floor and tightening the drawstring on my sweats. "I'm coming. Hold your horses."

I pulled open the door, a scowl firmly in place, expecting to find Walker. Instead, I was greeted by my mother. Her hair was pulled back into a lifeless ponytail, and dark circles shone under her eyes. She was usually the picture of casually put-together, but today, she wore workout pants and a worn hoodie. "Can I come in?"

I swallowed down the riot of emotions ranging from anger to grief. "Of course." I motioned for her to enter. My mom's steps faltered as she caught sight of the hole in the wall, but she said nothing. "Do you mind if we move this to the kitchen? I'm in desperate need of coffee."

"Of course." She headed in that direction. "Do you have any tea?"

I grinned down at the floor. "Do you think Jensen would let me live anywhere that didn't have a stockpile even though she knows I hate the stuff?"

A gentle smile pulled at my mother's mouth. "Of course, she wouldn't."

I pointed to one of the drawers. "It's in there. And there's a kettle above the stove." I was struck in that moment by how different it was for my mom to be in the space. Jensen knew where everything was, yet my own mother needed to be directed.

We both set to work silently—me with the coffee maker, her at the stove. It was as if we both needed a moment to ground ourselves in the everyday normality of simple tasks before taking on the elephant in the room.

"Do you have any honey?" my mom asked.

"In the pantry." I grabbed two mugs from the cabinet, setting one by the stove and taking the other with me to the coffee pot.

Silence continued to reign. But soon, both of our beverages of choice were complete, and we were taking our seats at the kitchen table. I had to tell her. With the scene last night, it was only a matter of time before she heard all the details. And soon, I was sure more stories would come to light. Uglier ones.

I took a deep breath. "He cheats on you, Mom. He's been doing it since I was a kid."

She met my gaze, nothing but defeat in her own. "I know."

My body jerked. "You know?"

She stared down into her tea, the silence in the room screaming as loudly as a siren. "I've always known." Her breath hitched. "I tried to fix things, to get him to go to therapy. None of it helped. And, somewhere along the way, I just accepted things for the way they were. The way they *are*."

Temper licked at my skin. "Do you have any idea how much

guilt I've been carrying around, keeping his secret? Since I was eight years old and walked in on him with some woman in the barn." Mom's head snapped up. "The shit he filled my head with. How horrible I felt for keeping it from you. Should I tell you? Would it do any good? Would you blame me for hurting you?"

"Oh, honey, no." My mom reached across the table to grab my hand, but I pulled it out of her reach. Her fingers curled in on air as she took her hand back. "I've made a mess of everything."

Tears filled her eyes. "I know you think I'm weak, putting up with his drinking and now this." I started to speak, but my mom held up a hand to stop me. "And I understand why. I thought I was doing the right thing. Doing my best to keep my family together." Her voice cracked, and my heart broke right along with it. "And now I've lost you both."

I couldn't quite bring myself to reach out and take her hand, but I couldn't leave her alone in this either. "Mom, you haven't lost me."

She lifted her eyes to meet mine. "Haven't I?"

I sat back in my chair, my back teeth grinding together. "I just can't be around him anymore. If last night proves anything, it's that. I have to let you two do what you think is best for whatever marriage you have. I'll do everything I can to keep a relationship with you, but I won't be coming to the ranch anymore."

"I kicked him out."

My mouth opened and closed, but no words came out. Never in my life had my mom sent my dad packing. "You kicked him out? Can you even do that?"

One corner of Mom's mouth quirked up. "Your grandfather must have seen through Craig's doting son-in-law act more than I'd guessed because he didn't leave the ranch to me in his will. He left it to *you*. I'm just the caretaker until your fortieth birthday."

This time, my jaw simply fell open. Pieces clicked into place. My grandfather had died five years ago, and it was right around then that my dad's asshole behavior kicked up another degree. "Mom, that's not what I want. I'll sign it back over to you."

She shook her head. "The will protected us and the ranch really. Your dad was always more interested in the ranch than me. Sure, he loved me, in that puppy-love kind of way when you're young and naïve. But the ranch, *that* was always his true love. It's why he took my last name instead of vice versa. He said it was to keep the Harris history alive. But I think it was more about having the prestige the name carries around here."

My mom took a sip of her tea. "You should've seen how pissed he was when he found out about Dad's will. I'm sure that's part of why he's been so hard on you. To him, you walked away from the thing he wanted more than anything when you took a job with the Forest Service."

My jaw clenched. "I love the ranch. Grandpa knew that. I just couldn't live my life under Dad's thumb. I knew that from the time I was thirteen. I had to go my own way."

Mom nodded. "I know that. And I haven't told you enough, I'm so proud of you. Of what you do. Of the man you are."

There was a burning in my chest. "Mom, why didn't you tell me any of this was going on?"

Her shoulders slumped. "I was hoping I could fix it all. That, somehow, I could make us a family again. The way it was in the beginning."

I kept my tone gentle but firm because she needed to truly hear my next words. "For that to happen, he'd have to *want* to be a part of our family. And he doesn't."

A single tear spilled over. "I see that now. Walker didn't share much about what happened last night, but your father spilled some, and I've had friends call this morning to share the rest." She straightened her shoulders. "I have an appointment with a lawyer in an hour. I'm going to file for divorce."

My chest seized. I'd wanted her to take that step for so long, but now it felt wrong. Like I had forced it somehow. "You don't have to do that for me."

She nodded, wiping under her eye. "I'm doing it for all of us."

I reached across the table and grabbed her hand. "I hope this is the first step to you finding some happy."

My mom gave me a watery smile. "I think it will be." She squeezed my hand and then released it. "Speaking of happy... Walker mentioned when he dropped off your father last night that Jensen was over here taking care of you."

That familiar mask slipped into place. "We're friends, Mom."

She took another sip of tea. "Friendship is the best foundation for a relationship."

It was as if someone were slowly impaling me with a hot poker. I wanted it so badly, this thing that seemed almost within my reach, but I was so damn terrified that I'd fuck it all up the same way my father had. But maybe, just maybe, there was hope for us yet.

CHAPTER
Thirty-Four

Jensen

T HE SUN SHONE DOWN, AND I TIPPED UP MY FACE SO I
could soak up the rays. The flash of mild temperatures
had held, and I was going to appreciate every moment
of it.

A small muzzle sniffed at my shoulder. I smiled but didn't
turn my head. "Hey there, Ember." I kept my voice low and
stayed seated on the bucket I'd flipped over in the small paddock area she had at the equine center.

Life wasn't getting any simpler. Cody's threats still hung over
my head, I had no idea whether or not this thing with Tuck was
going to blow up in my face, and no one had figured out who
was going after the wild mustangs. But I was doing what Grams
had advised. I was holding onto the good.

And a big part of that was time with my horses. Ember
edged just a bit closer, taking another sniff. The fracture in her
leg wasn't as bad as we'd first thought, and I hoped to take her
home and introduce her to Phoenix soon. I had a feeling Phee
would be happy to play surrogate mama to this sweet foal.

While Ember had gotten used to having people around,

she didn't fully trust anyone yet. I'd give her all the time in the world. Thankfully, I had more time now that I had Kennedy at the Kettle. She hadn't mastered the baking aspect of the job yet, but it still gave me a couple of hours in the middle of each day to visit Ember and my herd at the ranch.

Ember took another step. If I reached out, I'd be able to stroke her side. I resisted the urge. Something told me this relationship had to come on her terms. I dipped my head, trying to send the message that I was deferring to her.

Ember sniffed at my hair and began to gum at it with her lips. Not biting, not nuzzling, maybe just trying to figure out who or what the heck I was. I couldn't hold in the soft laugh or the huge smile.

I slowly raised my head, meeting her curious gaze. "That can't taste very good." Slowly, so very slowly, I raised my hand to her cheek. Ember let me stroke her soft face twice before she backed away. I let her go.

She eyed me as though waiting for my anger at her retreat. I gave her nothing but my wide smile and the freedom to go. Her muscles eased, and she began nibbling at the hay on the ground.

"She's better with you than anyone else. You really do have a way with them, Jensen."

I turned at the sound of Dr. Neill's voice. "They have a way with me, too."

It was true. During the time I'd been working myself to the bone, too proud to ask for help, I'd sacrificed time with my horses. But having it again, I was reminded of how right my instincts could be. I just had to tap into that other sense, that deeper gut view of the world. And, slowly, I was starting to trust it again.

Dr. Neill brushed the hair from her face. "I think she'll be ready to go home with you in just a few weeks now."

I stood and ducked between the paddock rails, careful to keep my movements slow. "That's great news. I think it will really help her. I think being with Phoenix might help, too."

Dr. Neill watched Ember munch on more hay. "You might be right. She's healing well, but she needs companionship."

My chest tightened at the thought of all Ember had lost. "Phee knows what it's like to lose a family in a traumatic way. I think they might just be kindred spirits, those two."

Dr. Neill smiled. "Let's hope you're right. I've got to make my rounds, but call if you need anything."

"I will." I reached out and shook her hand. Turning back towards Ember, I leaned on the fence rail. "I've got to go, pretty girl, but I'll be back soon. Before you know it, you'll be home for good."

Ember raised her head at the sound of my voice, seeming to assess what I had said. She didn't appear convinced. That was all right. We had all the time in the world.

I wound my way through the paddocks and stalls, comforted by the familiar sounds and smells of the horses. A bird called overhead as I crossed the parking lot towards my SUV. My thoughts drifted to Tuck, as they did so often lately. Sometimes, it was just a flash of those Arctic blues in my mind's eye. Other times, it was a memory of something funny he'd said. Something sweet he'd done for Noah.

And if I were really lucky, it was a phantom feeling. As if his teeth were grazing my ear. His tongue trailing down my neck. His lips closing around my—the bird called from above again, and I realized I was about to walk smack into a parked car that wasn't mine.

Get ahold of yourself, Jensen. I straightened my path, shaking my head. I beeped the locks to my SUV as I approached and paused to grab a flyer shoved under one of the windshield wipers. I pulled open my door as I unfolded the paper.

I froze, my blood turning to ice.

Stop saving them, or you're next.

Drawn next to the messily scrawled text was a rifle scope target.

I jerked around, my gaze jumping from vehicle to vehicle, but there was no one paying me any attention. A handful of people headed to or from cars, staff members and horse owners dotted the rows of outdoor paddocks and fields, but not a single person looked in my direction.

I shakily slid into the driver's seat, closing the door behind me and pulling out my phone. I hit the most recent contact.

"What're you wearing, Wilder?"

"Tuck?" I hated that my voice trembled on the single word.

All playful amusement left Tuck's tone. "What's wrong? Where are you?"

I swallowed against the emotion in my throat. "I'm at the equine center visiting Ember. And someone left a note on my car. A threat."

"I'll be there in twenty. I want you to go inside and sit in the office. Tell them what happened. I don't want you alone. Have you called Walker?"

My eyes scanned the parking lot before I pushed open the door and got out. "No. I called you first."

"I'm gonna call him as soon as I hang up with you. It'll be a toss-up who gets there first."

I nodded and then realized that he couldn't see me. "Okay." I jolted a bit as something hit me. "Tell him to check my horses before he comes out here. Tuck, what if something happened to the herd? Oh, God. Ember." I lost all fear for myself as I realized whoever had left the note might be on the equine center grounds. I started to run for the facility.

My hand shook as I took a sip of water from the cup Dr. Neill had given me. But it was no longer from fear. It was from anger. Ember was fine, my horses at home were okay. Extra bodies were keeping an eye out now. But some asshole had threatened me and the creatures that held such a large piece of my heart. My blood was boiling.

"Wilder." The voice cut through the equine center's office like a whip.

I stood, water sloshing out of my cup and onto my hand. I set it down on the counter just as Tuck pulled me into his arms.

"Are you okay?" The words were a roughened whisper against my hair.

I nodded. "I was freaked. Now, I'm just pissed."

Tuck pulled back, his hands going to my arms, his gaze tracking over my face. "Did you see anyone?"

I blew out a breath. "No." My gaze tracked out to the parking lot. "I looked around as soon as I read the note. There were plenty of people, but no one seemed especially interested in me."

That muscle in Tuck's cheek ticked. "Where's the note?"

I inclined my head towards the counter. "No one's touched it but me."

Tuck released me and turned, bending over the counter to study the note. His body tightened as he read it, and when he straightened, the movement was stiff and stilted. "Wilder."

I edged closer, fisting his shirt in my hand. "I'm fine."

He hauled me against him. "Wilder." The single word was pained.

"I'm fine," I repeated, unsure of what else to say to ease him. "I'm safe."

"And we're keeping you that way."

"Is she okay?"

My brother's voice had us startling apart.

I brushed the hair back from my face. "I'm fine. Just pissed."

Walker strode over to the counter, glanced at the note, and cursed. His head snapped in my direction, his finger pointing. "No more rescue operations until we find this guy."

I opened my mouth to speak, but he kept right on going. "I don't want to hear it. It's too dangerous."

I threw up my hands on an exasperated sigh. "If you would shut up and listen for one single second, I was going to say that I didn't have the resources to take any more horses at the moment anyway."

Walker's jaw worked. "Well, good."

Tuck cleared his throat. "If you two are done bickering, can we focus on getting this note to a crime lab and figuring out how we're going to keep J safe?"

"She's never going to be alone, that's how."

I sighed and began rubbing my temples. "I'm not stupid. I'm going to take precautions, but I'm not living with some big, hulking shadow."

"Jensen—" My brother started.

I held up a hand to cut him off. "No. Come up with another option." I reached out and squeezed Walker's arm. "I love you, but I need some air right now. I'll be with Ember."

I strode out of the office and towards the paddocks. The sun still shone down, and I let the rays seep into my back as I rested against the fence. Ember was still happily munching away. At least, she was safe.

"We just don't want anything to happen to you."

I didn't turn at the sound of Tuck's voice. "I know. But I can't live my life with someone constantly hovering over my shoulder. I already have a hand helping with the horses every day." I turned to face him. "I need my moments alone, or I'll go crazy."

Tuck reached out and slid a strand of hair behind my ear. "I get it. I just want you safe."

I let my head fall to his chest. "Compromise?"

He trailed a hand up and down my spine. "Tell me what you're thinking."

"A ranch hand comes up with me to feed and make sure there's nothing suspicious going on, but he leaves afterward. And I don't open or close the Kettle alone."

Tuck's hand slipped beneath the fall of my hair, gently pulling my head back so our gazes locked. "Deal. But Walker and I are also adding cameras to all the gates at the ranch. The feed will go to your phone, so you'll be able to see and hear whoever you're letting in."

I took a step closer, our bodies flush against each other. "If it makes you feel better, fine."

"It does." He gave my hair another little tug. This time, it sent sparks of pleasure down my spine. "I want to kiss you so bad right now, I can taste you on my tongue."

My belly clenched. "I want your mouth on mine."

Footsteps sounded, and Tuck released me. "Fuck."

There was no lying to myself now, I wanted more. I wanted Tuck's hand in mine as we walked down the street. His arm around me at a movie. His lips on mine whenever we damn well pleased. I just had no idea if he would ever want the same.

CHAPTER
Thirty-Five

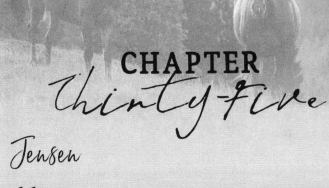

Jensen

"YOU'RE DOING POPCORN AND BROWNIES AND cookies, right?"

The hopeful tone of my little boy's voice had a smile tipping my lips. "Is it New Year's Eve, or is it New Year's Eve?"

A massive grin spread across Noah's face. "It's New Year's Eve."

I pulled the cooling brownies over to slice them. "Have you decided what movie you want to watch?" Every year, Noah and I had the same tradition—as many treats as our bellies could handle and a movie marathon. I always told him he could stay up as late as he wanted, but he'd yet to make it past ten.

Noah climbed up onto his stool so he could oversee the brownie slicing. "*Karate Kid*."

I fought the groan that wanted to surface. Since Noah had started karate lessons, I'd watched that movie more times than I could count. "You sure about that choice?"

Noah's head bobbed up and down so fast I was worried he might give himself whiplash. "I want to learn the fight sequence at the end."

I started lifting brownies onto a platter. "Then *The Karate Kid* it is."

A knock sounded at the door, and Noah jumped off his stool, racing for the entryway.

"Wait!" My voice held a thread of panic that had Noah skidding to a halt and looking confused. "Let me get it. We don't know who it is."

Usually, I had no problems with Noah answering the door. Our ranch had always been fenced and gated. No one got in without a code or someone buzzing them in. But between Cody's threats, the graffiti on my barn, and the note I'd gotten yesterday, I'd been more than a little on edge when it came to Noah's safety.

"It's me, guys," a voice boomed through the door.

Noah executed some sort of excited jump kick and bolted for the door. "It's Tuck, Mom! Come on!"

"Okay, okay, you can answer it." I wiped my hands on my apron. There was no reason to be nervous. I'd seen Tuck almost daily for most of my life.

Noah pulled open the door, revealing Tuck holding two grocery bags full of stuff. "Happy New Year's."

Noah jumped up and down. "It's not New Year's yet. Not till midnight. This year, I'm gonna make it till then. Whatcha got, Tuck?"

Tuck chuckled. "I couldn't come to the New Year's Eve epic junk food movie fest without a contribution." He started for the kitchen, Noah trailing behind, and gave me a wink as he passed. "I brought all my favorites. Sour cream and onion potato chips, Red Vines, Snickers."

Noah peeked into one of the bags. "That's awesome! Mom made brownies and cookies, and she's gonna make popcorn, too."

Tuck ruffled Noah's hair. "Then it sounds like all our bases are covered."

I shook my head. "It sounds like we're all going to be sick for days."

Noah pulled out a bag of chips. "But it'll be worth it."

Tuck and I both laughed. "So, what are we watching, little man?"

"*Karate Kid.*" Noah looked up at Tuck with uncertainty filling his expression. My heart cracked. My boy so wanted this man's approval.

Tuck's eyes widened. "Did you know that's my favorite movie of all time?"

Noah's expression morphed to one of wonder. "Really?"

"It's true. I watched that movie so many times growing up, I probably have it memorized."

Noah started bouncing on the balls of his feet. "I want to learn the fight sequence at the end."

"That scene is epic. We definitely need to watch it a few times to get that down."

Noah looked at me. "See, Mom? That's why I have to watch it so much, so I can get it perfect."

I smiled. "Whatever it takes."

"I'm gonna go find the movie, okay?" Noah charged out of the room before I had a chance to say anything.

I turned to Tuck. "What are you doing here?"

He moved in, giving me a swift kiss. "I wanted to spend New Year's Eve with you."

Warmth and something that felt a lot like hope filled my chest. "You didn't want to go to the saloon with Walker and Taylor?"

Tuck shook his head. "I'm where you are."

I looked across the sleeping boy sprawled between me and Tuck, a soft smile curving my mouth. Noah had made it to 10:35 this year. My boy was growing up. It wouldn't be long before he was up well past midnight.

As the credits to *The Karate Kid Part II* rolled, I started to rise.

Tuck stood quicker. "I've got him."

My movements stuttered. "Okay."

Tuck lifted Noah as though he weighed nothing more than the bowl of potato chips on the coffee table. I followed them up the stairs. Tuck made his way into Noah's room, and I snuck in front of them to pull back the covers so Tuck could lay him gently on the bed. Knowing how the night would likely go, I'd made Noah get in his pajamas before we started the second movie.

I pulled up the covers and snuggled Noah's favorite bear next to him. I pressed my lips to my son's hair, inhaling deeply the scent that was uniquely Noah's. "Love you," I whispered.

As I rose, Tuck grabbed my hand, leading me into the hall. "You're an amazing mom."

I shook my head. "You've seen us when we're a basket-case mess. I could do better."

Tuck framed my face with his hands. "It's not about things looking perfect all the time. It's about loving him and doing everything you can to give him the best life possible. You do that every single day."

Three little words hovered on the tip of my tongue, urging me to say them, but something held me back. I brushed my lips against his, soaking up the heat and the feel of him. I could get lost in his kisses forever. I pulled back just slightly.

I couldn't say those three little words, but I could be brave enough to say *something*. "This is more." My gaze tangled with his, so many unsaid things dancing between us. "You've always been more. It's just taken me a third of my life to see it."

A brief flare of panic shone in Tuck's eyes, mixed with something that looked a lot like pain, but he seemed to rein it in. "I don't know if I can be what you need me to be."

I gripped his wrists on either side of my face. "You already are. All I'm asking is that we take this one day at a time and see where it leads."

"One day at a time." Tuck pressed his mouth against mine. "I can do one day at a time."

CHAPTER
Thirty six

Tuck

I TOOK A SIP OF COFFEE AS I PORED OVER PAPERWORK AT MY kitchen table. The stuff never seemed to end, and always found a way home with me. It didn't help that my head just wasn't in the game these days. My mind wandered often, and always to the same place. Jensen.

My Wilder was going to drive me to distraction. And I would die of death by paperwork. The conversation on New Year's Eve had freaked me out. No, honestly, it'd terrified me, but I was determined to push through. We'd crossed a line that couldn't be uncrossed, and I wanted to make this work. I'd give anything to make it work.

My phone buzzed somewhere on the table. I patted the different stacks of paper, trying to find it. It buzzed again. My hand connected with something. I lifted a pile and hit accept without taking note of who was calling. "Hello?"

"Tuck."

I set down the stack of papers. "Hey, Cain. Happy New Year."

"Happy New Year. You get up to any trouble on New Year's Eve?"

I grinned down at my coffee as I thought of my evening. "I hung out with Jensen and Noah."

There was a moment of silence. "Walker know about that?"

My morning coffee soured in my gut. One thing I hadn't put a lot of thought into was how Walker would react to my seeing his sister. I hadn't put much thought into it because I'd planned for this to be temporary. But now that we were trying for more, I would have to tell him, and it wasn't going to be pretty. I cleared my throat. "I'm not sure."

Cain grunted.

I gripped the handle of my mug a little tighter. "What? Do you have a date with him after this for a gossip session?"

"No, but I was going to call him now that he knows I've been looking into Jensen's situation."

I straightened. "Did you find something?"

"I found the motherload."

I waited for him to continue, but he didn't. "Well, what the hell did you find?"

Papers shuffled in the background. "A little appreciation wouldn't be remiss."

I let out a growl. "Okay, thank you oh high and mighty hacker, sir. I'm so grateful for your nefarious ways. Now, will you tell me what the fuck you found?"

Cain chuckled. "That's the spirit." He paused for a moment. "Your boy is in deep."

If Cain and I had been in the same room, I probably would've punched him. I couldn't handle his cryptic teases. "In what sense?" I asked through gritted teeth.

"Let's start at the beginning. Cody Ailes has a weakness for gambling. It doesn't matter what it is—cards, horses, the fucking lotto. If there's a game of chance, he wants in."

I rubbed a hand over the scruff on my jaw. "Well, that explains the foreclosed house and all the debt."

"It gets worse."

Something in Cain's tone had my gut twisting. If Ailes had put Jensen and Noah in danger by coming to Sutter Lake, I was going to kill him.

The sound of fingers on a keyboard came over the line. "The gambling started early, before he even turned twenty-one."

I wondered if Jensen knew anything about that. Something told me she didn't. That had never been her scene.

"He graduated college early but didn't walk."

My jaw tightened. "Yeah, because he was too busy walking away from the nineteen-year-old girl he had just knocked up."

Cain ignored my outburst. "He moved to Philadelphia." That was just about as far away from Oregon as you could get and still stay in the continental US. "The gambling got worse, and he ended up on a loan shark's radar."

"Fuck." I rubbed at my temples where my head was starting to pound.

"That's when things got interesting. After the loan shark's guys put Cody in the hospital, the dude gave him a job."

My hand dropped from my head. "What?"

"I know. I guess the loan shark wanted someone familiar with *all* the various gambling action in Philly, and Cody definitely was. He was the inside man at a number of establishments all over the city. That helped for a while. Cody was able to offset what he gambled away by what he raked in for the loan shark."

I leaned back in my chair. "Something tells me things didn't stay that way."

"Do they ever when it comes to addiction?"

Cain's words had my father's face popping into my mind. I gritted my teeth. "No, they don't."

"Cody started losing more than he could cover. But here's the thing about doing business with lowlifes, there's always more of them hanging around who are happy to *help* you out. Cody started selling for a dealer. He sold at card games and at the race track."

My gaze went unfocused on the pile of paper in front of me. "I do not like where this is headed."

"You shouldn't. Yet again, the new gig kept Cody's head above water for a bit, but he got too bigheaded. Started sitting at higher-stakes games and losing. Big. Soon, they were taking his car, his house, anything the collectors could get their hands on. Credit cards were maxed out, and the people he lost to don't mess around." Cain paused. "He has two weeks."

"Two weeks for what?"

"Two weeks to deliver five hundred thousand dollars, or they come looking. And they won't be putting him in the hospital this time."

"Fuck!" I stood, my chair tipping back and crashing to the floor. "We've got to get him out of here. They can't figure out the tie to Jensen and Noah."

"I know, man. I'm about to email you all the leverage you need. Tell him you'll hand it over to the cops. Or worse, his boss. That should get him gone. If Cody's smart, he'll turn state's evidence and get himself into Witness Protection. Some of those guys he was working for are seriously connected."

My laptop dinged, and I clicked on the screen. "Got it. Thank you, Cain. I mean it."

"Always, brother. You know that. I'm going to call Walker in thirty. That gives you about an hour head start to get Cody out of town before Walker commits murder."

I grabbed my keys from my counter. "You know where he's staying?"

Cain scoffed as if what I'd said was insulting. "That shitty little motel at the edge of town."

I headed out my front door. "Room number?"

"One sixteen. Just do me one favor?"

I beeped the locks on my truck. "What's that?"

"Try not to get arrested or killed, would you?"

I pounded on the motel room door. It was a miracle that just that action didn't knock the whole thing down. There was no answer. I pounded again. "Open the fucking door, Ailes, or I'll take this interesting folder of information to the cops."

The door swung open. Cody stood there looking hungover and pissed. "What the fuck is your deal, man?"

I gave his chest a hard shove, sending him in reverse a few steps to finally fall back onto the bed. "Oh, I'm going to tell you what my *deal* is. You walk out on your responsibilities as a man. That's your problem. But you bring the fucking shitstorm that you've made of your life to my woman's door? In *my* town? Now, *that* is very much my fucking problem."

Cody's face paled. "I don't know what you're talking about."

I let out a laugh, but it was cold and ugly. "Stop playing games, asswipe. I've got a folder of photos and documents that could send you to jail for at least a decade or two. I'm guessing if they made their way into your boss's hands, you'd be saying goodbye permanently."

Cody pushed to his feet. "You can't threaten me."

I arched a brow. "Can't I? I've got people who will get that information to the cops *and* your boss if you haven't left town in one hour. I don't care where the fuck you go as long as it's out of the state of Oregon forever. When the paperwork comes through about terminating your rights to Noah, you won't fight it. You're going to do the first decent thing you've ever done for that kid and stay gone. Jensen is never going to hear from you again. Am I clear?"

Cody held up his hands in a gesture that was meant to be

appeasing or pleading but instead looked pathetic. "Just hear me out, man."

"You've got sixty seconds."

He started pacing. "I need the cash. Jensen has more than she needs. And from what I've seen and heard around town, your family does, too. Just get me the money, and I'll stay gone forever."

This guy was a total and complete moron. Did he really think I believed his bullshit? "We give you one penny, and you'll only come back for more. Not to mention, there isn't one damned thing you've done to earn it."

Cody's face screwed up into an ugly scowl. "And either of you have? The only thing you've done is gotten born into a rich family."

That muscle in my cheek began to tick. "How about we work for a fucking living? Jensen works herself to the bone almost every day trying to provide a good life for your son. What have you ever done?"

Cody threw up his hands. "God, that bitch must have developed a golden fucking pussy since I had her—"

I couldn't hear the rest of his words because the blood roaring in my ears was too loud. Every ounce of control I had simply snapped. And I lunged.

Just as my fist met Cody's jaw, the door burst open, and Walker was there, tearing me off Cody.

I struggled to break free of Walker's hold. "Let me go!"

Walker held firm. "Once you've calmed down. When Cain called and said you were going to run Cody out of town, I knew we were in trouble. I know I have a hot head when it comes to my sister, but you're even worse."

I swallowed hard. "I'm okay now."

Walker slowly released his hold and slapped me on the back.

Cody sat up from where he'd been sprawled on the floor. "I'm going to fucking sue your ass."

Walker smirked. "I don't know what you'd be suing him for. I saw the whole thing. Tuck was clearly defending himself. You can't sue just because you got your ass handed to you in a fight."

I grinned at Walker. "Well, thanks, Walk."

"Anytime, bud."

Cody pushed to his feet. "Get out of my room, you freaks."

My face went stony. "You've got one hour."

Cody flipped us the bird. "I want to get out of this hick town anyway."

Walker and I left the room and strode across the parking lot.

Walker paused for a moment, looking back at the motel. "You wanna wait him out? Make sure he leaves?"

"Of course."

Walker inclined his head. "I've got coffee in my truck. I was on my way to the station when Cain called."

I followed Walker towards his rig. "What I could really use right now is a whiskey."

Walker chuckled. "That I can't help you with."

I climbed into the truck. "Then coffee will have to do."

Walker poured some of the beverage into the thermos's cap and handed it to me. "Thanks for handling Ailes."

The muscles between my shoulder blades tightened. "Of course."

Walker met my gaze. "Really hear me. It means the fucking world that you care about my sister as much as I do."

This was it. The perfect moment to tell him that Jensen and I were more than just friends. I opened my mouth to say just that, but my throat held the words hostage. *Why couldn't I tell him?*

CHAPTER
Thirty-seven

Jensen

"**A**RTHUR, YOU'RE A FLIRT." I GRINNED AS I COUNTED out my favorite customer's change.

Arthur gave Kennedy a wink. "Well, what do you expect when you keep hiring gorgeous women?"

Kennedy handed Arthur his muffin. "Anytime you're ready to propose, I'll be here waiting."

Arthur chuckled. "I'd better go get that ring."

We watched as Arthur walked over to join his bridge cronies. Kennedy sighed. "I love that man. They just don't make them like that anymore. Did you know that he stayed until closing the other day because there was just one other man in here and he didn't want me to be alone?"

"He's a good egg." I glanced up from the register. "You weren't uncomfortable working alone, were you?"

Kennedy waved a hand in front of her face. "Not at all. I can take care of myself, but I thought it was sweet of Arthur to be so protective."

I smiled. "He's always looking out for *his girls*."

The bell over the door sounded, and my smile stretched wider as Tuck entered. My grin fell as I took in his face. He looked ready to commit murder. I motioned to Kennedy. "Can you handle the register for a minute?"

She straightened from rearranging the bakery case. "Of course."

I rounded the counter and gestured for Tuck to follow me into the kitchen. As soon as we were inside, I whirled on him. "What's wrong?"

Tuck ran a hand through his golden locks. "I need to fill you in on some Cody developments." My stomach pitched. "It's not a quick conversation. Can you take some time?"

I glanced out into the main room of the shop. The morning rush was over, the bridge crew was settled, and my mom would be in to help out in a couple of hours. "Let me check with Kennedy." I poked my head around the corner. "Kenz," I'd given her the nickname a couple days into her job here, Kennedy was just too dang formal. "Are you okay if I head out for a bit? My mom will be here in two hours to help with the lunch rush."

"Since all the baking is done for the morning, I'll be fine." Poor Kennedy still hadn't quite gotten the hang of baking.

She nodded. "I'll be fine. Take as long as you need."

Tuck gave Kennedy a chin jerk and headed for the door. I grabbed my purse and coat and followed. Tuck headed down the street towards where I could see his truck parked, his long strides dwarfing my own.

"Hey, behemoth, would you slow down?" I called.

Tuck paused, waiting for me to catch up. "Sorry, Wilder." He wrapped an arm around my shoulders. "I forget you're such a shrimp."

I pinched his side. "I am not a shrimp, you're just a freaking giant."

Tuck chuckled and guided me towards his truck, opening the door and helping me in. I watched as he rounded the hood of the vehicle, his strides purposeful and jaw still clenched. *What the hell is he about to tell me?* My insides seemed to twist themselves into a knot. I took a deep breath, trying to relax.

Tuck jumped in and started the rig. "Anywhere specific you want to go?"

I took a minute to study his face. "My horses."

Tuck nodded and headed out of town.

Our drive was silent. The urge I had to pepper him with questions on the walk to the vehicle vanished as soon as we started driving. Partly out of fear of what was to come. Partly because I just wanted to be with Tuck without bad news clouding the moment.

Tuck reached over and took my hand, twining his fingers with mine. His skin was rough, and I loved the feel of it against mine. His hands told the story of his life. Finely sandpapered from his work on the ranch and in the forest. A scar on his palm from when he and Walker had both gotten pocket knives for their tenth birthdays and decided that they needed to be blood brothers. Another on his finger from when a horse had kicked him and split it open.

I knew every story his hands told. And wasn't that the most precious gift? To know someone so deeply, so thoroughly that every detail of their skin was familiar. I loved this man. It would probably terrify him if I said the words aloud. But that didn't change a damn thing. I just hoped he could get used to it over time.

Tuck punched in the gate code and followed the gravel lane through the ranch to my pastures. The mustangs dotted the hillside, and something in me eased. He looked over at me. "Boulder?"

"Boulder." I slid out of the truck and took a moment to inhale the peace that flowed through the air up here. I could handle whatever he had to say.

Lips brushed against my temple, and my eyes flew open. Tuck was right there. Eyes blazing with a war of emotions, they flitted from one to the next so quickly I couldn't track them. I took his hand and squeezed, sending everything I felt through that one point of contact, hoping he would feel it even if he wasn't ready to hear it.

Tuck tugged me forward. "Come on."

We moved through the rails in the fence and headed for the boulder that was my favorite spot to sit. "You ready to tell me what's going on?"

Tuck grunted.

I hoisted myself up onto the rock. "Is that a no? Or is that an 'I've suddenly forgotten the English language that I've been speaking for over three decades?'"

"Stop being such a smartass."

I grinned over at him. "Now why would I want to do that?"

Tuck was silent for a moment. "Cody's gone."

The grin fell from my face. "Gone as in he took a trip? Gone like he went home? Or gone meaning you and Walker chopped him up into little bits and fed him to the pigs?"

Tuck chuckled and wrapped an arm around me. "Only you could make me laugh when talking about something that makes me fucking murderous."

I tipped my head back to study his face. "So, it was option three then. How do I keep you and Walker out of the clink?" I was trying to make light of it all, but in reality, my heart was hammering against my ribs, and my stomach roiled.

Tuck stared out at the horses below as they ran in formation across the pasture, Phoenix leading the way. "Cody was into some shit. It was bad. The people he is involved with are even worse."

I did my best to keep my breathing even. "How'd you find all this out?"

"Cain."

Of course. If my brother or Tuck needed dirt on anyone, that's who they called.

Tuck studied the forest surrounding the fields, seeing things that my eyes didn't pick up. "He got us enough information to force Cody's hand. He's gone. And it's for good."

I sucked in a breath. "I guess I should send Cain a muffin basket or something. Do billionaires like muffin baskets?"

Tuck gave my shoulder a firm squeeze. "Stop. You're making light of all this, which means inside, you're freaking out. Talk to me."

He knew me so damn well. Traitorous tears began to gather in my eyes. "Are Noah and I safe? Are these people going to come after us?"

Tuck shook his head and reached his hands up to frame my face. "No, Wilder. They have no idea you exist, and that's how it's going to stay."

I nodded into Tuck's hands, and he used his thumbs to wipe away my tears. "Thank you."

"For what?"

I turned my head so I could press my lips to Tuck's palm. "For getting him gone. For protecting Noah and me. You're a good man, Tucker Harris."

His body jolted as though the smallest bolt of lightning had hit him. "You deserve better."

My eyes bored into his, trying to make him understand. "I want you."

CHAPTER
Thirty-Eight

Jensen

THERE WAS A TUG ON THE BACK OF MY SHIRT. I LOOKED up from helping my mom slice veggies for our family dinner to see Noah.

"Mom, where's Tuck? I need him to help me with *The Karate Kid* fight."

I glanced over at my mom. "He's still coming, right?"

She shut the door to the oven. "He called this afternoon. Said he was still coming but that he might be a bit late. That case and all."

My stomach twisted. I wanted Tuck to find the person terrorizing the mustangs, but I hated that doing so meant that he was in danger every day until the guy was caught. I ran my hand over Noah's hair. "You hear that?" Noah nodded. "Maybe you can practice until Tuck gets here."

"Good idea." With that, he took off for the den on the other side of the house.

Grams, who was perched on a bar stool next to Taylor, took a sip of her wine. "Maybe I should go help him with his moves."

Taylor attempted to cover her laugh with a cough. My mom and I just let ours fly.

Grandma scowled. "What? I was a brown belt in my day."

"You were not," my dad called from the living area. "You took three weeks of classes and then got bored. Just like those hatchet throwing lessons you started a few months back."

She let out a huff. "Well, my teacher said I had a lot of promise. Maybe I'll pick them back up again and go with Noah. We can go for our black belts together."

Dad tipped his head back as if searching the heavens. "Lord, save me."

"Oh, shut it. Just remember who gave you life." Grandma's eyes narrowed on him. "I can just as easily take it away."

Walker thumped Dad on the back. "You better watch out, old man." He chuckled. "Come on, let's go out to the barn and you can show me that new Paint mare you picked up."

The men headed out, and we returned to cooking and sipping wine.

"Finally, some peace around here," Grandma muttered.

My mom dressed the salad and began to toss it. "If you're around to cause trouble, I'm not sure there's much hope for peace."

Grams threw up a hand. "No respect, I tell you."

Mom handed me the salad greens so I could add the veggies. "So, how is Tuck doing?"

My shoulders tensed. "What do you mean?"

She started pressing circular cookie cutters into the biscuit dough. "I heard Craig moved out. I've wanted to go visit Helen, but I wasn't sure if she'd be up for visitors quite yet."

My muscles eased a bit. "I think she'd like that. Tuck told me she and her lawyer filed the paperwork yesterday."

Grandma raised her glass. "Good for her. That man never deserved her." Her eyes cut to me. "That's the thing. Sometimes, you've got to weed through the bad eggs to find a good one. But once you do, you hold on tight."

My cheeks heated, and I became incredibly focused on my salad making.

Taylor slapped her hands down on the counter. "Okay, I can't take this anymore. What is going on between you two?!"

I froze. "I don't know what you're talking about."

Taylor threw up her hands. "Oh, please. I've seen the chemistry between you two from day one, but lately, it's different. Hotter."

"Definitely hotter," Grandma chimed in.

Taylor kept going. "I swear sparks fly off the two of you when you're in the same room. I'm pretty sure the only person who hasn't noticed is Walker. But that's because he's got his head in the sand about his baby sister."

I reached across the counter and grabbed Taylor's hand. "Please don't say anything to him."

Her eyes flared. "So, there's something to say?"

"Promise."

Taylor made a cross over her heart with her free hand. "I swear on my sisterhood membership card."

Grandma took another sip of wine. "That's legit."

I eyed Grandma and Mom. Both stared at me intently.

My mom reached out and grabbed my hand, giving it a squeeze. "What's going on?"

I collapsed onto the stool at the end of the bar. "I don't know. It started out casual. Just letting off some steam that I really needed an outlet for."

Grandma raised her glass in my direction. "You go, girl."

I sighed. "But almost immediately, it was more than that. I was an idiot to think that we could do the friends-with-benefits thing."

Mom slapped her spatula against the counter. "Don't you talk about my daughter that way. You are not an idiot."

God, I loved my mom. "It's just that he's always been my best friend. I mean, I know he and Walker have basically been blood brothers from the womb, but he's always been something to me, too. I can't describe it. He's just always been...*more*."

Mom nodded. "You two have always had a special bond." She smiled down at her biscuit dough. "When you were a baby and upset, Tuck could always get you to stop crying."

I turned to her. "I didn't know that."

She nodded. "When you hit high school and looked so much like a young woman, your father and I started to worry a bit about all those drives you took together. We kept waiting for him to ask you out. But it never happened."

I thought about how much I would've killed for a kiss or date during those high school years. When it never came, I'd just made peace with the idea that he didn't have those kinds of feelings for me. "I don't trust myself."

Grandma leaned towards me. "What do you mean, sweetheart?"

Hot tears pricked the corners of my eyes. "I've made such bad decisions when it comes to men. I'm scared that just me being in love with him is a sign I should run in the opposite direction."

Mom wrapped an arm around me. "Those experiences mean you know better than most. You know how you deserve to be treated. If those red flags surface, you're strong enough to cut the cord."

Grandma gestured with her wine glass. "And strong enough to cut his balls."

Taylor choked on her wine, and we all dissolved into laughter.

But a small ball of anxiety rolled around in my gut. I didn't know if I'd ever be strong enough to walk away from Tuck, even if the tides did turn. And what did that say about me?

CHAPTER
Thirty-Nine

Tuck

I SLAMMED MY TRUCK DOOR. A WHOLE LOT OF NOTHING was all I had to show for the wild horse case. I'd spent the day visiting with every single rancher who had leased land around Pine Meadow—and found nothing.

Rich, the rancher who'd had a few sheep stolen, had already brought the rest of his flock down for the winter and said he'd been avoiding the area like the plague since all the craziness started. David's brother, Bill, did his best to make introductions to other ranchers, but the group had closed ranks. None of them were wild horse supporters, so they had to assume that they were on a short list of suspects.

I did my best to be unassuming, to stress that I saw them as potential witnesses and nothing more. None of it helped. Not even Bill vouching for me got the ranchers to open up. I kicked at a piece of gravel.

"What'd that rock ever do to you?"

I looked up to see Jensen crossing the drive. Just the sight of her stole my breath. Her hair flew around her face, a bit wild, just like her. That dark shade of brown bringing out the golden hue of her skin. My chest seized. I wanted her more than my next breath.

Jensen held out a hand and led me around the house. As soon as we were out of sight, her lips were on mine, hungry, seeking, almost desperate. My own returned the frantic need. Tongues dueled, teeth tugged at lips, my hands got lost in her hair then wandered lower, gripping her ass. I needed more. All of her. I wanted to imprint myself on every last cell of her body. I pulled back with a gasp. "Have to stop now, or I won't."

Jensen took a few heaving breaths. "That was a hell of a hello, cowboy."

I grinned. "I like to keep you on your toes."

"Well, you've certainly done that." She peeked around the side of the house. "We'd better get back inside, or someone might come looking."

I grabbed her hand, tugging her forward. "Let's go."

Just as we headed up the stairs, the front door opened and Walker appeared, brows pulled together. I dropped Jensen's hand like a hot poker. "Where have you two been?"

Jensen cleared her throat. "I just wanted to get an update on the case before Tuck came inside."

Walker's gaze flicked to me. "Anything?"

I shook my head. "Not a damn thing. I swear this guy is a ghost."

Walker slapped me on the back as I passed. "No one's a ghost. If anyone can find this guy, it's you."

Guilt flooded me. Walker was the brother I'd never had. He trusted me. Believed in me. And here I was, basically lying to his face. *Fuck.* "Thanks, man."

"Dinner's ready," Sarah called from the kitchen. "Oh, good, you're here, Tuck." She studied the table. "I think I might have made too much."

I grinned and wrapped an arm around her. "I'm happy to help you out with that, Mama Sarah."

She squeezed my hand. "I'm sending you home with left-overs, too."

"Twist my arm."

Jensen pulled out a chair. "I'll invite Kennedy to come next time."

Sarah smiled at her daughter while motioning for me to take the seat next to Jensen. "That would be wonderful. That girl is just the kindest, and I hate that she's so young and all alone here."

I lowered myself into the chair. "How old is she?"

Jensen rolled her eyes. "She's twenty-two. The way Mom talks about her, you'd think she was fifteen."

Sarah took a seat across from us. "Oh, hush. Twenty-two is just a baby."

Jensen's gaze went unfocused. "Something tells me she's wiser than her years."

Maybe I needed to pay better attention when I went into the Kettle, figure out what this girl's story was. The last thing I needed was Jensen getting caught up in another dangerous situation an employee dumped on her doorstep.

Irma settled into the seat next to Sarah and grinned at me. "How ya doing, hot stuff?"

Jensen, who had just taken a sip of water, started choking.

I patted her on the back. "Are you okay?"

Jensen wiped her mouth with her napkin. "I'm fine." She glared at her grandmother. "Or I would be if someone would keep table conversation appropriate."

Irma took a sip of wine. "Oh, don't be such a stick in the mud. I'm allowed to appreciate a fine piece of man meat."

I chuckled. "I feel so used."

Irma pointed at me with a butter knife. "Buck up, sonny, and take it as a compliment. I've got good taste."

Dinner passed in its usual fare. Multiple loud conversations going on at once. Lots of laughter. Delicious food. And Jensen at my side. I reached under the table and squeezed her hand. Her eyes met mine and held, so much passing between us. Some I wasn't sure I was ready for.

"Noah, it's almost time to get ready for bed." Andrew stood and gestured for his grandson to rise.

"Aw, man," Noah pouted. "Can't Mom and Tuck take me?"

My eyes widened. Noah usually asked for Walker on nights like this. "Of course, we can." The table was more silent than usual as Jensen and I rose and left with Noah. I wondered if others were starting to put the pieces together.

We headed across the gravel drive. I held one of Noah's hands, and Jensen held the other. The boy swung between us every few steps, chattering away the whole time.

Jensen unlocked the door and pushed it open. "Noah, run upstairs and put on PJs and brush your teeth. Then Tuck and I will come and read to you."

We stood in the entryway while Noah ran upstairs. Drawers opened and closed. Water began running. Jensen and I stayed in place. Taking in the sweet simplicity of the moment.

"I'm ready," Noah called.

We headed upstairs. Noah wanted me to read him a book about Muhammad Ali, and Jensen to read him one about mountain lions. Then it was time for bed.

I ruffled Noah's hair. "Goodnight, little man."

Noah yawned. "Love you, Tuck."

A fist clamped around my heart. "Love you, too." The words came out choked, but they were there. This precious boy loved me. And I wanted nothing more than to give that back to him. To be the man he could depend on. That fist in my chest tightened again as visions of all the ways my father had let me down filled my mind.

I shook my head, trying to clear it as I forced myself to follow Jensen down the stairs. I could do this. I wasn't my father.

Jensen paused at the bottom of the stairs. "Thanks for being so good with him."

I tucked a strand of hair behind her ear. "He's the best."

She shuffled a little closer to me. "I think so. I wish you could stay."

I swept my lips against Jensen's. "I do, too." I kissed each temple, then her forehead. "I'll tell you what. I'll call you when I get home." I gave her a wicked grin. "Maybe we can have a little phone action."

Jensen fisted my shirt. "I guess I better go get that toy out of my nightstand."

My jaw fell open. "You don't have…"

She winked at me. "You'll find out soon enough."

I cut the engine on my truck. Other than the front porch light, the entire house was dark. I realized in that moment that it looked fucking lonely. And that's what my life had been. Sure, I'd had women warming my bed. I went to family dinners at the Coles', I saw my mom, I shot the shit with my co-workers. But I'd kept everyone at arm's length.

Until Jensen had wormed her way into my life and into my fucking heart. I guess it was nothing new. She'd always been there. Knowing me more deeply than anyone else. Seeing things others glossed over. But since we'd started this thing between us, it was like she'd come in and turned on the lights. Suddenly, I could see everything more clearly.

Tomorrow morning, I was going to go see Walker and tell him that I was in love with his sister. I'd take whatever hits he gave, but I wasn't going anywhere.

I slid out of my truck and headed up the stone path. My steps faltered, and my hand went to my Glock as I saw a figure hunched over on my front porch. The figure's head came up, and he sneered.

"There he is. The life-ruiner himself."

Fuck. "What are you doing here, Dad?"

He pushed to his feet, wobbling just a bit. "Aren't you going to invite your old man in? I got nowhere else to go. And whose fault is that?"

I started past him and up the steps. "You've never had a problem finding a place to stay before now. I'm sure you'll land on your feet."

Dad caught hold of my arm. "That ranch was supposed to be mine. You don't even appreciate the gift that was dropped at your feet. Not that you'd be worthy of it anyway."

I tore my arm out of his grasp. "There's only one person who's responsible for your life turning into a shitshow. You, Dad. You're the one who had everything at your feet. A wife who loved you. A son who adored you. A ranch to guide and grow. But it was never enough. You were always looking for more. More land. More control. More booze. More women. Nothing was ever good enough."

My dad's face twisted. "That's rich coming from you. My son, who is just like me. Aren't you always searching for more? Another adventure? A job with just a little more risk? More women? Hell, you've had half the females in the state. You're just like your old man."

My gut twisted, but I stayed silent.

Dad chuckled. "What? Cat got your tongue? I see you sniffing around that Cole girl. You are going to ruin her. She'll be nothing but a pile of tears and ash when you're done with her. And what's worse. She's got a kid."

My fists clenched and flexed as blood roared in my ears. "You don't know what you're talking about."

"Don't I?" He grinned at me, but the curve of his mouth had a feral quality to it. "I'm just going to kick back and watch. It's about time this town saw you for who you really are. The high and mighty Tucker Harris is really just trash. Trash that's gonna drag an innocent woman and her son down with him."

"Go sleep it off." I turned to head inside, but my movements were jerky. My palms were slick, and my hands trembled as I tried to shove the key into the lock.

My dad laughed. "Oh, boy, this is going to be so much fun to watch."

I glanced over my shoulder to see him walk down my front path and away from my house, a slight sway to his steps. I didn't have it in me to even make sure he got to wherever he was going safely.

I took a deep breath and slid my key into the lock and turned it. He was wrong. I loved Jensen. I could be faithful. I wouldn't get bored and turn to the bottle or other women the way my father had. I wouldn't ruin the best thing that had ever happened to me.

My phone buzzed in my pocket. I slid it out. Jensen's name flashed on the screen. I stared at the letters. Memories flashed through my mind. Her head thrown back in unrestrained laughter. The wonder on her face when she watched the mustangs. The way her skin seemed to hum beneath my touch. The kindness that lit her eyes when she helped Arthur with his cane. The pure love that poured out of her anytime she was around Noah.

Wilder was the best woman I'd ever known. The best I would *ever* know. She and Noah deserved so much more than a gamble. My finger hovered over the phone's screen.

I hit accept. "Jensen." My voice gave the slightest waver. "I can't do this anymore."

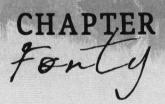

CHAPTER
Forty

Jensen

I SHOVED THE DRAWER OF THE REGISTER CLOSED A BIT harder than necessary. Okay, fine. A lot harder.

"Whoa, there. What's going on with you?" Taylor asked.

I glanced around the Kettle. Other than a couple in the far corner, it was just me, Taylor, and Kennedy. "Tuck ended things."

Taylor's mouth fell open. "What?"

"No explanation, no nothing. Would barely let me get a single word in before he hung up. And now, he's not taking my calls." I blew out a long breath. "I haven't heard from him in three days."

Tuck and I had eased into a routine of sorts. I saw him most days, even if it was just him popping into the Kettle for a baked treat. And we definitely spoke every day. Usually, multiple times a day. Without me realizing it, he'd become my touchpoint, my cornerstone. And I hated him a little bit for that. For giving it to me and then taking it away. My shoulders slumped. "I thought we were moving in the right direction."

Taylor rounded the counter and wrapped an arm around me. "You were moving in the right direction. This might just be a hiccup."

I shook my head. "It's not. He was supposed to call me the night of the family dinner after he got home. You know, for a *fun* phone call."

Taylor's brows rose. "Ah, one of those."

I nodded. "Instead of a sexy call, I got a two-sentence brush-off. Now, he's not returning my texts or calls. But I've seen his truck around town. I know he's fine."

"Not fucking cool." Kennedy leaned against the counter. "Sorry about the curse, but no other word would do."

Taylor raised her cup of tea in Kennedy's direction. "Amen to that, sister." She glanced at me. "Do you think he's just not ready yet?"

My blood began to heat. "The why doesn't matter. If there's one thing I've learned from the disaster that's been my love life, it's that people's actions show you way more about who they are than anything they will ever say." Hot tears pricked the corners of my eyes. "He's shown me very clearly that he doesn't want me. I have to hear that."

Taylor set her tea down on the counter and pulled me into a full hug. "I'm so sorry, honey. You deserve way better than this."

Kennedy rubbed a hand up and down my back. "I could always accidentally trip and spill scalding hot tea on him the next time he comes in."

I let out a snorted laugh as I straightened. "I'm lucky to have you both."

Taylor squeezed my arms before she released me. "This means only one thing."

I ran a finger under my eyes, trying to clear any sign of tears. "What's that?"

"We need a girls' night. Two, actually."

Kennedy straightened the stack of to-go menus on the counter. "Two?"

Taylor nodded. "Yup. The first entails the three of us in our

PJs, wine, chocolate, a chick flick that will make us sob, then a chick flick that will make us cackle. The second means us getting all dolled up, hitting up the saloon, having some cocktails, and getting our flirt on."

I grinned at Taylor. "You know Grandma Irma is going to want in on both of those."

Taylor clapped her hands together. "Oh, she's a must. That woman can get down."

Laughter erupted out of me as I remembered Grandma and Taylor's dance party in the kitchen a few weeks ago. My gaze caught on a figure across the street, and I stilled. My fists clenched.

Nearly three decades of friendship. The hottest sex of my life. Sharing things I'd shared with no one else. I deserved more than a disappearing act. I was owed a grown-up conversation. One where I was able to get a word in edgewise. "Kennedy, I need you to watch the register for a minute."

Taylor followed my line of sight. "Uh, J, I don't know if that's such a good idea."

I was already headed for the door. "It's probably a horrible idea." But I wasn't playing things safe any longer. I pushed open the door and moved down the walk. My strides grew quicker, my boots hitting the pavement harder with each step. With each contact, my anger grew. I was so sick of being tossed aside like yesterday's trash.

I gained on Tuck. Finally, I was within reach and tapped him on the shoulder. He turned, eyes going wide at the sight of me. "Hey, Jensen."

My hands balled into fists. "Hey, Jensen? Really?" He said nothing. "That's it? No, oh my gosh, you won't believe it, I was kidnapped by aliens, and they just returned me to Earth, and the first thing I did was come find you."

Tuck stood stock-still, not saying a word.

I fought the urge to curl in on myself. Never again would I give someone the power to make me feel less than. "Say something, you fucking coward." The words came out on a whisper, but I saw each one hit like a physical blow.

Tuck's mask slipped into place, and he shrugged. "When we started this thing, it was supposed to be casual. That's what I wanted. You pushed for more, but that's just not who I am."

Those hot, traitorous tears tried to rise, a mix of anger and betrayal. "This was more, and you know it."

That muscle in Tuck's cheek ticked. "This was friends scratching an itch. But it was a mistake."

I stared at Tuck, my gaze not breaking from his. "That's the first time you've ever lied straight to my face." He flinched. "But that doesn't matter. Because if there's one thing I've learned, it's to never waste a second of my time on someone who doesn't value all the amazing things I would bring into their world." Tuck said nothing. I nodded. "Right."

I turned on my heel and strode back to the Kettle. I forced my steps to be measured, unhurried. I didn't allow my shoulders to shake, even though tears streamed down my face. I would give Tucker Harris no clue that he had just ripped my still-beating heart out of my chest. And while emergency surgery could be done to make repairs, I knew things would never be quite the same.

I pushed open the door. Taylor and Kennedy both stood there, wide-eyed.

"Oh, shit." Taylor opened her arms, and I stepped into them. "He's a total moron."

"I know." My voice was muffled against her shoulder.

Kennedy rubbed my back. "He's the biggest moron who ever morraned."

I let out a small laugh.

Taylor released her hold on me. "He's going to realize that he made a big mistake."

I grabbed a napkin from one of the tables and wiped under my eyes. "I'm not so sure about that." I stared out the window to the empty street. "And even if he does, I think it's too late."

Taylor worried her bottom lip. "I fucked up. I almost ruined the best thing that ever happened to me. But Walker forgave me. And look at us now." Her new engagement ring caught the light as she talked.

I sighed. "You and Walker are different. You had just lost your mom. You were grieving and scared."

Taylor reached out and took my hand. "I was scared. So, I know what it looks like. And that man out there…" She gestured to where Tuck had stood on the sidewalk. "He's terrified."

My insides seemed to twist themselves into complicated knots. I'd seen hints of fear as Tuck and I had gotten closer, but I had no clue what they were about. And I wasn't sure that it really mattered at the end of the day. "If that's the case, then he needs to grow a pair and tell me he's scared. We could work through it together. But I can't do this alone. And, more importantly, I won't try. I've done it before, and I don't like the woman it made me into."

Memories assaulted me. Calling Cody over and over. Endless internet searches trying to find his new number. Hoping against hope that he'd somehow show up at the hospital when I went into labor. That he'd hear that I'd had Noah and suddenly realize he wanted to be a father. I wasn't ever going to put myself through that again.

Taylor squeezed my hand. "You don't have to do anything you don't want to do. Just keep an open mind as things unfold. I have a feeling growing up around his parents' relationship may have colored things for him."

Taylor had a point about that. I blew out a breath. I needed some space. Time alone to think things through. I turned back to the girls. "Taylor, I have a favor."

"Name it."

I glanced at the time on my phone. "Could you pick Noah up from karate at three?"

Little worry lines appeared on her forehead. "Of course. You're not planning to bash in Tuck's truck and get arrested, are you?"

Her question brought a small smile to my lips. "No. I just need some time alone. To sort everything through. Get myself together."

The worry lines on Taylor's face didn't fade. "You'll be safe?"

"I'm just going to the ranch. Spend some time with Phoenix and the rest of my girls."

Taylor smiled. "Sounds like a great plan. I'll grab Noah at three. Walker's off duty around then, so we can all go for ice cream or something. You can pick him up at our place when you're done. No rush."

I gave her a quick hug. "Thanks. I have my phone if you need anything."

I headed out the door. I'd let myself fall apart for a little while, and then I'd never cry another tear over Tucker Harris again.

CHAPTER
Forty-One

Tuck

"**F**UCK!" I SLAMMED THE FRONT DOOR OF MY HOUSE and plunged my fist into my newly plastered but still not repainted entryway wall. I pulled my arm out, drywall dust flying everywhere. I didn't care about any of it. Not the new hole in my wall. Not the mess on the floor. Not the blood dripping down my hand.

None of it.

Jensen wouldn't be showing up to make sure I was okay. She wouldn't insist on pulling out the first-aid kit to doctor my cuts. She wouldn't make me a homemade ice pack. And I sure as hell wouldn't be able to distract myself from the shitstorm that was my life by losing myself in her body.

And there was only one person to blame for that. Me. I'd ruined everything, just like my dad had said I would. But it was for the best. Like crash-landing your plane into a field instead of risking plowing into a building full of people. Everything would be so much worse if I fucked things up farther down the line. Jensen depending on me, Noah more attached.

I'd been right to pull the plug now. I was saving Jensen from myself. Eventually, she'd see that. Someday, we'd find our way back to friendship. She'd meet someone worthy of her, and it would tear at my insides, but I would be happy for her.

I walked into the kitchen and pulled a bottle of vodka from the freezer. I headed over to the sink and rinsed off my hand. I uncorked the vodka bottle with my teeth and hissed when the liquid hit my torn knuckles.

I set the bottle down on the counter and let my hand drip into the sink. I stared straight ahead, out the window and into the postage-stamp-sized backyard that I hated. This was my life now.

My phone buzzed in my back pocket. With my un-abused hand, I pulled it out. My brow furrowed. Why in the hell was Taylor calling me? My shoulders tensed, but I hit accept. "Hey, Taylor."

"You're a fucking idiot."

I sighed, placing the phone down on the counter and hitting the speaker button. "Well, hello to you, too."

"Don't give me that shit. I was rooting for you two. For weeks now, I've been practicing the speech I was going to give Walker to keep him from losing his shit when he found out."

My jaw clenched. "Well, now you can retire that speech."

Taylor let out a little growl. "I don't want to retire it! I want two people who I love very much to get their heads out of their asses and realize they're perfect for each other."

I gripped the edge of the counter, the action causing my split knuckles to reopen. "This is the best thing I could ever do for her. Walking away."

"Oh my God. Enough with the martyr crap already."

A small grin curved my mouth. "You know, you curse a lot for an elementary school teacher."

"Well, I'm not in front of a bunch of fucking ten year olds right now, am I? Actually, based on your emotional IQ, maybe I am. Why are you doing this?"

There was that familiar ticking in my cheek again. "Because I'm no good for her."

Taylor's voice grew gentle. "Why would you think that?"

I ran a hand through my hair, staying silent.

Taylor sucked in a breath. "Tuck, you're not your father."

I let out a chuckle, but it was cold. "That's not what he says."

"From the little I've seen and heard, your father is a drunk, a cheater, and an asshole. Why would you listen to a word he says? I'm sure he doesn't even believe half the shit that comes out of his mouth."

I twirled the bottle of vodka around on the counter, the same one that had been in my freezer for almost a year. "Doesn't mean he's wrong."

"Why do *you* think he's right?"

I drummed my fingers against the glass. "I like women."

Taylor snorted. "I like men. That doesn't mean I'm going to cheat on Walker."

I grinned at the counter. "I've had a bit more of an active sex life than you, Taylor."

"That *you* know of." She was quiet for a moment. "Has any woman grabbed your attention for more than just a fleeting, appreciative glance since you and Jensen started up?"

I thought back to the girl in the bar right before Jensen and I had gotten together. I couldn't even remember her name now. The truth was that every female paled in comparison to Jensen. They always had.

There was no body I craved more, not because it looked any particular way, but because it was hers.

There was no one I wanted to talk to more at the end of the day. I wanted her laughter, her tears. I wanted to know every thought that entered her head. That had never been the case with any other woman.

I had known for a long time that Jensen Cole was the only

woman for me. I'd just resigned myself to never having her fully.

"What if I hurt her?"

Taylor sighed. "The truth is, you will. You already have. But it's about how you mend those hurts. How you learn from them and try again."

My chest clenched. "I need to fix this."

"Yes, you do."

I tore off some paper towels from the roll on the counter and did my best to clean up my marred hand. "Is she still at the Kettle?"

"No. She left about an hour ago. Said she needed some time alone, to think. So, I'm on my way to pick up Noah from karate."

My heart stopped. "She shouldn't be wandering around alone right now. She knows that."

"Relax, Tuck. She just went back to the ranch. She wanted to be with her horses."

The vise that had settled around my chest relaxed just a bit. "Good." I paused. "Taylor?"

"I'm still here."

I let out a long breath. "Thank you."

A car engine turned over. "You can thank me by fixing this."

I grabbed my keys off the counter. "You got it."

I tapped end on the screen. I'd have a battle on my hands, but I wouldn't stop until Jensen had forgiven me. I just had to hold onto the flicker of hope I hadn't fucked things up beyond repair.

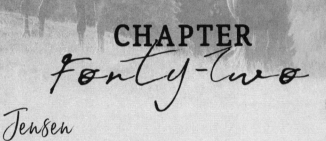

CHAPTER
Forty-Two

Jensen

THE DRIVE UP TO THE RANCH WAS QUIET. TOO QUIET. There was nothing to do but play the conversation with Tuck over and over in my head. Maybe I'd been wrong. So very wrong about him. Maybe I'd seen things that weren't there because I so badly wanted them to exist.

I hated the way my mind played tricks on me. That insidious doubt crept over everything and infected it with its poison. It made me question every moment Tuck and I had shared. What was real? What was merely a figment of my imagination? Maybe I'd never know.

I turned off the main road and onto our gravel drive that would lead me to my horses, my peace. The divots in the lane jarred my spine. If only that were enough to shake the memories of Tuck from my mind loose. An invisible fist seemed to squeeze my heart. How did I forget someone who had been woven into my life from the day I was born?

It had to be impossible. My only hope was that the pain would dull with time. When Cody left me, I'd thought the pain would take me out, I had been so devastated. When I learned the truth about who Bryce really was, I'd felt so dirty, I'd thought I would never get clean again.

But I'd persevered. I'd healed my damn self. For my son. For me. And then Tuck had come along, ruining my perfect plan of never letting another man into my heart. Tucker Harris had taken me out like a freight train. But there was nothing I could do to stop it.

Getting a taste of what life could have been with him, how sweet that existence would be, only to have it ripped out from under me. There was no coming back from that. The pain of a dream you could just barely touch with your fingertips, torn viciously from your grasp.

The only hope I had was to go numb. To turn off that part of myself that yearned for more. The part that remembered what it had been like to think I might get it.

I pulled my SUV to a stop outside my pasture, just in time to see my herd galloping across the field, Willow leading the charge. The elderly mare had come so far. Had proven that she had so much life left to live. Yes. This was what I needed. I slipped from the car and headed for the fence line. Ducking between the rails, I headed for my boulder.

Memories flashed. All the times Tuck had found me here. The endless conversations. Some about nothing at all. Others about the most important things we held deep inside for no one else to see. How could all of that have been a lie? I pressed my palms against the rock below me. I didn't believe it could be.

Phoenix nosed my shoulder. I turned, stroking her face. "Hey, Phee. You always know when I need a little extra love, huh?" She nuzzled in closer.

As I ran my hands down her neck, I watched the rest of the horses dance and play. Even Willow got in on the action, giving a little buck as she ran after a much younger mustang.

I sucked in a deep breath, letting the crisp pine air fill my lungs. I let my eyes close. I had so much. My son. My family. These beautiful horses. It would have to be enough. A flash of pain seared through my chest. Even my body didn't believe that lie.

My eyes opened at the sound of tires on gravel. I watched an unfamiliar truck pull up to the pasture. A man got out, cowboy hat hiding his face. And it looked like another was still in the vehicle.

My heart rate picked up just a bit. The man took off his hat, and my muscles relaxed. "Hey, Bill, what're you doing here?"

Bill ducked between the fence rails. "Afternoon, Miss Jensen. I was just coming by to check out a horse your dad trained. Might be adding her to my stable."

My mouth curved. "The Paint?"

"That's the one. She's a beaut." Bill looked out at the herd of horses in my pasture. "Why don't you train these mustangs? I know you've got the touch. You could sell them, make a decent living."

I gave him a kind smile. "I've trained a few, but not all of them are cut out for riding."

A flicker of a scowl appeared on Bill's face, but it was gone so quickly, I wondered if I'd imagined it. "Not a lot of purpose to them then, huh?"

My own scowl threatened. Phoenix edged closer to me as if recognizing the insult. "The purpose is life. Respect. Freedom."

Bill gave his head a shake. "At the cost of our ability to thrive?"

Phoenix danced at my side, almost trying to herd me away from Bill. I pressed my lips together and continued rubbing a hand up and down Phee's neck. "I think there has to be a balance, a way for ranchers to run their businesses successfully *and* for the mustangs not to lose any more of their home."

Bill tapped his hat against his leg. "I wish you could understand things from our perspective. Maybe you should come up to Pine Meadow with me, meet some of the smaller ranchers who are really affected by this."

A trickle of unease slid down my spine. It wasn't just because this man didn't see the value in my precious horses. It was something else. Phoenix let out a whinny. I took a step back, thoughts swirling and connecting.

Bill had a ranch between Sutter Lake and Pine Meadow. And he leased near where the mustangs resided. He'd been a stoic supporter of increasing the lands available to ranchers. He never raised his voice at those speaking on behalf of the mustangs, never called us names. But I remembered the flash of rage I'd seen on his face when there had been a town hall meeting about the proposal.

My stomach churned. Was I standing with the man responsible for all the heartbreaking loss my mustangs had endured? I took another step back, making a show of looking at my watch. "I'd better get going. I need to pick up Noah."

Bill studied me as he moved out of my path. "Of course. We can discuss the horses another time."

The muscles I hadn't realized were strung bow-tight eased. The events of the past few months had to be catching up with me, that was all. I gave Phoenix one more pat and headed for the fence.

I bent to duck between the rails when something flashed in my peripheral vision. Blinding pain hit me as my head knocked against the fence. I crumpled to the ground, everything around me blurring, my vision tunneling.

"I really wish you wouldn't have put those pieces together."

CHAPTER
Forty-Three

Tuck

I KEYED IN THE CODE TO THE GATE AND DRUMMED MY
fingers along the steering wheel as I waited for it to open.
My mind circled the same thing over and over. Jensen. How
could I convince her to give me a second chance?

My truck bounced over a ridge in the gravel road as I made
my way down the lane that curved around the ranch house and
towards Jensen's property. Movement flashed in the corner of my
eye, and my head jerked.

The shiny, dark brown coat shimmered in the sunlight as the
horse galloped down the road. I slammed on my brakes just in
front of the ranch house and jumped out of my truck. I held up
my hands. "Phoenix. Whoa, girl. It's okay."

She danced in place, throwing her head back in a whinny.

"What's wrong?" I glanced up towards Jensen's pastures, unease settling in my gut. "How'd you get out?"

The front door of the house opened, and Andrew strode out.
"How'd Phoenix get out?"

I slid closer to the mare. "I'm not sure. You seen Jensen?"

"Saw her drive past the barn, oh, I don't know, maybe two
hours ago?"

I pulled my phone out of my back pocket and hit her contact. It rang and rang before clicking over to the voice mail that hadn't changed in over five years. *You've reached Jensen...*

I tapped end on the screen. "Will you try her?" My hand tightened around the phone. I hated that my own stupidity meant that I didn't know if she was avoiding me or if she was actually in trouble.

Andrew arched an eyebrow but pulled out his phone to call his daughter. While I waited, I came around the back of my truck, searching out a halter and lead I knew I had buried in there somewhere. My fingers brushed nylon rope, and I pulled.

When I ducked out, there was a furrow between Andrew's brows. "No answer."

I handed him the rope and halter. "Can you get Phee? I'm going to drive up there and see what's up."

Andrew nodded. "I'll walk Phoenix up."

As Andrew took a few steps towards Phoenix, the mare danced away. I held up a hand. "Phee. It's okay." I pitched my voice low. "I gotta go find Jensen, so I need you to go with Andrew." The mare studied me and then took off at a gallop back towards the pasture. "Oh, fuck."

Andrew gripped my shoulder. "She's just heading home. We'll drive up and get her back in the pasture. See what's going on."

I climbed behind the wheel, and Andrew slid into the passenger seat. I was silent as we drove, my hands clenching the steering wheel.

"You think something's wrong, don't you?"

My gaze flicked to Andrew for a brief moment before returning to the gravel road. "I don't have a good feeling. But maybe I'm wrong. There's been a lot going on, and I've been on edge." I was never wrong about this kind of thing, but in this moment, I wished I were.

I pulled to a stop along the fence line. Phoenix paced back

and forth by a spot near the fence. Not the gate, but the space where Jensen and I usually ducked between the rails to head for her boulder. Maybe Phee could smell her there or something.

Andrew looked at me, real worry creasing his face for the first time. "Her SUV isn't here."

I slid from the truck. "You get Phoenix, I'll see what I can find."

This time, Phoenix allowed herself to be harnessed. I held up a hand, stopping Andrew from placing her back in the pasture. "Wait just a minute. I want to see what tracks I can find. If you let her back in, she'll just come straight over here."

Andrew nodded. "I'll hold her."

I slowly walked towards the portion of the fence that Phoenix seemed so interested in. My gaze skimmed across the ground, and my steps faltered. Two deep ruts gouged the dirt about eight inches apart. Drag marks.

I pushed down the panic that wanted to surface as that muscle in my cheek flickered. I crouched. My eyes ran over the trajectory. About two feet from me, the drag marks stopped. Just stopped. There were so many footprints, I'd never be able to find much direction there.

My gaze ran back over the drag marks towards the fence, trying to follow the path, attempting to get my mind to paint the picture of what had happened. My vision stuttered on a crack in the fence.

I rose, striding towards the fence, careful to avoid the path the crime scene techs might be able to get something out of. I crouched again, studying the wooden rail. It sagged in the middle. Dipped because there was a crack almost all the way through it. And blood. And in that blood were a few strands of hair. Hair so dark brown it was almost black.

My chest spasmed with a flare of pain so bright it stole my breath. *No. Fucking no.* The scene that played out in my head of someone hurting my beautiful girl was too vivid. I could see the fall, hear the scream as though she were right in front of me.

It was the same sound I'd heard when Jensen was sixteen. I'd been home from college on break, and Walker, Jensen, and I had gone on a hike. Jensen had stepped just a few feet off the trail to snap a photo of the scenery with her phone and stumbled on a coiled rattler.

That scream had turned my blood to ice. I'd never moved so fast in my life, grabbing hold of her t-shirt and yanking her out of striking distance. She'd shook in my arms, taking a good half hour to calm down, but she'd been fine. Now, I had no clue.

I pushed to my feet, hitting Walker's name on my phone.

Two rings. "Tuck. What's up?"

I heard Noah's giggles in the background.

Taylor's voice. "Noah, if you eat one more scoop of ice cream, you won't sleep tonight, and then your mom will never let me pick you up from karate again."

The boy's giggles turned to full laughter. "I won't tell Mom."

I opened my mouth to speak but couldn't. The words wouldn't come.

"Tuck? You there, man?"

"I need you to call in an APB." My voice was hoarse, gravelly, as though I'd smoked two packs a day for most of my life. "It's Jensen. Someone took her."

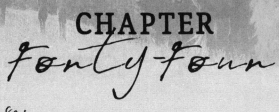

CHAPTER
Forty-Four

Jensen

MY ENTIRE BODY SEEMED TO PULSE IN A SORT OF whooshing pain. I let out a small moan. *What happened?*

I tried to lift my head, but the pain that sliced through it had lights flashing behind my eyes and me biting back a cry. *Had I fallen?* I couldn't remember, everything seemed so very hazy.

I kept my body still but slowly eased my eyes open. The space was entirely unfamiliar. Plywood walls. A single window that looked as if it hadn't been cleaned in the past decade. The floor was much the same—worn wood, dusty from infrequent use.

I needed more information. I braced myself and slowly rolled to my back. The pressure in my skull threatened to do me in. Above me were three slats of wood and a plastic-covered mattress. A bunk bed. I was on a bunk bed.

Nowhere I was familiar with had bunk beds. My heart rate picked up. Where was I?

I searched my memories. Flipping back and then forward and then back again. I'd been at the Kettle. I remembered the fight with Tuck. My heart gave a phantom spasm. I remembered walking across the street, tears streaming down my face and then…just nothing.

I squinted my eyes as though doing so would help me see my memories more clearly. All it did was cause my head to throb worse than before. There was a gaping black hole when it came to where I was and how I'd gotten here.

I eased back onto my side, taking in the room around me. I strained to see through the cloudy window. Trees. Ponderosa pines. A lot of them. Hopefully, that meant I wasn't too terribly far from home.

My gaze tracked over the space, and a memory flickered. A day when I was thirteen and Tuck had taken me to see the mustangs. There'd been a terrible thunderstorm, and Tuck had guided us towards one of the many Forest Service cabins scattered throughout the forest to wait it out.

Hope flared. Maybe I'd been with Tuck and had gotten injured. He could've stowed me here while he went for help. Had we made things right? God, I hoped so.

A voice sounded from somewhere. Then two voices.

"Dammit, Bill. This isn't what I signed up for." That voice, something about it tickled the back of my brain.

"Stop being such a pussy. I thought you cared about the cause."

"I do, but it's one thing to kill a few horses, it's a whole 'nother to kidnap the daughter of a family like the Coles. They're too connected. You do whatever you want, but I'm getting the fuck out of here."

A shot cracked through the air. My body jolted, and I bit down on my lip to keep from crying out. The sound of a heavy weight hitting the floor brought tears to my eyes.

Bill. It was as if the world had sped up and slowed down at the same time. Memories flipped through my mind, coming in short bursts and out of order until it all came together. Bill. The horses. Phoenix. The punch.

I forced my breathing to stay even, no matter how badly they wanted to come in quick, short pants. Bill had taken me. And he had a gun.

The price I paid for ignoring that voice that told me that something wasn't quite right. When would I learn to trust my intuition? Because when I thought back, there'd been similar instances with Cody and Bryce. Flickering doubts that I'd ignored.

When you silenced that voice within yourself enough, it stopped speaking. And just as I was coaxing it out again, I had to go and doubt it. Never again. I would get out of this, and when I did, I'd never mute that voice again.

Floorboards creaked. "Fuck!" Something crashed into a wall.

I jolted into a seated position, and the room around me swam, ripples of blurred shapes and colors. That was not good. I wasn't sure I could walk, let alone run. I needed a plan. A way out of here.

As my vision returned, I scanned the space. I needed something. Anything I could make into a weapon.

There was nothing. Unless you counted the mattress above me, and a desk and chair bolted to the floor. My heart picked up its pace once again as tears burned the back of my throat. Noah. My family. Tuck.

I had to find a way out. I couldn't lose them. Couldn't lose my shot at a perfectly imperfect life with them. Messy. Loud. Full of love. And color. And care. I'd fight tooth and nail for that life.

The door swung open, crashing into the wall. "Oh, good, you're awake."

There was a feral gleam in Bill's eyes. The kind you saw in a rabid animal's. The kind of beast you had no choice but to put down.

"What's going on? Did I fall?" I figured ignorance might buy me some time. Some answers.

He grinned at me, white teeth seeming to bite at the air.

"Don't play dumb with me, Jensen. I'm not Tuck, you can't lead me around by my dick."

I blinked rapidly, trying to think of a response.

Bill kept right on going. "Come on." He gestured with his gun for me to rise. "We've got a lot of ground to cover."

I stayed put. "Where are we going?"

"Just the perfect little spot I have picked out." He gestured with the gun again. "Get up." I stayed still. "NOW!"

I scrambled to my feet, and the world swam again. I reached out and grabbed hold of the top bunk to keep myself upright. "I'm not sure I can walk."

Bill muttered a curse. "You're going to have to." He jammed the gun against the small of my back. "Walk."

My first steps were wobbly. As I reached the doorway, the sight of blood pooling under Tom's body had my stomach threatening to heave. "They'll catch you. If you leave him here, they'll catch you."

Bill chuckled. "I'll bring him outside, and the scavengers will do all I need. A quick scrub of the floor, and no one will be the wiser."

"I'm expected at home." I hated that my voice trembled as I said the words. "They'll know something's wrong."

Bill clucked his tongue as he pushed me out the front door of the cabin. "But it'll be too late by then." He sighed. "You've always been irresponsible, Jensen. Coming up to these woods alone all the time. In a day or two, they'll find your SUV at one of the trailheads. And no one will be the least bit surprised when they find your body at the bottom of a ravine."

CHAPTER
Forty-Five

Tuck

I PACED BACK AND FORTH AS CRIME SCENE TECHS MILLED around the parking area, the fence, and the pasture. The horses seemed to do the same, snorting and whinnying, picking up on the frenetic energy of the people invading their space.

"There might be some other explanation." I knew Walker didn't believe the words coming out of his mouth, but he needed something, *anything* to hold onto.

I ran a hand through my hair. "We need a direction." If they'd stayed on foot, I'd have a shot, something that I could track. But disappearing drag marks most likely meant a car. All I could do with that was wait for the next sign. I fucking hated waiting.

I started pacing again. I had to keep moving. It was the only way to keep the guilt at bay. That curling, thick cloud eating away at my insides. Because I should've been with Jensen. If I hadn't been such a colossal asshole, she wouldn't have needed to be alone. She would've brought me with her. My fists clenched and flexed, the energy humming through me seeming to crackle through my fingertips.

Walker pulled a phone out of his pocket that I hadn't heard ring. "Cole." Pause. "Where?" I froze. "We'll be there in twenty. Call in SWAT."

My blood turned to ice. "What?" The single word was a harsh command. I didn't give a fuck.

"They found her SUV. A trailhead up by Pine Meadow."

My brows pulled together. "That makes no sense."

Walker shoved the phone back into his pocket. "She wouldn't go up there alone, would she? Not now."

I shook my head. "She wouldn't. And we've got blood and hair." The vise around my chest constricted with each word. "Someone took her. They just used her vehicle to do it." Which meant they didn't have their own, unless there were two unsubs.

I scrubbed a hand over my face. I refused to believe more than one person could be at this. "Walker, have your dad do a head count of all ranch staff, see if he's missing anyone. I'm getting my maps out of my truck. I want to see what's around there."

Walker's jaw hardened, but he gave a chin jerk and strode towards his father. I unlatched my tailgate and pulled out a tube of maps. I thumbed through them, searching for the one I needed. My hands trembled a bit. We'd find her. She'd be fine.

I spread the map out over my tailgate, my eyes scanning the paper. Within a minute, I had three possibilities. Potential hidey holes where this fucker could possibly keep J. If he'd gone to all the trouble of taking her away from the ranch and leaving the vehicle at Pine Meadow, she had to be alive.

Walker leaned against the tailgate. "What do you have?"

"I've got three spots for us to check out." I pointed to the areas on the map. Two Forest Service cabins and a cliffside overhang where someone might just think they could hide a person from prying eyes. "We need to go now."

Walker nodded. "I'll follow in my rig."

I rolled up the map I needed and slammed the tailgate closed. I was going to find my girl.

"No. You wait for SWAT." David's voice cut through the speaker on my truck like a whip.

My hands clenched around the steering wheel as I envisioned them wrapped around my boss's throat. "It's going to take at least another hour for SWAT to assemble. That hour could change everything."

He knew the words I *wasn't* saying. That one hour could mean the difference in whether we found Jensen alive. I gripped the wheel harder.

David cleared his throat. "I'm sorry. I know she's important to you, but we have procedure for a reason. It's to keep you safe, and her. Wait for SWAT."

"Fuck procedure. I'm not waiting." I couldn't live with myself if I did.

David's tone hardened. "You do that, you're out of a job. That's disobeying a direct order."

"I'll just have to take that chance." I hit end on my phone just as I pulled into the tiny trailhead parking lot. This trail didn't get a ton of use, and if we hadn't been looking for J everywhere we could think of, it might've been days before this was called in. Weeks, even.

Walker swung in beside me, and we both jumped out of our vehicles. A sheriff's deputy strode up. I gave him a chin jerk. "What do you have?"

The deputy's hands rested on his gun belt. "A whole lot of nothing. Vehicle's locked. No signs of struggle. It's like she just went for a stroll."

My jaw worked. "She didn't."

Walker squeezed my shoulder. "We're going in. Tell SWAT we have our sat phones whenever they get here."

The officer's eyes flared just a bit. "You're not waiting for the rest of your team?"

That muscle in my cheek began to tick. "There isn't time." I turned back to my truck, making quick work of grabbing my pack and checking the gun at my hip. I was ready.

I glanced over at Walker to see him tightening the straps of his own pack. "Let's go." I inclined my head towards the trail.

We began walking in total silence. I took the lead, my gaze constantly scanning, looking for any signs that someone had ventured off the trail. There was nothing.

"Walk me through the plan."

My eyes continued scanning. I fought the urge to move quicker, but I couldn't afford to miss a single sign. "First, we hit the first cabin. Then, we split up. I'll head for the overhang." I blew out a breath. "You know the signs to look for."

"I don't have the gift you do. But I'm good, Tuck. I know what to look for." There was frustration and just a touch of hurt in Walker's tone.

"Fuck. I'm sorry, man. I know you got this." I paused in my progress, crouching to examine a broken branch and check for footprints off the trail. Nothing. I kept going.

"No apology needed. We're both fucking stressed."

Understatement of the century. The forest thinned a bit as we reached the cabin. I unholstered my gun as I caught sight of a truck parked outside.

Walker and I worked in silence, needing only a few hand gestures to communicate the plan. That was the thing about working with someone you'd known from birth, they knew the way you thought, how you would react, and they always had your back.

We crept towards either side of the door. I gave a swift nod, and Walker kicked it in. "Sutter Lake PD. Oh, fuck."

There was a tearing sensation in my chest at the sight of all the pooling blood. *No. Fucking no.* Walker stepped to the side, and a body appeared. A male body. *Not Jensen. It's not Jensen.*

Walker quickly cleared the only other room, but I could do nothing but stand there, staring. *It could've been Jensen.* I shook myself from the fog. After a shot to the head, the man was unrecognizable.

I strode back outside, quickly circling the cabin, looking for any signs of life. There was nothing. I made my way back to the truck to find Walker on his phone, calling in the license plate.

Walker hit a button on the phone and shoved it back into his pack. "Tom Woodward."

My brow furrowed as I tried to place the name. "He works at Double J Ranch, right?"

"He does. Was pretty outspoken about the mustangs, too."

I muttered a curse. "He's not in this alone. Someone was with him, and that someone obviously doesn't care much about the loss of human life."

Walker tapped the side of the sat phone. "I'm trying to get some additional information, and crime scene techs are on the way."

"Right now, it doesn't matter *who*," I growled. "It matters *where*. I'm heading for the overhang. You head for the other cabin. We can't wait around here doing nothing."

"You're right." Walker stuffed the phone into his pack, then met my gaze. "Don't get killed, okay?"

I shot him a cocky grin. "Bullets have nothing on me." I held his gaze for one second longer, then took off.

I wasn't following a marked trail, it was more a worn path that led to the edge of a ravine I'd be able to follow to the overhang. This land was like a second home, but there were still too many unfamiliar places. I needed to rely on landmarks.

My steps faltered, and I retreated a few paces. Crouched.

Examined the underbrush. "Sonofabitch." Lying on one of the brambles was a cluster of blue threads. The same shade as the sweater Jensen had been wearing earlier today.

I pushed to my feet, fighting the urge to run. I kept my progress measured, my eyes scanning the space around me. Another cluster of threads. My girl was so fucking smart. She knew I'd come looking for her, and she was leaving me a trail.

I pulled out my phone and dialed Walker. He answered on the second ring. "I've got signs of her." I relayed my position.

"I'm on my way. It's gonna take me a bit, though."

I scanned the woods around me. "Move slow and be quiet as a mouse. They could be anywhere."

"Got it."

I hit the button to end the call, shoved the phone into my pack, and pulled my gun. My steps were steady and as quiet as I would be when tracking an animal. Except, this time, I followed a trail of blue threads.

"I need a break. Please. My head."

I froze at the edge of the forest. Jensen. I'd never experienced anything like the relief I felt at hearing her voice. I wanted to charge forward, put a bullet between the eyes of whoever had done this. I stayed still, hidden under cover of the forest, the only option to hide as the trees melted away to a rocky ravine.

"Fine." The voice was so familiar. "I guess I'll just have to send you over right here."

Jensen screamed, and I lunged.

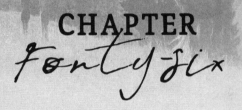

CHAPTER
Forty-Six

Tuck

THE WORLD SLOWED. EVERYTHING HAPPENED IN heartbeats. One pulse of that life-controlling organ after another.

Jensen. A gun to her head. A hand squeezing her neck as a man shuffled her back towards the ravine's edge.

One wrong move was all it would take to wipe her from this Earth. All I could think about was how I had wasted so much time. So much damn time listening to my father's lies, letting them color my life. Allowing them to steal my shot at happiness.

Never again. I was going to find us a way out of this mess.

I aimed my gun. "Bill, you don't want to do this." That kind and concerned interest I'd seen in him was nothing but a façade.

A sneer stretched across his face. "Don't I? You and your girlfriend here have been sticking your nose in matters that are none of your concern. I tried to warn you off. Gave you chance after chance. But, no, you just couldn't listen."

My jaw clenched. "Your brother know about this?"

Bill stiffened. "David has nothing to do with this."

I inched forward. "Of course, he does. You've been killing horses on land he's in charge of safeguarding."

Bill's eye started to twitch, and his hold on Jensen tightened. "Those fucking vermin are ruining the livelihoods of human beings. Don't you think people are just a little more important than horses? They tear down fences, eat grass that is supposed to feed livestock, take up valuable space that other ranchers could be using. They have to go."

"This is not the way to make that happen." My gaze cut to Jensen. She was struggling to pull air into her lungs. My grip on the gun tightened. "Ease up your hold there."

Bill let out a cackle. "Now, why would I do that?"

"Because if you don't, I will put a bullet in your fucking brain." And I would. No hesitation. I wanted to do it right now, just for his grip on her neck, one I knew would bruise.

Bill stepped more fully behind Jensen. "Nope, nope, nope. You're gonna toss your gun over here, or you're going to watch all the blood drain from your girlfriend's body."

The minute I tossed my gun to Bill, Jensen and I were both done for. I looked at Wilder. She motioned downward with her eyes. I squinted. She made the motion again. I adjusted my grip on my gun. My Wilder, so fucking smart. "Bill, let's just take a breather here. Don't do something you're going to regret."

His hand closed harder around Jensen's throat. "I'm not going to regret a fucking thing—"

Jensen dropped like a ton of bricks. The move startled Bill so much that he lost his hold on her, and I got my opening. I exhaled and squeezed the trigger. I wasn't taking any chances. Right between the eyes.

I knew I would feel no guilt for taking the life of the man who was trying to steal my future. Attempting to snuff out the brightest light to ever walk this Earth. No one would do a damn thing to hurt Jensen if I could do anything to stop it.

Bill crumpled in a heap to the side of Jensen. Her gaze flew to him and then to me. "I knew you had me."

Her words took flight in my chest, warmth spreading. I was a better man because I knew her. Because I loved her. "Are you okay?"

She nodded. "I'm—"

"No!" The word was a guttural cry. I turned to see David charging through the woods, rifle raised. "You!"

"David, get yourself in check. I had no choice. He was going to kill Jensen." Time slowed as pieces fell into place. None of my team members were behind David. He was completely alone. He hadn't wanted Walker and me to search for Jensen. Not because he was worried about our safety, but because he wanted time to cover for his brother.

David shook his rifle at me. "All this for some fucking horses? You bleeding-heart animal rights sissies."

"You were in on this?" I couldn't quite get the pieces to compute. David had always been an asshole. But this?

"I don't give a flying fuck about the horses one way or the other. I was just trying to protect Bill." His gaze dropped to his brother, tears filling his eyes. His gaze snapped up to me, and so did the barrel of his rifle.

I needed time. Time to figure out how to get us out of this. "Why? What was the point of all this?"

The rifle began to shake in David's hand. "Did you know we grew up in Hettiesburg?"

"No, I didn't." Hettiesburg was one of the poorest communities around Pine Meadow.

David swiped a hand over his brow while keeping his rifle steady with the other. "My dad struggled to keep a small flock of sheep on some leased land. One year, those damn horses took down the fence, and we lost half the flock. Never been hungrier than I was that year. Bill just didn't want any other families going through what we did. What's so wrong with that?"

I eased forward a step, my mind racing, trying to find a way out of this. "There's nothing wrong with wanting to make sure families have food on the table."

David aimed his rifle at my head and took a step closer. "Then why did you fucking kill him?"

I went with the honest truth, hoping against hope that it might get through the crazy to the small, sane part of David I hoped was somewhere inside. "Because he was trying to take my family from me."

"Lower the gun." Jensen, God bless her, had worked Bill's gun out of his grasp and now had it trained on David. He froze. "I've got better reaction time than you. You don't want to test me."

I saw a slight tremor in Jensen's hold and wondered if she really could pull the trigger if she had to. Jensen was such a protector of life in all forms, I knew it would destroy her to have to end one. She pushed to her feet. "Lower the gun. Now."

David hesitated for a moment, his gaze flicking from me to his fallen brother and then finally Jensen. I saw the moment the fight left him. His shoulders slumped, and the end of the rifle dipped.

I charged forward, grabbing the gun from his hold. "Get on the ground, hands behind your head."

David slowly lowered himself to the ground, assuming the position he'd ordered so many to take over his career.

I turned to Jensen, her hands were violently shaking now. "Hand me the gun, Wilder." She obeyed, but the movements were robotic. Shock was setting in. I holstered the gun she gave me and kept my own trained on David. "I need you to get my cuffs from my pack." I slid the bag off one shoulder and then the other.

My gaze didn't stray from her as she searched through it. She was okay. Just watching her move, watching her chest rise and fall, eased me a bit. She was okay.

Now, I just needed to figure out how I could get her to forgive me.

CHAPTER
Forty-Seven

Jensen

WALKER PULLED ME INTO A HARD HUG. THE FORCE of it caused me to let out some sort of strangled *oomph* sound. His hold on me only tightened. "Don't you ever do that to me again."

"Sorry?" I mumbled into his shoulder, but it came out as more of a question. It wasn't exactly my idea to get kidnapped.

He released me from his hug but kept hold of my shoulders. "Not as sorry as you're going to be when you get home. Mom and Dad are fit to be tied. You were supposed to have someone with you when you were with the horses."

"Shit." It didn't matter how old you were, something about upset parents waiting for you always sent a flood of dread through your gut. "Did you have to tell them?"

Walker raised a single brow. "Do you really think they didn't already know? Wouldn't find out?"

He had a point. My eyes traveled around the vast array of law enforcement personnel. Forest Service, county sheriff, Walker, and a couple of his deputies, the medical examiner, and EMTs. My gaze caught on Tuck, who was talking to the sheriff and someone from the Forest Service.

I wanted desperately to run over there and affix myself to him like some sort of spider monkey or land-capable octopus. I needed to touch him. To make sure he was okay. To see if *we* were okay. Walker had shown up moments after Tuck had cuffed David and ushered us back to the Forest Service cabin where the emergency vehicles could make it in. Tuck and I hadn't exactly had time to talk.

"Jensen? Earth to Jensen?" My brother gave my shoulders a little shake.

I blinked a few times. "Sorry, what?"

His brow furrowed. "The EMTs want to take a look at you." He gestured towards the ambulance.

"I'm fine—"

"You are not. I'm pretty sure your head is going to need stitches." Walker ushered me towards the flashing lights and away from Tuck.

My chest tightened with each step. My breathing picked up its pace. By the time we reached the EMTs, I was practically hyperventilating.

Worry filled Walker's expression. "What's wrong?"

"Could, uh, could you get Tuck?" I hated that I was even asking, but I'd beat myself up about it later.

Walker looked from me to Tuck and then back again. "Uh, sure."

The EMT gestured for me to sit on a stretcher and placed a blood pressure cuff around my arm. I watched as Walker reached Tuck and gestured towards me. Tuck's head snapped in my direction, and he immediately strode away from the other officers without saying a single word.

His strides ate up the distance in no time. "What's wrong?"

I felt color rising to my cheeks. I licked my lips. "I just wanted to make sure you were okay. Maybe the EMTs should check you out, too." I couldn't bring myself to tell him the whole truth.

That I didn't want to be farther away from him than absolutely necessary.

"Ma'am," the EMT interrupted. "I'm going to need to take a look at your head."

Tuck took a step back, and that familiar tightening in my chest returned. Tuck must have noticed because he rounded the stretcher so he was standing at my back. "I'm right here, Wilder. I'll always be right here." He rested his hand on top of mine on the gurney, his fingers lacing with my own.

That fist around my chest loosened just a bit. The EMT began prodding at my head, and I winced.

"Hey, watch it, buddy." Tuck's voice cracked like a whip.

The poor EMT took an instinctive step back. "S-s-sorry."

I squeezed Tuck's hand. "He's just doing his job."

"Well, he could be a little gentler about it."

The EMT slowly stepped forward again. "I'll try and be more careful."

I gave him a sympathetic smile. "You're doing fine."

He nodded jerkily. "I think you're going to need stitches."

I sighed. "I really don't want to go to the hospital. And needles aren't exactly my favorite thing." Tuck chuckled behind me, and I elbowed him. "Are you *sure* I need stitches?"

The EMT bit his bottom lip. "I have the glue here, but you'll have to let me clean it first, and that won't be fun without a numbing agent."

Anything was better than needles. "Do it."

Tuck moved in closer. "Wilder—"

I squeezed his hand hard. "I don't want to go to the hospital. I don't want needles."

"Okay," he whispered. "You pass out on me, and I'll be really fucking pissed."

I chuckled. "I'll do my best."

The EMT pulled out a kit of some sort and started organizing an array of things I didn't want to look at too closely. He looked from me to Tuck and back again. "This is going to hurt."

I nodded and held Tuck's hand tighter. "Distract me. Tell me what's going on with David."

Tuck let out a sigh that ruffled the hair on the back of my head. "He's on his way to county lockup."

"I can't believe—" The sting of the alcohol against the gash in my forehead stole the words out of my mouth and the air out of my lungs.

Tuck squeezed my hand in a rhythm I knew was meant to distract me from the pain. Three squeezes. Pause. Another three. Pause. "You're doing so good, Wilder. So fucking strong. Like always."

"Fuckity freaking fudge sticks fuck!" I'd found my voice again, and I wasn't afraid to use it.

The EMT winced as if preparing for Tuck to rip him a new one. Instead, Tuck just chuckled. "At least I know you're getting back to normal."

I inhaled through my nose and out through my mouth as the burning fire on my head eased. "Back to normal because of my creative cursing?"

Tuck leaned in closer. "I love your creative cursing."

My breath caught. "I'm glad." *I'm glad? Really, Jensen? That's the best you've got?* I blamed the head injury.

I felt Tuck straighten, but he kept hold of my hand.

Walker filled my line of sight. "What's the verdict?"

"They're gluing her back together," Tuck offered.

Walker's gaze flicked to our joined hands. He paused for a moment and then shook his head, grinning. "You worried she's going to pass out on you again?"

"The thought had crossed my mind."

The EMT started messing with my wound, and I bit down on my lip to keep from crying out. "This will just take a few seconds."

I forced my eyes closed, and Tuck picked up the rhythmic squeezing of my hand.

Walker cleared his throat. "Tuck, the Forest Service wants your official statement when you're done here."

Tuck grunted his agreement.

Walker pushed on. "When the EMTs are done with J, I want to get her home, but you can send whoever by to take her statement later."

I held my breath. Waiting. Hoping that Tuck would protest. Insist on taking me home himself. Better yet, on not leaving my side. I hoped that this would be the moment he would tell my brother and everyone else that his place was by my side. Instead, there was nothing but silence.

CHAPTER
Forty-Eight

Tuck

I SWIPED THE PALMS OF MY HANDS DOWN MY JEANS AS I climbed out of my truck outside Jensen's guest house. I'd fucked up. Pretty much at every turn. And I knew it.

But the look on Jensen's face when I'd agreed to let her brother take her home from the crime scene...that had gutted me.

I just hadn't known where we stood. And the last thing I'd wanted to do was have that conversation in front of Walker. I blew out a long breath and started for the door.

I'd checked in with Walker on my way home from the Forest Service station after an afternoon of interviews, statements, and a whole lot of *how the hell did this happens*. He'd told me that Jensen was resting and that his parents were keeping Noah for the night so she could sleep in.

She was alone. Now, I just needed to see if she'd let me through the front door. If she didn't, I'd stay outside and wait. I was done messing up where Wilder was concerned. It was time for her to know that I was here to stay.

"About time you got here."

My hand went to the gun holstered at my hip before my brain recognized Irma's voice. "Jesus, that's a good way to get shot."

Irma rose from the rocker on the front porch. "So's abandoning my girl in her time of need. And being an idiot." Her eyes narrowed at me. "I still got pretty good aim, you know."

"Message received." I glanced at the door. "Walker said she was alone."

Irma followed my gaze. "She wanted to be, but I couldn't quite make myself leave her that way." She looked at me. "But now that you're here, I can." She started down the steps. "Don't fuck this up, cowboy."

I blew out a long breath before I rapped on the door. I'd do my best not to fuck things up any worse than I already had. The sounds of a television came from inside. Then the faint sound of footsteps. The door opened.

Jensen stood there, hair falling in loose waves around her face, those amber eyes blazing with a mixture of hurt and anger. She wore tiny sleep shorts and a tank. The outfit made zero sense for the dead of winter, and as the cold air hit her, those nipples I loved so much hardened.

My cock jerked. *Fuck.* This was not the time. I pushed inside, not waiting for an invitation. "You need to put something else on."

Jensen's hands came to her hips. "Excuse me?"

I grabbed her hand and tugged her toward the stairs and her bedroom. "It's too cold for you to be wearing that."

"Tuck, my house is about seventy degrees."

I ignored her protests and kept leading her towards her room. "Don't care. You've been through a lot, and the last thing you need on top of that is to get sick." I released my hold on Jensen when we reached her space, and I went straight for her dresser, pulling open drawers until I found the one with her sweats. I pulled out the biggest, bulkiest ones I could find and held them out to her. "Here, put these on."

Those adorable little worry lines appeared between her brows. "Tuck?"

I placed the clothes in her hands, forcing her to take them. "Put on the sweats."

Jensen's gaze met mine. "Why?"

A muscle in my cheek ticked. "Because I don't want you to get sick."

"Why?"

I let out a growl. "Because I fucking care about you, all right? And the last thing I want is something else happening to you on my watch."

She let the sweats drop from her hands and stepped closer. "Tuck, none of this was your fault."

I stepped back, shaking my head. "You know damn well that's not true. I've made a fucking mess of everything."

Jensen edged closer, moving me back towards her bed. She pressed down on my shoulders. "Look at me."

I ground my teeth together but tipped back my head so I could meet her gaze.

She cupped my face in her hands. Hands that were incredibly soft even though she worked them to the bone day in and day out. Hands that tended scraped knees and checked fevered brows. Hands that shoveled manure and calmed skittish horses. Hands that soothed my soul and twined with mine so perfectly, it was as if they were always meant to be there.

I pressed my cheek into her palm, my scruff pricking her skin. I wanted to bury myself there. Under her flesh. Crawl as deep as possible so she could never dig me out. "I'm so sorry."

Jensen took one hand and brushed the hair away from my face. "There's only one reason you'd have to say that."

"I think there are plenty of reasons, but what would yours be?"

Tears filled her eyes, and I wanted to slit my own throat. "If you're trying to leave me again." A single tear crested over, tracking down her cheek. I reached up and swiped it away with my thumb. "I have to warn you now. You can try and leave, but I'll just follow. I've been chasing you since the day I could walk, and I don't think that's ever going to change."

An image of a dark-haired little girl wobbling after me filled my mind. "I never want you to stop. The thing you don't realize is that I've been chasing you right back."

More tears fell down Jensen's cheeks, and she inhaled a shaky breath. "I need to tell you something, but I don't want you to say anything afterward."

My brows pulled together. "Okay…"

"Tucker Harris, I've loved you since before I knew what the word even meant. That love has shifted and changed through the years. Because, what I didn't realize, was that love is a living, breathing thing. I've loved you as a brother, as a friend, as my first crush, as my lifeline, as the person who sets my soul free. You call me Wilder, but it's you who helps me be that way. I'm never more free to be who I am than when I'm with you."

A vise gripped my chest, squeezing to the point of pain. I hadn't earned her love, but she'd given it to me anyway. So freely, and asking for nothing in return. I may not deserve her, but I was going to do everything in my power to live a life in celebration of that most precious gift.

I opened my mouth to speak, but Jensen held a finger to my lips. "Don't. Don't say anything. I don't want you to say it just because I did. And if you don't feel it yet, I don't want to know right now."

Fuck. I'd caused my wild girl so much doubt. I hated myself for that. I opened my mouth again, but this time, Jensen took it in a slow kiss. "Don't talk. Just feel."

She didn't want me to tell her how I felt. Wasn't ready to hear it. So, I'd show her. With my hands, my mouth, my body. In every way I could, I'd show her.

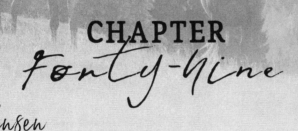

CHAPTER
Forty-Nine

Jensen

MY HEART HAMMERED IN MY CHEST. ITS BEATS sending shockwaves throughout my body. I knew Tuck loved me in whatever way he was capable. I trusted it, trusted myself. But more than anything, I needed him to know that I loved him regardless of whether he could say the words or not.

My love was not some fickle thing dependent on roses and chocolates or dates on Friday nights. My love was feral, chasing him down and never letting go.

The thing Tuck didn't realize was that he'd been *showing* me that he loved me for as long as I could remember. I didn't need the damn words.

Tuck shot to his feet, sweeping me off mine. My legs wrapped around his waist, our mouths colliding, pouring out all the things words could never express. His tongue darted into my mouth, probing, stroking, tempting, teasing. He was comfort and fire all at the same time.

Tuck turned so he could lay me on the bed. The movement was gentle, almost reverent. His hands lingered beneath me as his gaze traced my face. There was so much in his eyes, but he said nothing. He bent, pressing his lips to my left temple, then the right, and finally, my forehead.

Tears filled my eyes again. I wanted that trio of kisses for the rest of my life. My hand stroked his face, and I lived for the prickle of his stubble against my palm, against my thighs. My belly clenched.

Tuck rose above me, his hands traveling from my back to my stomach. His fingers traced the outline of my nipples through the thin cotton of my tank top. I shivered. His circles grew smaller and smaller until they pressed against the finest points of my breasts.

A single finger slipped beneath the strap of my tank, pulling it down until my breast came free. He repeated the action on the other side. Tuck pushed the camisole lower, granting him full access.

He cupped my breasts, massaging, kneading, stroking. Every time I thought I could predict the type of touch that would come next, he surprised me. His fingers found their way to my nipples, rolling them into tight buds, flicking one, then pulling the other deep into his mouth.

I let out a gasp. That move was one of my favorites. My body knew what it meant. The accompanying rush of wet between my thighs had me squirming.

Tuck released the nipple and tugged my tank lower, catching my sleep shorts with it. The graze of his knuckles over my thighs sent chills up my spine. My body wept in anticipation. He lowered himself to his knees, dragging the last remnants of my clothing with him.

He settled himself between my thighs, placing one leg over each shoulder. Then he simply stared. Gazing at that most secret part of me as though it held all the answers in the world. He inhaled deeply, and I instinctively tried to close my legs. He held them open, shaking his head at me with a wicked grin.

Tuck ran his nose over one thigh, then the other, his scruff sending little fireworks off in my nerve endings. His tongue ran over my core. His strokes were lazy as if he had all the time in the world, and he wanted to explore every inch of me.

The tip of Tuck's tongue traced my opening before dipping inside. I clenched around him, wanting more, needing more. He retreated, continuing his lazy figure eight at my center. Each pass sent him closer to that bundle of nerves, but not quite close enough.

When he finally dipped a digit inside, I nearly wept. My fingers fisted in his hair, twisting and tugging. I was in no way gentle, but I couldn't seem to help myself. His tongue flicked over my clit, and I moaned. He did it again and again. Flicking, sucking, pressing.

His fingers stroked me higher, that cord inside tightening. I fought it off, not ready yet. Not wanting the climb to end. He sucked hard.

"No," I panted.

Tuck released me, a puzzled look on his face.

I eased my hold on his hair, running my fingers through it. "I want to come with you inside me." Tuck stood, unbuttoning his shirt. His movements were unhurried as he kept his gaze locked with mine. I took a deep breath. "No condom." Tuck froze. "You're safe, right?" He nodded slowly.

I knew Tuck would never risk me if he weren't sure. I also knew that he understood what this meant to me. This piece of myself I was giving him. "I'm on the pill. And I trust you."

That did it. The slow, measured unbuttoning was forgotten. His fingers tripped over the final few buttons until he finally ripped the shirt off. He kicked off his boots while unfastening his jeans. And then he was before me. All smooth, tanned skin over hardened muscle. I would never tire of looking at him.

Tuck bumped against my opening, leaning over me so he

could take my mouth as he entered me. His lips barely left my skin as he took me. My mouth. My neck. My ear. My cheek. My nipple. My temple. They went wherever they pleased, the softness of his lips surrounded by the prickle of his stubble causing a riot of sensations I'd never get enough of.

His lips finally released me as he thrust deeper, hitting that magical spot inside, over and over. I tried to hold on. Small tremors wracked my body. My fingers dug into Tuck's back as my muscles started to shake. Just a little longer, a little higher.

Tuck's back arched as he thrust one last time. That curve of his body sent me soaring. Lights sparked across my vision, and everything around me seemed to fracture and then knit itself back together in a whole new way. A way that was so much better than before.

I sucked in air, my chest heaving, trying to get ahold of the world around me. As I came back to myself, I realized that Tuck had done just as I asked. He hadn't said a single word since I told him that I loved him. And yet, he'd said it all.

CHAPTER
Fifty

Tuck

NOTHING WAS BETTER THAN WAKING UP TANGLED WITH Jensen. She was like an octopus when she slept, all her limbs somehow twining with mine. My body didn't mind one bit. It somehow seemed to fit perfectly with hers.

I could feel her heart beat against my palm. The steady rhythm eased me. She was here. Safe. Whole.

Jensen stirred, arching back and letting out a little moan.

My hold on her tightened. "Careful with those noises you make, Wilder."

She stilled for a brief moment and then turned in my arms so she could press her lips to my throat. "Morning."

I rose up on an arm, brushing the hair out of her face, careful to avoid the wound on her head. "Love waking up with you."

Jensen grinned up at me. Her smile was so wide, so un-guarded, it was like taking a roundhouse kick to the solar plexus. "I don't hate it."

I pressed my lips to her temple. "We're doing this."

Jensen placed a hand on my chest. "My stomach just flip-flopped."

My hands continued to wander, tracing lines on her body that only I could see. "I think we should tell Noah first."

Jensen pushed me to my back and straddled me, the sheet falling to her hips. "He's going to be excited."

My fingers dusted over the dip and curve of her waist. "I'm not above bribing him."

Jensen let out a laugh. "I don't think that will be necessary." She bit her lip, those little worry lines peeking out on her brow.

I reached up, rubbing at the creases. "What's wrong?"

Her shoulders slumped just a bit. "Walker."

My hands dropped to her hips. "I have to talk to him after we tell Noah. Today."

Jensen's fingers traced circles on my chest. "I don't get to be a part of that conversation?"

"I need to tell him first." I sighed. "He's going to be pissed, and I need some time to make him understand that this is more." I cupped her face in my hands. "That this is everything."

She turned her head so she could kiss my palm. "Okay. But if he pulls his overprotective bullshit, I'm banning him from the Kettle."

I chuckled, rolling Jensen to her back and hovering over her. "You fight dirty."

She grinned up at me. "You have no idea."

My head dipped lower. "I guess I better find out."

I stepped between Jensen's legs as I took a sip of coffee. She wrapped them around me, careful to avoid the gun holstered at my hip, and set her cup of tea on the counter. "I hate that you have to go into work today."

I groaned. "It's not on the list of things I'm looking forward to."

She laughed, plucking my coffee cup out of my hand and

setting it on the counter. "What's it gonna take to make you a tea drinker?"

I chuckled and then tucked a strand of hair behind her ear. "At least a dozen more showers with you." Just the image of Jensen on her knees in the shower that morning, water streaming down her curves, had my dick twitching against my zipper. I'd had her twice that morning, and I still wanted more. I had a feeling I'd never get enough.

Jensen leaned in closer. "I think that can be arranged."

I dipped my mouth to hers, my tongue teasing her lips apart.

"What the fuck?"

I started at the sound of Walker's voice.

His eyes darted from me to his sister and back again. "Someone want to tell me what the hell is going on here?"

Jensen hopped off the counter. "I think it's pretty obvious. Tuck and I are seeing each other. We were going to tell you today."

Walker started laughing, but it had an ugly cast to it. "Are you delusional, J? Tuck doesn't date. He fucks and moves on."

Jensen flinched as if he had hit her with a physical blow.

I stepped forward. "Not cool, man. I know you're pissed at me, but don't take it out on her."

Walker's jaw clenched. "Don't tell me how to talk to my sister." He side-stepped me and met Jensen's gaze. "What are you thinking?"

Jensen squared her shoulders. "I love him."

Walker scoffed. "You love him? And how does he feel about you?"

Jensen shook her head. "That's none of your business."

Walker threw up a hand. "Just what I thought." He whirled on me. "And you. I trusted you. You know what she's been through, and you decided that lining her up as your next fuck buddy was the thing to do?"

Each sentence might as well have been a kick to the gut. I

had known Walker would be upset, but hearing what he really thought of me…it killed something inside. I forced myself not to let it show. Jensen was the most important thing right now. I held up a hand. "You need to calm down."

Walker shoved at my chest. "The last thing I need to do is calm down. *You* need to get the hell off my family's property."

That muscle in my cheek began to tick. "I don't think that's your call."

"The hell it's not." Walker started shoving me towards the door, but I stood my ground.

"Stop!" Jensen screamed it so loudly, I'd bet her family next door could hear. She gave her brother a hard push. "This is my house. You don't get to decide who stays here. Just like you don't get to decide who I let in my bed and in my life. Tuck is your best friend in the world, and you just treated him like he was shit on your shoe. You're the one who's leaving."

Walker's jaw hardened. "You're making a big mistake. And this time, I'm not going to be here to pick up the pieces." With that, he took off out the front door. A few seconds later, I heard his truck tear down the drive.

Jensen slumped against me. "I never knew he thought that little of me."

I wrapped her in my arms. "He doesn't. He's just losing his mind right now. He'll come around." I did my best to keep my breathing even and to not tighten my hold on Jensen too much. I'd never wanted to deck my best friend more in my life. He and I were going to have a come to Jesus talk, and it wasn't going to be pretty. But he *would* hear me.

The sound of tires spitting up gravel came from outside. Jensen sighed. "What now?" She slipped from my arms and headed to the front door.

I followed her out onto the porch. The way the sun was coming up over the ridge, I could only tell that it was a truck barreling our way. *Fuck.* What did Walker want now? It skidded to a stop, and a figure hopped out. Whoever it was, was silhouetted against the light, but the voice... I recognized that voice. But it wasn't Walker's.

"You fucking bitch." The figure's arm raised. Metal glinted in the sun.

I didn't think. I shoved Jensen out of the way. A crack. Searing pain. And then nothing at all. Just an endless sea of black.

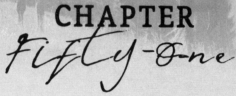

CHAPTER
Fifty-One

Jensen

HE WAS FALLING. THE MOVEMENT SEEMED TO GO ON forever. Each inch he fell, ripped at the muscle and sinew around my heart.

He hit the ground with a thud, his body almost bouncing with the impact. I didn't think, I just moved. Right to Tuck's side. Where I was meant to be.

Blood seeped from his chest. *No. No. No.*

"Goddammit!" The yell came from Cody's direction.

It seemed impossible, but I'd forgotten he was even there. Cody raised his gun again. It was as if some other force took over my body. I reached for the Glock at Tuck's hip, pulling it from its holster. I squeezed the trigger. A second time. I wasn't taking any chances.

Cody slumped to the ground. I felt nothing. Just a numb buzzing that seemed to overtake me. I set the gun on the ground and applied pressure to Tuck's wound. Then I screamed.

My dad was already out the door with his rifle, having heard the shots. He took off at a dead run towards me.

"Call an ambulance!" Tuck's blood seeped through my fingers.

That was wrong. Bad. That needed to stay in his body. I pressed harder on the wound. That's what they did in movies. But what if it was the wrong thing? What if I did something that killed him? I squeezed my eyes closed and prayed. I willed the blood to stay in his body, for his heart to keep beating.

My father slid down next to me. "Ambulance is on its way. Is he breathing?"

The question tore at my heart. That ragged muscle and sinew. "I don't know."

Dad leaned over Tuck, placing his ear next to Tuck's mouth. "He's breathing, but it's very shallow."

I stared at the blood seeping out between my fingers. "How long?"

Dad swallowed audibly. "They said fifteen minutes."

The ranch had always been one of my two favorite places in the world. But in that moment, I hated it. Why didn't we live in a city? Somewhere an ambulance was seconds away. "What else can I do?"

My father's voice caught in his throat. "You're doing it. Do you want me to take over?"

"No." The word came out as a sharp warning. No one could touch Tuck until the EMTs got here. If I was touching him, if I was holding his blood in his body, I could keep him alive. I tried to gentle my tone. "You should check on Cody."

What did it say about me that I hoped I'd killed him? How was I that person? I guess I was that person for Tuck.

My father jolted as if just realizing that there was another person involved. He jogged over to Cody's fallen form. I watched as he pressed two fingers to Cody's neck. His eyes narrowed and then closed. When they opened again, he shook his head.

My shoulders relaxed the barest inch. Then I froze. Something was wrong. Tuck's body was too still. "Dad! I don't think he's breathing."

My father ran over and dropped to his knees. "You keep pressure on the wound. I'm going to start chest compressions."

I kept my hold as firm as possible, my dad's jolts to Tuck's chest, sending more blood seeping through my fingers. *Please don't leave me. Please don't leave me.* I said it over and over again in my mind. Then I began mouthing the words silently. A chant, a prayer, a call to the Universe to keep this beautiful man here.

Sirens sounded. *Finally.* The ambulance raced up the drive, and EMTs hopped out. One of them, I didn't know his name, almost tripped at the sight of Tuck. He knew him. The guy quickly got himself in check and began barking orders.

"Ma'am, I need you to step back," a female EMT told me.

"I-I can't. I'm holding pressure on the wound. He'll bleed too much."

"It's okay, I'm going to take over now so we can get him to the hospital."

I nodded, the action jerky. As soon as I released my hold on Tuck's chest, the blood pooled. The EMT took my place, blocking my view, but it was too late. I knew it in my bones. Tuck was dying.

I stared down at my hands. So much blood. The liquid began to turn tacky, almost thick. Because blood wasn't supposed to be on the outside of your body.

My breathing picked up its pace. I couldn't seem to get enough air into my lungs. They burned with the effort.

"Breathe, baby girl, just breathe." It was my mom.

"N-N-Noah?" Noah couldn't see this.

My mom rubbed a hand up and down my spine. "Irma's got him in the den watching a movie. He doesn't know what happened." She tried to usher me a few steps forward.

I refused to move, shaking my head. "No."

She kept her voice incredibly gentle. "I just need to wash the blood off your hands so we can get in my SUV and follow the ambulance."

I didn't move from my spot a mere five feet from Tuck. My mom disappeared. But soon, she was back with a bucket and a rag. I didn't even recognize the items until she began carefully wiping away the blood. Each swipe of the cloth sent tears spilling over.

"I can't lose him, Mom."

"Oh, baby." She wrapped her arms around me. "They're doing everything they can."

"We have to go, now." It was the male EMT who said it.

My father stepped forward. "We're going to follow."

I moved closer to them all, my gaze not leaving Tuck's face that had far too little color. "Is he going to be okay?"

The EMT grimaced. "It depends on how quickly we can get to the hospital."

CHAPTER
Fifty-Two

Jensen

Beep. Beep. Beep. I tried to take comfort in the sound. It meant that Tuck's heart was still beating. He was breathing. But I kept trying to interpret each *beep*. Was that one shorter? What did that mean? It was an endless cycle.

I traced circles on the back of Tuck's hand with my fingertip. His heart had stopped three times in the past forty-eight hours. But it had started beating again four times. Four was my new favorite number. I drew it on the back of Tuck's hand. "You're too damn stubborn to give up. I know you. I know you better than anyone, and you won't let a bullet take you out."

I lifted his hand and placed it against my cheek. The hand that told the story of his life. I wanted it to have more stories to tell. I wanted the skin to sag and be peppered with age spots. I wanted one of those fingers to house a band of metal. But most of all, I wanted it to twine with mine for the rest of my days.

Maybe I was crazy. The man hadn't even told me that he loved me. But I felt it to the depth of my soul. Tears began to splash, soaked up by the hospital blanket.

"You really love him, don't you?"

I started at the sound of Walker's voice. I laid Tuck's hand back on the bed but kept my fingers woven with his. I wasn't letting go. "I don't have the energy for this, Walker."

"I didn't mean it like that." When he stepped closer, I saw that his face was ravaged. Guilt had done a number on him. But Walker's last words to Tuck had been ones of anger, of scorn, and now, his best friend lay in a hospital bed fighting for his life.

Tuck was breathing on his own, but he hadn't woken up yet after the surgery. The longer he stayed under, the smaller his chances for a complete recovery got. My heart gave a painful squeeze. "So, how did you mean it?" I wasn't quite ready to let my big brother off the hook. Maybe if he'd have been there instead of leaving in a grown-up hissy fit, things would've gone differently.

Walker took a few tentative steps closer, gripping the rail at the end of the bed. "I just didn't see it." He shook his head, a hint of a wistful smile playing on his lips. "Taylor says I'm deaf, dumb, and blind when it comes to you two. Maybe she's right. I've played it back a million times in my head. From when we were kids to now—"

"It wasn't always...*this*." I didn't have a word to encompass what Tuck and I were now.

Walker stared down at Tuck's frame. "I know that. But you two have always had a special bond. I just didn't realize how deep it ran."

More tears spilled over, tracking down my cheeks. I made no move to wipe them away. They were a measure of my love for the man who lay in this bed. "He's always seen me on a level that others didn't."

Walker's Adam's apple bobbed as he swallowed. "You do the same for him."

"I hope so." I stared at Tuck's face, tracing the lines of it with my gaze. "I don't know for sure."

"I do." Walker sighed. "The thing I should have known from

the second I saw you two together is that he never would've gone there if you weren't everything to him."

The tears came faster now, curving over my cheeks and dripping off my chin.

Walker shuffled his feet and glanced down. "I'm sorry I was such a grade-A asshole. I'll never forgive myself for what I said."

There was an implied *if he doesn't wake up* at the end of that statement. I squeezed my eyes closed. "I'm scared."

Walker opened his mouth to say something, but my gasp cut him off. Tuck's hand had tightened around mine the barest amount. A second time. A third.

"He's squeezing my hand. Go get a doctor."

Walker jogged out of the room and down the hall.

I leaned over the bed. "Tucker. Open your eyes. Please."

His eyes moved as if trying to open but weren't quite able to see the action through. Tuck's hand squeezed mine again, a little harder this time. One. Two. Three.

"Please, baby."

Tuck's lids fluttered open.

My tears fell fast and hard. "Never been happier to see those baby blues."

Tuck opened his mouth to speak, but a garbled croak came out instead.

I reached over to the table and grabbed the cup of water with a straw. "Here, have a small sip. They said you can't have too much or you'll get sick." I lifted Tuck's head so his mouth could reach the straw. His gaze held mine the whole time. Finally, I pulled the cup away. "Let's see how that does. How do you feel?"

Tuck stared at me for a moment, staying silent. "Love you, Wilder." His voice was hoarse, but the words couldn't have been clearer.

My breath caught, and the tears that had slowed started up in earnest again.

"I've always loved you." He cleared his throat, wincing at the pain but pushed on. "I couldn't tell you. I thought I'd only bring misery and pain into your life in the long run."

I shook my head. "No."

Tuck squeezed my hand. "But I told you in my own way. Every time I touched you three times. Every time I squeezed your hand three times. Every time I kissed each temple and your forehead. That's what I was telling you. One touch for each word I couldn't say."

My mind raced, trying to place the first time he'd given my hand a trio of squeezes, or the first time he'd given my ponytail three quick tugs, but I couldn't. He'd been doing it for as long as I could remember.

"It wasn't always this kind of love. But I have loved you from the first moment I laid eyes on you. And now I'm going to tell you out loud, every day for the rest of my life. I love you, Jensen Evelyn Cole."

I wanted to tackle him. Kiss him everywhere my lips could reach. But I had a feeling that was bad for people with holes in their chests. I pulled my hand from his grasp and cupped his face. I kissed one temple, the other, and then his forehead. "There has never been a day I didn't love you. And there never will be."

CHAPTER

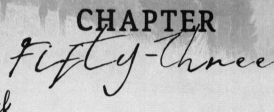

Fifty-Three

Tuck

THREE WEEKS LATER

"WHO KNEW ALL IT TOOK WAS ME GETTING SHOT for you to be okay with me dating your sister."

Walker scowled at me as he helped me out of the truck. "It's not funny yet." He paused. "Not sure it will ever be."

"Sorry, man." I winced as my feet hit the ground. I was so fucking happy to be out of the hospital, but my body still had a long road of recovery ahead. And it was frustrating as hell.

Walker studied my face. "You okay?" He offered an arm to help me walk.

I pushed it aside. "I'm fine. Stop hovering."

"I'm not hovering. I'm just making sure you don't end up in the hospital again."

"You guys are like two bickering old men," Jensen called as she headed down the front steps of her guest house.

The doctors had refused to release me unless someone could stay with me. My mom had immediately offered to move me in with her, but Jensen had stood firm. My little Wilder had wanted me with her, and she wasn't taking no for an answer. There was a small den off the living room of the guest house, and as soon as I was out of the woods medical-wise, she had set to work making it into a room for me.

I hated everyone fawning all over me, but Jensen was the one who was easiest to handle. "Get over here, Wilder."

Jensen slid under my arm, and I turned my face so that I could brush my lips against hers. She stayed there, guiding me up the path, supporting me under the guise of just wanting to be close to me. "I'm so glad you're home."

Noah bounded out the front door. "Tuck! You're here! I decorated your room for you. I drew out the whole fight sequence from *Karate Kid*, and Mom helped me hang it over your bed. She said we can watch one of the movies tonight if you feel up to it. Do you feel up to it?"

I let out a chuckle. The action caused a pulling on my chest, but it didn't hurt nearly as bad as it had a week or two ago. "I'm definitely up for it."

The first time Noah had seen me in the hospital, he'd fallen apart, sobbing in his mom's arms. That had hurt almost more than the gunshot wound to my chest. It had taken some time, but after some convincing, he realized that I was going to be fine. He'd taken to the idea of me coming to stay with them and the small bits of affection I'd shown to his mother remarkably well.

We were building the beginnings of a family. I squeezed Jensen's shoulder, halting her movement, and swept my lips against hers again. "Love you," I whispered against them, so low that no one else could hear.

"Gross," Noah whined.

Walker chuckled. "I agree, little man."

Noah scrunched up his face. "Are you guys gonna be lovey-dovey like all the time now?"

Jensen laughed. "Well, I kind of love him, so the chances are good."

Noah's little fists landed on his hips. "I have one rule then."

I grinned. "Sock it to me."

Noah's expression grew serious. "No kissy stuff during *Karate Kid*."

I let out a bark of laughter and had to hide the wince that wanted to come after. "That's a deal."

Noah nodded. "Good." He turned on his heel and marched towards the house.

Jensen started us forward again. "I need to warn you. There's someone here to see you."

My steps faltered. "Who?"

She looked from me to the house and back again. "Your dad."

My jaw clenched. My father had come to the hospital, but I'd told Jensen and my mom that I didn't want to see him. I just didn't have it in me. But I knew I'd have to talk to him eventually, and I guessed now was as good a time as any. "Okay."

Jensen let out a breath. "Good." We made it up the steps, and I had to pause to catch my breath. "Do you want to be set up in your bed or in the recliner in the living room?"

"Recliner," I grunted. I hated how my body was currently betraying me.

Walker opened the front door, and Jensen guided me through to the living room. My father jumped to his feet as soon as we appeared. "Tucker."

He looked different. But I couldn't quite place how. His face appeared almost thinner. His eyes clearer.

"Hi, Dad."

No one moved for a few seconds. Then Jensen ushered me towards the recliner. "I'm just going to get him set up in the chair, and then I'll leave you two to talk."

It took a couple of minutes to ease me into the oversized furniture. And by the time I got there, I was breathing heavily.

Worry filled Jensen's expression. "Are you okay?"

I squeezed her hand three times. "I'm fine. You remember what the doctor said. It's going to take some time for me to get my strength back."

Jensen nodded slowly just as Walker appeared with a couple of bottles of water. "Here you go." He handed one to me and the other to my dad.

My dad took the bottle from Walker, and his hand shook. "Thank you."

Jensen met my gaze and mouthed "*I love you*." Then she and Walker left.

My father and I were silent for a good sixty seconds.

He fiddled with the wrapper on his bottle of water. "So, the doc says you'll make a full recovery as long as you do the physical therapy they're recommending."

I nodded. "He predicts I'll be back to one hundred percent in a month or so."

"That's good. Real good." Dad finally met my gaze. "I'm glad you're going to be okay."

"Me, too." The silence returned, stretching out and making itself comfortable. I could only take it for so long. "What are you doing here, Dad?"

That familiar muscle in his cheek ticked. "You didn't want to see me in the hospital, and I wanted—"

I couldn't let him finish. "No, I didn't." My father's body gave a little jerk. There was so much more that I could say. How he'd torn my family apart. How I'd let him poison my mind. But those three words were enough. I didn't owe him any more.

His hand tightened and relaxed around his water bottle as though he were trying to calm himself. "It was a wakeup call."

My brows pulled together. "What was?"

My father stared down at the table, his gaze going unfocused. "Getting the call that you'd been shot. That they weren't sure if you were going to make it." His voice grew rough. "Then, when you wouldn't see me…"

His voice trailed off, and my chest tightened. I refused to let this hit of emotion lower my shields. I couldn't risk it. Dad pushed on. "Thank you for letting me see you now." I nodded. "I want you to know." He took a breath. "I stopped drinking."

My eyes widened. "You did?"

He nodded. "Been going to meetings. I'm seeing things clearer now." He looked down at his hands. "I'm trying to take things one day at a time like they say to do, but I wanted you to know."

I swallowed hard. "I think that's good. And I'm glad you told me."

My dad rose, wiping his hands on his jeans. "I won't take up any more of your time. I just wanted to check on you."

I cleared my throat, remembering how it had felt to know that Jensen loved me even when I least deserved it. "Dad?" He paused on his way to the door. "Maybe you could come back next week. We could play some cards."

My dad smiled. I couldn't remember the last time I'd seen that expression. "I'd like that."

I cleared my throat. "See you in a few days, then."

"In a few days, son."

As soon as the front door closed, Jensen was back. "Was it okay?"

I blinked up at her. "He stopped drinking. He's going to meetings."

She smiled. "He told me. I think that's going to help a lot."

"I hope so." I patted the side of the recliner. "Come here."

Jensen eyed my chest. "Are you sure?"

"Yes, I'm fucking sure, get over here."

She scowled as she slid in next to me. "Watch your language, you big behemoth."

I wrapped my arm around her, not giving a shit that the action tugged at my still-healing chest. "I'll watch it, Wilder." I listened for a second but didn't hear any noise. "Where is everyone?"

Jensen burrowed into my side. "Walker took Noah outside."

I looked down and arched a brow. "So, we're alone?"

She shook her head. "Don't get any ideas. The doctor said three more weeks."

I grinned. "I can still feel you up, though." I palmed her breast, and her nipple beaded under my touch. I groaned. "Okay, maybe that's a bad idea."

Jensen laughed. "Maybe." She was silent for a moment. "It feels right with you here."

I tucked a strand of hair behind her ear. "What does?"

"My house." She tilted her face up to look in my eyes. "It's always kind of felt like a temporary stop. I'd never planned on being here for long, but with you here, Noah playing outside, it feels like a home."

My mouth curved. "I'm glad." Tears welled in her eyes, and I wiped them away with my thumb. "Hey, now, what's all this about?"

"I don't want you to leave."

My brow furrowed. "Then, I won't."

A shuddering sob tore through her. "I was so scared."

"Baby." I held her more tightly to my chest. "I'm fine. And I'm not going anywhere."

She hiccupped a breath. "Promise."

I kissed her hair. "You're stuck with me for good. And you know how stubborn I am. So good luck getting rid of me."

Jensen relaxed into me. "I probably won't always be, but right now, I'm glad you're so dang stubborn."

I chuckled, then leaned forward to brush my lips against one temple, then the other, and finally her forehead. "I love you." I'd told her every day since I'd woken up, and I was keeping my promise to tell her every day for the rest of our lives.

Epilogue

Jensen
ONE YEAR LATER

"**W**AKE UP, WILDER."

I let out a moan, and not the kind that gave me the warm and fuzzies. "Go away. Too early."

Lips grazed one temple, the other, and then my forehead. "Rise and shine, sleepy head."

I rolled over to find Tuck standing over our bed, dressed in jeans, boots, and a jacket. I glanced at the clock on the nightstand. "It's six o'clock." Normally, I was fine with early rising, but it was my day off, and Tuck had kept me up well past my bedtime last night since Noah had been at a sleepover.

Tuck had never moved out after his gunshot recovery. He'd moved seamlessly into my bedroom and our lives. I kept waiting for Noah to freak out. But he never did. Tuck had finally reminded me that he'd been in Noah's life from the day he was born. Now, he was just around more. At some point, I'd have to tell Noah what had happened with his birth father, but he was still way too young.

Tuck tugged on my hand, trying to get me to sit up. "I have something I want to show you."

I growled at him. "You couldn't show me at a reasonable hour? Like eleven, after you've fed me some brunch?"

Tuck chuckled. "It'll be worth it. I promise."

I pushed out of bed, heading for the closet. "It'd better be."

Tuck stared at my ass as I went. "For this view? Already worth it."

"Not for me," I called from between the racks of clothes.

"Give me time, Wilder. Just give me time."

I pulled on clothes, not paying attention to what I grabbed as long as it was warm. When I emerged from the closet, Tuck laughed. "What?"

He pointed at my shirt and then my sock-clad feet. My flannel shirt was misbuttoned, and I had on two different socks. I shrugged and rebuttoned the shirt. Tuck held out a coat. "Don't want you catching a cold."

He hadn't grown any less overprotective over the past year. If anything, he was more so. But we'd found our rhythm. He'd figured out a way to stand beside me when I needed him instead of always being in front. But I knew if I ever needed him for something, he'd be there.

And our relationship wasn't the only one to find its groove. Tuck and his father had found their way, too. It wasn't perfect, but it was so much better than it had been. Craig had stayed sober from the day of Tuck's accident on. He'd never gotten back together with Helen, but that had been the best thing for them both. They were getting along better now than I had ever seen.

"Need caffeine," I grumbled.

Tuck chuckled as he led me down the stairs. "I've got you covered." On the table by the door were two travel mugs. He handed me the one with the tea string peeking out.

I inhaled the brew. Cherry blossom green tea. My favorite. "You're marginally forgiven."

Tuck laughed harder and guided me out the door. "Let's see if I can get all the way there."

I mumbled something about breakfast in bed for the rest of the year as we made our way to Tuck's truck.

He opened the door and eyed me up and down. "Are you still asleep? Do you need me to lift you in?"

I stuck out my tongue and hoisted myself up into the truck. He shut the door gently and rounded the vehicle. I'd never get tired of looking at him, his long strides eating up the space. Broad shoulders. Lean muscle. Golden hair. And those devastating baby blues.

Tuck winked at me as he got in. "Checking me out, Wilder?"

"Always."

He turned over the key. "I like it."

I laughed. "So, where are you taking me before the sun has even risen?"

"You're just going to have to wait and see." He reversed, but instead of heading out onto the road that led to the ranch's exit, he took the lane that led up to my horses.

My brow furrowed, but I didn't say a word. I knew he wouldn't tell me anything if asked anyway. Tuck wound around the ranch until we reached the pasture. He parked and turned to me. "Wait there."

My stomach flipped at the smile on his face. It was one I didn't see often. It almost looked giddy. "Okay."

Tuck rounded the hood and pulled open my door, helping me down. "Come on."

I knew the sun was on its way because there was just enough light for us to navigate the terrain. We slipped through the rails on the fence and headed to the boulder. Tuck hopped up and patted the space between his legs for me to join him. I did.

I leaned back into his chest, soaking up his warmth and the feeling of safety, love, and freedom. What he gave me was just like the spirit of these horses. We'd been broken, but now we had a safe place to rest and a person who helped us be truly free. "I love you," I whispered.

He kissed the top of my head. "That's good."

I laughed. It was such a Tuck thing to say. "Why is it good?"

"It's good because I just bought the ranch over there." Tuck gestured at the land to our right, the one that bordered both the Cole and Harris ranches.

My jaw dropped. "You bought the Holmes spread?" That ranch was ten thousand acres of prime real estate.

He nodded against my head. "Between that, the piece of land my mom wants to gift us, and your property here, I think we could build a pretty amazing wild horse sanctuary and still have space to build a home."

My heart started to beat faster, and tears gathered in my eyes. "That's my dream."

"I know." He whispered the words against my ear as he reached out for my left hand. "I never want another sunrise to go by without you knowing I want forever with you." Cold metal slipped over my finger. "Marry me."

The ring sparkled against the first tendrils of sun coming over the mountains. I gasped. It was gorgeous, an antique setting with intricately woven designs, and a diamond that was far too big. I turned my head so I could see into Tuck's eyes. "There's nothing I want more."

Our lips met in a kiss that was a mesh of love, need, comfort, and the promise of forever. Tuck pulled away first, cupping my face. "I want to adopt Noah. He's already mine in my heart, but I want him to be mine on paper, too."

The tears that had gathered in my eyes spilled over now. "You're going to make him the happiest boy on the planet."

I scrambled to my feet on the rock and yelled out over the land where we would build our beautiful life. "I'm marrying Tucker Harris."

Tuck stood behind me, laughing as the herd of horses let out a symphony of whinnies. "You're crazy."

I turned in his arms. "But you like me that way."

He brushed his lips against mine. "I love you just as you are, as you were meant to be. Wild and free."

THE END

ENJOY THIS BOOK?

You can make a huge difference in *Beautifully Broken Spirit's* book life!

Reviews encourage other readers to try out a book. They are critically important to getting the word out about a novel and mean the world to every author.

I'd love your help in sharing *Beautifully Broken Spirit* with the world. If you could take a quick moment to leave a review on your favorite book site, I would be forever grateful. It can be as short as you like. You can do that on your preferred retailer, Goodreads, or BookBub. Even better? All three! Just copy and paste that baby!

Email me a link to your review at catherine@catherinecowles. com so I can be sure to thank you. You're the best!

BONUS SCENE

Want a little peek into Jensen and Tuck growing up? By signing up for my newsletter, you'll get this bonus scene. Plus, you'll be the first to see cover reveals, excerpts from upcoming releases, exclusive news, and have access to giveaways found nowhere else. Sign up by going to the link below.

www.subscribepage.com/BBSbonus

ACKNOWLEDGMENTS

If you've read my books before, you know I'm an acknowledgments junkie. I love having that little bit of insight into an author and their journey on a particular novel. Who lived the process with them, dried their tears when things got tough, cheered when they typed "THE END", and all the things in between.

I'm so incredibly fortunate to have so many people on my "team". The first thank you always has to go to my mom. She gave me my insatiable love of books and is my biggest supporter. Thank you for everything, Mom!

Writing can be lonely at times, but the internet can be a beautiful place and if you're lucky you'll meet some of the most amazing women you can imagine. Ones who will encourage, share wisdom, and generally keep you from rocking in a corner when things get tough. Thank you to all the amazing authors who have been supportive in every way possible. An extra special thank you to Alessandra, Devney, Meghan, Emma, and Grahame…I'm so grateful to have you in my life!

To my fearless beta readers: Angela, Emily, Ryan, and Trisha, thank you for reading this book in its roughest form and helping me to make it the best it could possibly be!

The crew that helps bring my words to life is pretty darn epic. Susan and Chelle, thank you for your editing wisdom and helping to guide my path. Julie, for catching all my errors, big and small. Hang, thank you for creating the perfect cover for this story. Stacey, for making my paperbacks sparkle. And Becca, for creating trailers that give me chills.

To all the bloggers who have taken a chance on my words... THANK YOU! Your championing of my stories means more than I can say. And to my launch and ARC teams, thank you for your kindness, support, and sharing my books with the world.

Ladies of Catherine Cowles Reader Group and Addicted To Love Stories, you're my favorite place to hang out on the internet! Thank you for your support, encouragement, and willingness to always dish about your latest book boyfriends. You're the freaking best!

To my own personal cheering squad: Gena, the Lex Vegas ladies, Lyle, Nikki, Paige, and Trisha, thank you for endless encouraging conversations and lots of laughs. So grateful to have you in my corner.

And a very special thank you to Carol, who was the first to tell me about the Ochoco wild mustangs, answered a million questions about these beautiful creatures, and shared her own rescued mustangs with me.

Lastly, thank YOU! Yes, YOU. I'm so grateful you're reading this book and making my author dreams come true. I love you for that. A whole lot!

ALSO AVAILABLE FROM
CATHERINE COWLES

Further To Fall

Beautifully Broken Pieces

Beautifully Broken Life

ABOUT
CATHERINE COWLES

Writer of words. Drinker of Diet Cokes. Lover of all things cute and furry, especially her dog. Catherine has had her nose in a book since the time she could read and finally decided to write down some of her own stories. When she's not writing, she can be found exploring her home state of Oregon, listening to true crime podcasts, or searching for her next book boyfriend.

STAY CONNECTED

You can find Catherine in all the usual bookish places…

Website: catherinecowles.com

Facebook: facebook.com/catherinecowlesauthor

Catherine Cowles Facebook Reader Group: bit.ly/
ccReaderGroup

Instagram: instagram.com/catherinecowlesauthor

Goodreads: goodreads.com/catherinecowlesauthor

BookBub: bookbub.com/profile/catherine-cowles

Amazon: https://www.amazon.com/author/catherinecowles

Twitter: twitter.com/catherinecowles

Pinterest: pinterest.com/catherinecowlesauthor

Facebook Group: bit.ly/AddictedToLoveStories

Made in the USA
Middletown, DE
16 October 2021